M000004891

liquididea press
PORTLAND, OREGON

Praise for Avogadro Corp

"The Singularity Already Exists... Chilling and Compelling."

—Wired

"Awesome, thrilling, and very, very real. In a world where self-driving cars and AI stock-traders are becoming real, Hertling's AI Singularity may be just around the corner. You need to read this book!"

–Ramez Naam, author of *Nexus*

"A tremendous book that every single person needs to read. In the vein of Daniel Suarez's *Daemon* and *Freedom™*, William's book shows that science fiction is becoming science fact."

—Brad Feld, *managing director Foundry Group,*
cofounder Techstars

"An alarming and jaw-dropping tale about how something as innocuous as email can subvert an entire organization. I found myself reading with a sense of awe, and read it way too late into the night."

—Gene Kim, *author of* The Phoenix Project

"A highly entertaining, gripping, thought inspiring book. Don't start without the time to finish—it won't let you go."

—Gifford Pinchot III, *founder Bainbridge Graduate Institute,*
author of The Intelligent Organization

Praise for other books by William Hertling

"Holy Cannolli! Go buy this book."
> —**Brad Feld**, *managing director Foundry Group*

"An insightful and adrenaline-inducing tale of what humanity could become and the machines we could spawn."
> –**Ben Huh**, *CEO of Cheezburger*

"A fun read and tantalizing study of the future of technology: both inviting and alarming."
> –**Harper Reed**, *CTO of Obama for America*

Avogadro Corp

Avogadro Corp

The Singularity is Closer than it Appears

SECOND EDITION

WILLIAM HERTLING

Second Edition
Paperback ISBN: 978-0984755707

Keywords: artificial intelligence, singularity, technological singularity, science fiction, programming, general purpose artificial intelligence, strong artificial intelligence, robotics, near future

For Rowan, Luc, and Gifford

PROLOGUE

David Ryan stood on tiptoes and craned his head over the crowd. He smiled at the sight of his wife's blonde hair, only ten feet away. Turning sideways, he pushed into a gap between a sequined dress and a suit. An arm jostled him, and champagne sloshed towards the rim of the three glasses he balanced in both hands. Shuffling through the dense crowd, he finally rejoined Christine, who stood chatting with Mike Williams, his lead developer and good friend. He handed them their drinks with relief.

A banner year at the world's largest Internet company meant another no-holds-barred Christmas party, continuing a longstanding tradition. Avogadro Corp had again rented the Portland Convention Center, the only venue large enough to hold their ten thousand Portland employees. A jazz band played on stage, part of this year's Roaring Twenties theme, while usually reserved geeks danced and became inebriated on free alcohol. Glasses chimed in toasts, lights flashed, and laughter sounded from everywhere.

David glanced at Christine, stunning and exotic in a black sequined flapper dress. He smiled, happy to be celebrating, and with good cause, too: his project was successful, he was married to a smart, funny woman, and he had a great friend and technical lead in Mike. He had every reason to be happy.

David took a self-congratulatory sip of champagne and Mike nudged his arm, sending the drink over the rim. "Here comes Sean," Mike said, eyebrows raised.

A bit of awe and hero-worship made for a moment's hesitation. Sean Leonov, cofounder of Avogadro, was something of a demigod. A brilliant scientist who not only designed the original Avogadro search algorithms and cofounded the company with Kenneth Harrison, he also continued to write research papers while helping lead the company.

"Well, David, Mike, Christine—Merry Christmas!" Sean said, demonstrating the amazing memory that was one of his many talents. He clasped David's shoulder and shook hands with Christine and Mike. He turned to David and smiled. "It's been a while since we talked, but I heard through the grapevine about your progress. When do we get a demo?"

"Any time you want, we're ready. The results are more promising than anyone expected."

"I'm glad. Send me an email, and I'll have my admin set up a meeting. Now, I hear Ops is complaining about the servers you need."

David groaned inside. Ops, short for Operations, was the Avogadro department responsible for maintaining and allocating the all-important servers. More than a million computers spread across nearly a hundred data centers around the world hosted all of Avogadro's websites and applications. Ops was also David's Achilles' heel right now.

David loosened his jaw and struggled to keep his voice calm. "We're consuming somewhat more resources than projected. But we *are* functionally complete, and user testing shows ELOPe's effectiveness is higher than expected. Resource utilization is our last major hurdle. When you see the results, I think you'll agree the resources are worth the investment."

"It's not the money I'm worried about," Sean said, "but the scale. I've already pulled strings to get the project onto the production servers for more horsepower. But before you release, you've got to fix these scalability issues. Hundreds of millions of eager customers will hit the application on day one."

David winced. Sean's tone made it clear he expected David to solve the problem.

Sean turned to Christine. "So how's the gaming business?"

She smiled. "Good. We're building on a new RPG with a free-form magic system. User-designed spells. It's gonna kick butt."

"How do you balance power so the spells don't get out of hand?" Sean asked.

"That's the cool part," Christine said. She went on about the self-balancing system she'd invented that correlated magical impact with spell cost.

David tuned out of the conversation and fumed inwardly at Sean's comments about Ops. His project was going to change the face of email—hell, *all* communications—forever. Server resources should be inconsequential by comparison.

Sean chatted with Christine for a minute about her work and then said quick goodbyes as he noticed someone he wanted to talk to.

After Sean left, David turned to Mike. "Damn Gary and his whining. He's going to sabotage the project before we even get a chance to prove success. Why can't he just leave us in peace?"

Christine put a hand on his arm. "With a presentation to Sean, you'll have more management support. Gary is not going to kill your project or he'd have done it already. "

"But—" David began.

"But nothing. You're a few months from release, and then the server resources are someone else's problem." She smiled and raised one eyebrow playfully.

David returned the smile without much conviction. She was right on a theoretical level, but it didn't change his anger at Gary Mitchell, the Vice President of Communication Products.

Six months earlier, when David realized ELOPe needed far more computing resources than the typical R&D projects, he'd gone to Sean, who quickly gave David's team access to the production servers in the Communication Products group. They had massive spare capacity, and it was an easy choice.

Gary Mitchell had resented Sean's decision, arguing an R&D project could compromise the stability of production servers. He remained vocal in his opposition over the last half-year, and since he couldn't take out his frustration on Sean, he took it out on David and his team. Eager for any excuse to get ELOPe booted from what he regarded as his own backyard, Gary scrutinized their every action.

"Hey, you can hardly blame him," Mike said. "We're using five hundred times more processing power than we predicted, which has got to be a record for any research project. We're like a black hole for computational resources."

David ignored his lighthearted tone. Amid the glitter and glamour of the party, and despite their efforts to cheer him up, a burning resentment rose in David's stomach. The project was an ideal match for his technical skills, in an area he was deeply passionate about, and also strategically important to the company. It was the kind of perfect storm that came along once or twice in a career, if you were lucky. Damn it, he just wanted the thing to succeed.

He swallowed his champagne in a gulp. "I've given ELOPe everything and we're so close. I'm not going to let this opportunity get away from me."

CHAPTER 1

D avid arrived at the executive conference room ten minutes early, his throat dry and butterflies in his stomach. He struggled to keep his mind focused on preparing for the presentation, pushing aside his nervousness. Project managers rarely, if ever, presented to the entire Avogadro Corp executive team.

He was the first to arrive, which meant he could set up without pressure. Syncing his phone with the room's display took only a few seconds. There was no overhead projector here, just a flush-mounted panel in the wall behind him. He ran his hand over the polished hardwood desk and leather chairs. It was more than a small step up from the plastic and fabric in the normal conference rooms.

David took some comfort in the ritual of getting coffee. He poured two raw sugars into a steaming mug and smiled at the lavishly-stocked buffet containing everything from tea and juice to breakfast pastries and lunch foods. Avogadro was an egalitarian, geek-culture company, but top executives had their perks.

Still no one had arrived, so he wandered around the room admiring the view. The dominant feature was the Fremont Bridge over the Willamette River. In the foreground, loft buildings dotted the Pearl District and, to the right, taller structures marked Portland's downtown. Directly to the east, close to where the upper slopes of Mount Hood lost themselves in dense cloud, the early morning sun broke through a rent in the overcast, sending shafts of light to paint the city orange and rose. He was just wondering if he could see his own house in northeast Portland when he heard a welcoming "Hello David."

Sean Leonov entered alongside a tall, dark-haired man, whom David at once recognized from photos and articles: Kenneth Harrison, Avogadro's other cofounder, respected throughout the company. Sean shook David's hand and introduced them.

Other senior vice presidents started to file in, and Sean briefly introduced each in turn. David shook hands or gave nods as appropriate, his head swimming with names and roles.

For a few minutes, a cocktail party atmosphere reigned as people grabbed food and coffee and socialized. They gradually took seats, arranging themselves in something resembling a pecking order around Sean and Kenneth. One seat at the head of the table was conspicuously empty.

When the bustle of arriving attendees died down, Sean stood. "I've already introduced you to David Ryan, the lead for the ELOPe project. I hired David two years ago to prove the feasibility of a radical new feature for AvoMail. He's done an incredible job, and I invited him here to give you a look at what he's developed. Prepare to be amazed."

"Thank you, Sean," David said, walking to the front of the room. "Thanks, everyone, for coming."

He thumbed his phone to project his first slide, a black and white of a secretary leaning over a typewriter. "One of the early corrective technologies was Liquid Paper," he said, to chuckles from the audience. "Highly innovative in its own time, it allowed typists to reduce the rework associated with correcting an error. But correction fluid was nothing compared to the spellchecker, a tool that both detected and corrected errors automatically." In the background, the slide changed to a photo of a man using a first-generation personal computer.

"Years later, as processing power increased, grammar checkers were invented. First generation software detected only trivial mistakes, but later versions evolved to both detect and fix a wide range of problems including purely context-dependent issues. These corrective technologies started out in word processors and gradually worked their way throughout the whole suite of communication tools from presentation editors to email." He paused, enjoying the storytelling.

David focused his attention on one executive at a time, making eye contact with them before he moved to the next. "Today, the standards of business communication have changed. It's not enough to have a grammatically checked, correctly spelled email to be an effective communicator. You must intimately know what your recipients care about and how they think in order to be persuasive, using the right mix of compelling logic, data, and emotion to build your case."

Pleased to see he had everyone's rapt attention, he went on. "Sean hired me two years ago to test an unproven concept: an email language optimization tool to help users craft more compelling, effective communications. I'm here today to show you the results of our work."

He flipped slides again, popping up a timeline.

"In the first twelve months, through data mining, language analysis, and recommendation algorithms, we proved the feasibility of the core building blocks. Then we set about in earnest to integrate those pieces in the Email Language Optimization Project, or ELOPe."

David clicked again, and now the wall display showed a screenshot of AvoMail, the popular Avogadro web-based email. "From an experience perspective, ELOPe works like a sophisticated grammar checker. As the user edits an email, we make suggestions about the wording in the sidebar.

"Behind the scenes, complex analysis is taking place to understand user intent and map their goal to effective language patterns we've observed in other users. Let me give you a very simple example you might be familiar with. Have you ever received an email from someone in which they asked you to look at an attachment, but they forgot to attach the file? Or perhaps you were the sender?"

He heard wry chuckles and a few hands went up in the audience.

"An embarrassing mistake that no longer occurs because Avo-Mail looks for occurrences of the words 'attachment' or 'attached,' and checks if a file is present before sending the email. Through language analysis, we've improved the effectiveness of the user's communications."

A woman vice president raised her hand. David struggled and failed to recall her name, and settled for pointing to her.

"That's a simple example of looking for keywords," she said. "Are you talking about a stock set of phrases?"

A

"No, we don't rely on keywords at all," David said. "I'll explain the process, but I'd like to use a more complicated example. Imagine a manager asking for additional project funding. The decision maker will want a justification for the request. What's the benefit to the company of the investment? Maybe a quicker time to market, or a higher return. Perhaps the project ran short of funds and is in danger of being unable to complete."

David relaxed a little at the sight of nodding heads as the carefully chosen example resonated with his audience of executives. "ELOPe can analyze the email, determine the sender is asking for funding, know the request should be accompanied by a justification, and provide effective examples."

David flipped to an auto-play slide. The short video kicked into motion, demonstrating a manager writing an email asking for an expanded budget, as suggested justifications popped up on the right-hand side. Each example already incorporated details gleaned from the original message, like the project name and timeline. David waited while the minute-long video played, noting the soft exclamations of amazement coming from the group. He smiled to himself. As Arthur C. Clarke said, "Any sufficiently advanced technology is indistinguishable from magic." Well, this was magic.

David paused to let the video sink in before resuming. "We provide fully customized recommendations, because each person is motivated by specific kinds of language, styles of communication, and reasons. Let's use another example. An employee is going to ask for an extended vacation; he'd like to make a compelling case for granting his request. What will motivate his manager? Should he mention he's been working overtime, or that he needs to spend time with his kids? What if he's planning to visit the Grand Canyon, a place his manager associates with good memories?

"The answer," David went on, as he paced back and forth in the front of the room, "depends on the person you're emailing. So ELOPe customizes its analysis not only to what the sender is asking for, but for what the recipient is motivated by."

David noticed Rebecca Smith standing in the doorway listening to the presentation. In a sharp tailored suit, her reputation hovering about her like an invisible aura, the Avogadro CEO made for an imposing presence. Only her warm smile left a welcoming space in which an ordinary guy like David could stand.

She nodded to him as she came in and took her seat at the head of the table.

"What you're describing," Kenneth asked, "how does it work? The natural language processing ability of computers doesn't even come close to being able to understand semantics. Have you had a miracle breakthrough?"

"At the heart of how this works is the field of recommendation algorithms," David said. "Sean hired me, not because I knew anything about language analysis, but because I was a leading competitor in the Netflix Prize. Netflix recommends movies you'd liked to watch. The better they can do this, the more you as a customer enjoy using their service. Several years ago, Netflix offered a million-dollar award to anyone who could beat their own algorithm by ten percent.

"What's amazing and even counterintuitive about recommendation algorithms is that they don't depend on understanding anything about the movie. Netflix does not, for example, have a staff of people watching movies to categorize and rate them to find the latest sci-fi space action thriller I may like. Instead they rely on a technique called collaborative filtering, where they find other customers like me and analyze how *those* customers rated a given movie, to predict how I'll rate it. Sean's insight was that since natural language analysis struggles to understand semantics, it would be best to start with an approach that doesn't rely on understanding, but instead one which utilizes patterns."

When David received nods from the audience, he went on. "ELOPe parses billions of emails, comparing the language used and how the recipient reacted. Was the response positive or negative? Compiled over thousands of messages per person, and millions of people, we can find a cluster of users similar to the intended recipient of an email and analyze how they respond to variations of language and ideas to find the best way to present information and make compelling arguments."

Now there were puzzled looks and half-raised hands as people around the room tried to ask questions. David forestalled them with one hand. "Hold on for a second. Let me give you a simple example. Let's imagine a person named Abe who, whenever he receives messages mentioning kids, responds negatively." David spread his arms, getting into the story. "ELOPe has to predict how Abe will react to a new email. If the message mentions kids, which Abe historically has a negative reaction to, then it's a good bet the new email will be received unfavorably. If Abe was your boss, and you were going to ask him for vacation time, spending time with your kids isn't a good justification."

He heard a few laughs.

"So there's no semantic analysis?" Rebecca asked. "We don't know why he dislikes kids?"

"Correct. We have no idea why Abe feels the way he does," David said. "We just observe the pattern of behavior."

"What if my manager hadn't received any emails about kids?" Sean asked. "How could we predict how he would respond?"

David grinned. Sean knew the answer and was just helping him along. "Let's say we have another user, Bob, who hasn't received any messages about children. However, ELOPe groups together Bob,

Abe, and about a hundred other individuals based on their almost identical responses to most topics, such as the activities they do on the weekend, the vacations they take, how they choose to spend their time. Let's say this group of people are ninety-five percent similar. That is, across all the topics they've responded to, they are ninety-five percent likely to have the same sentiment in their response: negative or positive. This is what we call a user cluster."

Heads nodded.David went on.

"If other members of the cluster received emails about kids, and they responded negatively, then ELOPe will be ninety-five percent certain Bob will behave the same way. Of course, situations are rarely so cut and dry, and it is a *statistical* prediction, which means that five percent of the time ELOPe will be wrong—but most of the time the analysis will be right. So if your boss was Bob, you still shouldn't mention kids when you ask for vacation.

"Joking aside, ELOPe is working, and we've tested the software with users. On average, favorable sentiment in reply emails increases twenty-three percent with ELOPe turned on compared to the baseline. That's twenty-three percent more vacations granted, twenty-three percent more people agreeing to go on dates, twenty-three percent more people getting their work requests granted."

Rebecca stared at him. "Wait a second. Going on dates? So you've got someone out with another person, someone they wouldn't have otherwise been with. That seems manipulative, even risky."

David's stomach threatened to leap into his throat as his internal danger meter flared into the red. He noticed Kenneth, startled by Rebecca's objection, leaning over to speak quietly to Sean.

The dating example was so damn controversial. The next few minutes would make or break his project. If Kenneth and Rebecca decided against him, he'd lose Sean's support and ELOPe would never be released.

"Hold on. Maybe I chose a bad example." David held up both hands. "Who's taken a Myers-Briggs personality workshop?"

As expected, everyone raised a hand or nodded in assent. Myers-Briggs or something similar was standard fare for every manager in big companies. "Now, what was the purpose of the workshop? It's not just to find out whether you're an introvert or extrovert, right?"

"To work effectively with others," Sean said.

"Working effectively means what?" David paused. "Learning how others communicate and think, like who is likely to appreciate a data-driven argument versus an emotional argument, or who likes to think out loud versus having time to respond to written arguments."

He scanned his audience, forcing himself to stay upbeat and chipper even though he feared group opinion could go against the project at this point. "Is that manipulative? Do we take a Myers-Briggs workshop to manipulate people, or do we do it to be able to work more effectively with them and spend less time in arguments and disagreements?"

A few of the VPs turned to Rebecca, waiting for the CEO to respond. She hesitated, then nodded. "It's helpful. I can see that. I've been through more than my fair share of those workshops."

"And if two individuals took Myers-Briggs together, they'd get to know each other better. Perhaps those people would not only work together better, but as a side effect they might be more likely to have an enjoyable date. What we're doing with ELOPe is giving everyone the same benefits they would get from an expensive workshop. We're empowering human beings to become better communicators and collaborators, something everyone wants."

The tension in the group dropped noticeably, and the audience was once more dominated by nodding heads.

"Remember, we're measuring sentiment in these messages," he went on, pacing back and forth in front of the display again. "It's not a grudging assent: people are having and maintaining more effective and cooperative ongoing communication when our tool is enabled. Once, spellchecking was the big innovation that leveled the playing field between people of good or bad spelling ability. Now we're leveling the playing field for writing—enabling people of all abilities to create powerful, well crafted communications."

There was quiet for a minute, then one of the executives asked, "What's the timetable for releasing this?"

Discussion went on for another fifteen minutes, but the topics were all implementation details and business return on investment questions.

At the end of David's presentation, Sean walked him to the doorway while the executives helped themselves to another round of coffee and food. "Good job," he said privately to David, as he ushered him out. "I'm confident they'll vote to go live when you're ready."

As the door closed behind him, David leaned against the wall outside the conference room. The experience had been draining. Then he chuckled. The dating example had been contentious, but it was better to raise the issue and address it early than leave the topic lingering. He was sure the presentation had won them over. The language analysis on his slides that he ran last night in ELOPe predicted a ninety-three percent favorable response.

—⁂—

"Gary, it doesn't make sense to optimize until after we're done."

While David handled the all-important presentation with the bigwigs, Mike patiently defended their resource utilization with Gary Mitchell. Mike wondered, not for the first time, if David had arranged the meeting with Gary to conflict with the executive meeting so Gary wouldn't attend the briefing.

Mike sighed. Give him a team of developers to motivate, a thorny bug to fix, or a new architecture to design, and he'd be happy. But he hated organizational politics. David owed him one for this.

"Of course," he went on, "we'll only use a fraction of the number of servers after we optimize. We'll work on efficiency improvements when the algorithm is done. Optimizing now would hurt our ability to improve the effectiveness. This is basic computer science."

"Mike. Mike."

Mike rolled his eyes at Gary's condescending tone, a safe maneuver since Gary appeared to be studying the ceiling. Gary leaned back in his chair, arms behind his head, white dress shirt stretched over his belly, jowls hanging down under his chin. Mike wondered how Gary had ended up at Avogadro. He needed only a cigar and ashtray to be at home as a 1950s General Motors vice president.

"I know your project got special approval from Sean to use production," Gary said. "Those servers are responsible for running Avogadro's day-to-day operations." He straightened and stared at Mike, jabbing a fat finger in his direction. "You're eating up so much memory and bandwidth on AvoMail that I've had to twice bring in additional capacity. You know what happens if AvoMail goes down? Millions of customers abandon us, and I get chewed out by Rebecca Smith." He stood and walked over to the operation dashboard updating in real-time on the wall display. "Hell, I can measure the loss if we slow down by even half a second. You spike CPU usage, we lose revenue."

"Gary, we—"

Gary tapped the dashboard and ran right over him. "Like every other R&D team, you think your project is manna from Heaven. Meanwhile, I gotta keep things running here, and ELOPe is making us run critically short of capacity. Approval from Sean or not, I'm in charge of Communication Products, and I have ultimate responsibility for ensuring absolutely zero downtime. You've got two weeks to get your server utilization down, or I'm cutting off your access to my production servers. And if you have another spike, I'll shut you down instantly."

"Listen, Gary, we can—" Mike started.

"I don't want to hear excuses!" Gary shouted. "We're done. I've had this discussion with David repeatedly. Two weeks. You go tell David. Goodbye." Gary shooed him out of the office with his hand like an errant cat.

Mike stood, then stormed out, blowing past Gary's startled admin. Resisting the urge to slam doors, he stalked down five floors, fuming with unspent anger. He crossed the street and went down a block, then up again into his own building.

He slowly relaxed during the walk, one benefit of the sprawling campus. Avogadro Corp had expanded so much they now spanned seven city blocks in the northwest part of Portland, on the site of an old trucking company.

As the company and their profits grew over the last fifteen years, they put up one new structure after another, so fast the employees couldn't keep track of who or what was where. Mike had seen three new buildings go up in the few years since he started.

There was an ongoing curiosity among the employees to discover what the different buildings contained. Most of the campus was quite normal, but there were some oddball aspects, like the telescope observatory opened by randomly chosen employee access cards, and the billiard room that changed floors and buildings. Mike had seen that one himself. Whether the trick was managed by moving an actual room, Facilities staff carting off the contents, or duplication, no one knew. Of course the engineers at Avogadro couldn't resist a puzzle, so they'd tried everything from hiding Wi-Fi nodes to RF encoding the furniture, with ever more puzzling results.

There was a half-serious belief among some employees that one of the executive team had a Winchester-house complex. Mike had visited the San Jose fixture once, during his college days. Built by Sarah Winchester, widow of the firearms magnate, William Winchester, she had the house under constant construction from 1884 to 1922, believing she would die if the work ever stopped. The idea that a similar belief plagued one of the Avogadro executives, driving them to do the same to the company campus, brought a smile to Mike's face. On the whole, however, he figured the curiosities were a game to entertain engineers. It takes something extra to retain brilliant but easily bored geeks.

The smile disappeared as Mike crossed the second floor bridge back to R&D and thought of David. He'd blow a gasket at the news of Gary's ultimatum.

Their recommendation algorithm, which sounded so simple when David explained the idea to a nontechnical person, depended on crunching vast quantities of data. Every email thread had to be analyzed and correlated with millions of other emails. Unlike movie recommendation algorithms, which were clustered using less than a hundred characteristics, it was orders of magnitude more complex to do the analysis on emails. They needed a thousand times more computation time, memory, and all-important database access. Coming out of the meeting, Mike had no doubt Gary had reached the limit as far as available resources were concerned.

Unfortunately, Mike had been less than honest. He shrugged, uncomfortable with himself. When had it become necessary to lie in his job?

The reality was that he, David, and other members of the team had been working for months to optimize ELOPe. Sadly, the current server-consuming behemoth was the best they could do. There weren't going to be any more efficiency gains, and therefore no way to meet Gary's ultimatum.

Mike sighed. David would be seriously upset.

—⁓—

A busy morning kept Mike hopping from one urgent issue to the next, despite his desperate need to talk to David. Hours later, with the most critical problems resolved, Mike ran into David's office before anything else could interrupt him.

"Got a minute?" he asked in a cautious tone, poking his head around the door.

"Of course."

Like all the engineers' offices, David's had room for three or four guests, as long as everyone was friendly and used deodorant. A big whiteboard spanned one wall, and north-facing windows held a view of heavily-wooded Forest Park. Mike was sure the six-month-old setup was less effective for working together than last year's lay-out when the team was in one big open space, but he enjoyed the change. Besides, the office would be different again next year.

Mike recounted the meeting with Gary Mitchell. David's face grew grim before he even finished. "Then he kicked me out. What could I say even if I had the chance? There *aren't* any more efficiency gains."

David sat at his desk, fingers steepled, staring into his darkened monitor. It was a bad sign when he stayed in statue-mode for over a minute. Tux the Penguin, the Linux mascot, which Christine had bought David after one of their first dates, wobbled over David's display in the ventilation system breeze. "So two weeks is our deadline. What do you want to do?" Mike prompted, after he'd endured as much of the painful silence as he could stand.

"Pare down the number of developers we have working on fixes and algorithm improvements," David said, having apparently reached some conclusion. "How many people can you dedicate to optimization?"

"I'll focus full-time," Mike said, starting to count off on his fingers. "Certainly Melanie," he added, referring to one of their best software engineers. "Figure two or three other folks. Probably five in all. But, David…" He looked him square in the eyes. "We're not going to make any improvements. We've tried everything."

"All right, starting with the five of you, get focused on performance full-time," David said, ignoring Mike's protest. "After we hit our next release milestone on Thursday, we'll see where we stand."

Mike sighed and left the office.

CHAPTER 2

"How's the project going?" David asked, popping into Mike's office on Thursday morning. He perched on the windowsill, glancing outside at Mike's view of the football-field-sized granite calendar that mapped the history of the universe into a single calendar year. A bunch of new hires were getting their orientation on the month of December. Damn, but Mike had the best view from the floor. He turned back to Mike, hoping he'd have some good news.

"Excellent," Mike said, finally pulling his eyes from the screen. "Everyone finished their tasks for the iteration, code is checked in, and integration tests are running. We'll know in a few minutes if everything passed."

"No, on the performance front," David said, his voice sharp even to his own ears.

Mike raised his eyebrows and glanced at the door.

David sighed and threw a crumpled-up sticky note toward the garbage can. Mike didn't like it when he yelled and had given him the "appropriate work environment" lecture numerous times.

"If we don't have a performance gain, we've got bigger issues than the checkpoint."

"I'm not expecting anything, I'm afraid," Mike said, glancing down to where David had missed the basket. "Dude."

"You had people on optimization, right?"

Mike picked up the paper. "Yeah. We poured through profilers, analyzed every bit of network traffic and database queries. We tried dozens of options, focusing on our bottlenecks. Melanie even rewrote our in-memory representation from scratch. Everything we did either had no effect or made the performance worse. We backed out most of the changes and kept a few of the minor tweaks. The net gain is less than one percent. I'm sorry. We've been banging our heads against this for months. I know you want a miracle, but it's not going to happen."

"Damn." David scanned Mike's full-wall whiteboard. One end had a checklist of features, fixes, and enhancements planned for the current release. Interspersed around the rest of the wall were box diagrams of the architecture, bits of code, and random ideas. David stared intensely, as though the solution to their performance problems might be found somewhere on the board.

"It's not there, I looked," Mike said.

David grunted, admitting that Mike guessed his thoughts. Mike had been smiling when David came in, and now he appeared as glum as his boss. David's disappointment was contagious.

"I hope you're not thinking of canceling the snowboarding day," Mike said. "We've had one for every other release. And there's fresh snow."

David glanced out the window. December drizzle. That meant powder on the mountain. Damn. This project was too important to give everyone a day to play. "We've got to --" He turned back and trailed off mid-sentence at the expression on Mike's face.

"The team is expecting the trip," Mike said. "Some of the guys were here until two in the morning getting their work done. They deserve their day off, and they'll return refreshed and ready to tackle the performance issues. You can't ask people to give their all and not give them something back."

David's mouth opened and closed like a fish, as he bit back what he was going to say. His stomach clenched in frustration and he turned to stare out the window. "Do you have any sense of the pressure I'm under?"

Mike nodded.

"I guess one day won't make that much of a difference with something we've been struggling with for six months," David said. "But when we get back, I want one hundred and ten percent focus on performance. Take everything else off the backlog."

—m—

David leaned over and slapped the button on the alarm clock. He rolled onto his other side and looked at Christine, who was still sleeping. He kissed her on the cheek, watched her breathe for a minute, and slid out of bed. Dressing quickly in the dark, he slipped downstairs where his duffel bag and snowboard were waiting by the door.

A few minutes later, Mike pulled up quietly in his Jetta, exhaust vapors puffing out of the tailpipe in the cold morning air. David brought his equipment out. Wordlessly, Mike opened the trunk and helped David load the gear. David climbed into the passenger side, and smiled. The glow of the dashboard illuminated two steaming coffee cups.

"You're fucking brilliant," David said, taking a sip.

"You're welcome. The snow report said six inches of fresh powder on the mountain. Should be good."

"Where's the rest of the team?"

"Ah, most of them are driving up in Melanie's new truck," Mike answered. "I thought the two of us would drive together and give them a break from their manager and their chief architect."

David smiled. "You're getting people-wise in your old age."

"I'm not old yet. I'm certainly not an old married man like you."

It was about an hour's drive to Mount Hood. For a while they rode in companionable silence, heading east on I-84, enjoying the coffee and early morning light.

"Where do you want to be in a couple of years?" David asked, breaking the quiet.

Mike glanced sideways. "Whoa, dude. That's a weighty question for oh dark thirty." He paused to consider. "You know, I'm happy now. I'm working with awesome people on the most interesting project I can imagine. I've got a good manager, even if I have to keep you in line from time to time."

David grinned.

"I like what I'm doing," Mike said. "I don't think I could ask for more. More servers, maybe."

They both chuckled.

"How about you?"

"I've been thinking about what I want to do next." David was quiet for a moment. "Worrying about Gary and his deadline keeps me awake at night, gives me plenty of time to ponder the future."

"Man, don't get stressed. We'll solve the problem. Or we won't, and Sean will give us additional servers somehow. ELOPE's not worth losing precious sleep over. We all need more of that."

"It's not just the servers. Yes, of course I want ELOPe to be released and the project to succeed. Being hired to run ELOPe was a huge break for me." David paused and shook his head. "No, the real problem is I don't want to be under anyone's thumb like we are with Gary. We're doing all the work here, and sure we'll get some credit, but in the end, the profit and kudos will go to Gary Mitchell. Meanwhile, we have to take shit from him."

Mike paused. "What are you thinking?"

"We build on the credibility we have right after we release ELOPe to get the support to do a big project from the ground up. A brand new product for Avogadro that won't be subordinated to Gary. Something that can change the world."

Mike nodded. "Sure, that would be nice, but—"

"Not just nice," David cut him off. "It's what I'm meant to do. I know it deep in my bones."

Mike glanced at David but bit back whatever he was going to say.

"Did I ever tell you about my dad?" David started after some minutes of silence.

"You two used to build stuff in your garage together."

"After the army, he went to work as a machinist. He brought home a bunch of old tools the factory was throwing out, refurbished them, and we used to build stuff, anything really, in the shop in the garage. I was the only kid around who fabricated birdhouses out of steel."

"Sounds cool. I never built anything with my father."

"It was cool. He was always inventing new things. My mother would complain about the ironing board, and he'd build one from scratch. He was an inventor through-and-through."

"Like you."

"Exactly. But the difference is he worked in the same factory for thirty years. Paid for me and my sister to go to college and then died on the job, doing the same machinist work he'd been doing the day he started."

"I'm sorry."

David shrugged. "It was five years ago. When he died, they replaced him with a CNC machine. An automated metal cutter. You understand? He was an amazing man, but he's gone."

Mike was quiet for a minute. "We all die eventually."

"I want to make a dent in the universe," David said softly. "Just a small dent, and get some credit for it."

—m—

Sixty miles east and an hour later, Mike slid down the lift ramp and snapped into his bindings. David had already started down the run. Mike jumped to get forward momentum and followed him down the mountain.

He didn't understand David. Blindingly brilliant, David was fun to be friends with. On the other hand, his drive and focus on what was over the horizon caused him to lose sight of where he was. The story about his father was touching, but David missed the fact that his father sounded like a happy man, someone who enjoyed his life.

Damn. David had shrunk to a small black blob on the slope far ahead. Mike bent further to pick up more speed, and the cold mountain air whistled through the vent holes in his snowboarding helmet.

The difference in perspective, even when he and David were immersed in the same situation, amazed him. This was the best time of Mike's career. Sure, folks like Gary came along, adding to the challenge. David, faced with the identical state of affairs, took personal affront at Gary's influence. Worse, he saw ELOPe as merely a stepping-stone to something bigger. What about the results of this project, or friendship, or enjoying the journey?

Mike turned the board sideways to stop. When he crunched to a halt, it was utterly silent in the cold mountain air. The ski run split here, and David was already out of sight. Which way did he go?

—⚍—

Mike walked into David's office. "Got a minute?"

It was late Tuesday evening, just three days before Gary's deadline. David had sprung for pizza and most of the team worked through dinner. The department budget had less than a buck left, since David's purchase of a small pool of servers a few weeks ago, implying David paid for the food out of his pocket. The engineers were slowly trickling home now and finally Mike could share the bad news without an audience.

"Sure, just let me wrap this up." David poked and prodded his computer into submission. "What can I do for you?"

Mike turned a guest chair around and sat backwards. "We can't make Gary's ultimatum. Nothing we can pull off before the end of the week is going to make a significant difference. I've had the whole team focused on performance. We've run trials of every promising idea and we've improved by a mere three percent." He crossed his arms and waited for David to respond.

David sat, hands steepled in front of him, staring out the window, the glass a curious meld of room reflections and lights from outside. David's room ran the RoomLightHack, developed by an Avogadro engineer to override the automatic light switches. The hack had been improved over time, making it possible to dim the room's LEDs. David had them set somewhere between moonlight and starlight.

A minute passed, and it was obvious David wasn't going to say anything. His tendency to become uncommunicative exactly when the stakes were highest drove Mike crazy.

Another long minute went by, and Mike started to mentally squirm. "I wish I could find something," he blurted, "but I don't know what. There's this brilliant self-taught Serbian kid who's doing some stuff with artificial intelligence algorithms, and on his home PC, no less. I've been reading his blog, and he has some novel approaches to lightweight recommendation systems. But there's no way we could duplicate what he's doing before the end of the week."

Mike was really grasping at straws, and thin ones at that. He hated to bring bad news to David. "Maybe we can turn down the accuracy of the system. If we use fewer language-goal clusters, we can run with less memory and fewer processor cycles."

Mike was startled by David's soft voice floating up out of the dimness. "No, don't do that."

David smiled in the glow of his display. "Listen, don't worry. We've got a few days. You guys keep working. The executive team loved the demo a couple of weeks ago. We don't want to fool around with the accuracy when ELOPe impressed everyone so much. Keep the team working on performance but don't touch the system accuracy. I'll get the resources we need some other way."

"Are you sure?" Mike asked.

"Yes, I'm sure. I'll get the servers." He suddenly sounded confident.

Mike left puzzled. The deadline was a couple of days away. What could David possibly have in mind?

—⚍—

After Mike left, David stood up and wandered over to his window. The wet pavement glistened in the glare of streetlights. The Portland Streetcar stopped outside the building, picking up a few last stragglers.

On the one hand, Gary was an idiot with no vision. ELOPe would run on the very product Gary had responsibility for, Avogadro's email service. AvoMail would gain a killer feature when ELOPe was ready, and though David might receive accolades, Gary's group would profit through added users and additional business. If Gary supported the project in even the most minor way, he'd get massive publicity and credit.

On the other hand, if he were in Gary's shoes, he'd probably worry about outages, too. But, damn it, some things were worth the risk.

So how could he resolve the apparent conflict? Gary wouldn't approve running ELOPe on production servers because the software consumed excessive resources. The R&D server pool lacked sufficient computing power by several orders of magnitude. So either ELOPe had to become more efficient, which didn't seem possible, or they needed a new group of servers to run on, or the email server capacity must be bigger.

The technical challenge of resource use appeared intractable. But getting more or different servers was a *people* problem, a question of convincing the right managers of what was needed. He paced the office, deep in thought, until—yes. That would do it.

David sat back down at his computer. He stretched his arms, moved a few scraps of paper out of the way, and prepared to get to work. He opened up an editor and started coding.

Hours passed in a blur.

David looked at the computer clock and groaned: almost four in the morning. Christine would kill him. She forgave his all-consuming work habits, but she gave him hell when he pulled all-nighters. He'd be irritable for days until he made up the sleep, and she'd be pissed at him for being grumpy.

Trying again to milk the last drop from his cup, he debated the merits of another coffee right now. Well, he had nothing to lose at this point. He stood up, a painful unbending of his spine after more than six hours of hacking code. Every minute had been worthwhile: he'd almost solved the resource problem.

Mug in hand, he padded down the eco-cork floored hallway in his socks. He filled the mug with coffee, added sugar and cream, then stood for a few minutes in a daze, letting the hot beverage warm him. He glanced up and down the hallway, black and tan patterns on the floor swimming in his fatigued eyes. The drone of the late evening vacuum cleaners a distant memory, it was eerily quiet in the office now, the kind of stillness that settled over a space only when every living being had been gone for hours. David wasn't sure what that said about him. He shuffled back to his desk.

Hunched over his keyboard, David peered again at the code. The subtle changes were masterful, the sort of work he hadn't done since the early days of ELOPe, when just he and Mike did all the development. He needed to be extremely careful about each line of code he changed. A single bug introduced now would be the end of the project, if not his career.

A little more than an hour later, he reviewed the changes line by line for the last time. Finally satisfied, David committed his changes to the source code repository. It would be automatically deployed and tested. He smiled for the first time in hours. Problem solved.

CHAPTER 3

G ary Mitchell took the Avogadro exit ramp off the Fremont Bridge and pulled up to the parking gate, the light from the car's headlights bouncing off the reflective paint on the barrier in the early morning darkness. He waved his badge at the machine. The gate rose up, and Gary drove into the empty garage, a hint of a smile on his face.

It was two days before the deadline to pull ELOPe off the server. David and Mike hadn't done anything to drop usage. In fact, he'd woken to blaring alerts from his phone: there'd been small CPU spikes all night long, and a big one this morning about five, right around the time the East Coast workday was starting.

The idiots had come within a hairsbreadth of overloading the whole system. Fortunately, AvoMail adapted dynamically, cutting back polling frequencies and slowing the delivery of mail, but they'd been close to a full outage.

Gary alternated between anger and glee. He'd never had significant downtime on his watch, and didn't plan to. But this time David had brought them so close to disaster that Gary could justify sending the email he'd been wanting to write for months, telling Sean he was kicking ELOPe off production.

He would have liked to pull the plug first and *then* send the message, but that was pushing the line with Sean.

It was the first time in a while Gary had arrived at the office this early. He found the empty building disquieting. He pushed the feeling aside and thought about emailing Sean, bringing a smile back to his face.

A few minutes later, Gary passed his secretary's vacant desk and entered his own office. His computer came to life, and he went straight to AvoMail to compose the email to Sean.

```
From: Gary Mitchell
To: Sean Leonov
Subject: ELOPe Project
Time: 6:22am
Body:
Sean, just to give you a heads up. I have no
choice but to pull production access for the
Email Language Optimization Project. They're
consuming 2,000 times the server resources we
allocated, and spiked usage this morning,
```

```
causing degraded service levels for ninety
minutes.

We gave them carte blanche when we had excess
capacity because it's your special project.
However, they consume so many resources we
routinely dip into reserve capacity, and
service degradations like the one they caused
today lose us commercial accounts every time.

I spoke to David and Mike about their server
utilization many times, but they did nothing
to get usage down. I gave them a final warning
two weeks ago and have seen no improvements.

Effective tomorrow at 9am, I'm revoking
production access for ELOPe.
```

Email finished, Gary sat and stared for a minute. Was he too obviously gloating? He didn't think so. He hit send.

Time for coffee. He sauntered down the hallway whistling.

—ɯ—

John Anderson let his heavy messenger bag slide to the floor and shrugged out of his wet raincoat before hanging it on a wall hook behind his desk. He dropped into his chair, the pneumatic shock absorber taking his weight without complaint, and sighed at the prospect of another day in Procurement processing purchase requests. A tentative peek at his inbox revealed more than a hundred new emails. His shoulders slumped a little and he reached for his coffee.

This week he had the kids, so he had to drop them off at school before work. Since Portland's crazy school system meant the best public schools were all elective, he and his ex-wife had to choose among a dozen different schools. They ended up with the Environmental School. His kids loved the place, and so did he. Unfortunately, they lived in Northeast Portland, the school was in Southeast, and work was across the river in Northwest. His normal twenty-minute commute turned into an hour-plus on the days he dropped the kids off, which meant he'd arrive late at work, his smartphone beeping and buzzing as emails piled up. He loathed starting the day with a backlog. The consolation prize was that the kids' school was right next to a Stumptown Coffee. John sipped at the roasted Ethiopian brew, the dark, bittersweet warmth bringing a smile to his face.

As the coffee brought his brain into gear, he found the will to tackle his inbox. He was brought up short by a puzzling email from Gary Mitchell. Sent earlier this morning, the email asked him to divert five thousand servers. John read the email three times in its brief entirety.

```
From: Gary Mitchell
To: John Anderson
Subject: ELOPe Project
Time: 6:22am
Body:
Hi John,

Sean Leonov asked me to help out the ELOPe
guys. They need additional servers ASAP, and
we're running out of extra capacity here.
```

Please accelerate 5,000 standard servers out
of the normal procurement cycle, and give them
to IT for immediate deployment. Assign asset
ownership to David Ryan.

Thanks, Gary Mitchell

Normally when a department wanted new servers, they put in a purchase request. Parts were bought, shipped to Avogadro data centers, assembled into the custom servers Avogadro used, and installed onto racks. Then another group took over and installed the operating system and applications used on the servers. Depending on the size and timing of the order, it would take anywhere from six to twelve weeks from the time they were requested until the servers were available for use.

When a department needed servers in a rush, they requested an exception. That process would take servers already purchased for another group and in the pipeline, and divert the servers to the department that needed them urgently. Replacement computers would be ordered for the first group, who would have to wait a little longer.

Diversion requests weren't uncommon; no, the puzzling part wasn't the request, but that Gary would send an email. Only the procurement app could be used to order, expedite, or divert servers, a fact Gary should know since he routinely requested more servers.

He put his hand on the phone and then took it away. A call to Gary would eat up at least fifteen minutes. Regardless of what the procurement rules were, whenever John tried to explain them to anyone, they would argue with him. The higher up in the company they were, the more they would argue, as though their lofty organizational height carried potential energy that could override the rules. A quick email would save John from getting his ear chewed out.

> From: John Anderson
> To: Gary Mitchell
> Subject: Email Procurement Forms
> Gary,
>
> We can't do a server reallocation exception
> based on an email. I couldn't do that for 5
> servers, let alone 5,000 servers. Please use
> the online Procurement tool to submit your
> request:
> http://procurement.internal.avogadrocorp.com,
> or have your admin do it for you. That's the
> only process for procurement exceptions we can
> use. We can approve your reallocation
> exception if you follow the existing process
> and provide appropriate justification.
>
> Thanks,
>
> John Anderson

John continued to work through his backlog of emails. The number of new messages in his inbox would give the casual observer the impression he had been gone from work for a week, rather than just the late start he had gotten dropping off his kids. He took another sip of coffee and continued to work through the pile. The rest of his day, like every other, would consist of endless rounds of coffee and emails. Gary's message might have been a little unusual, but it was quickly forgotten amid the deluge of other issues.

—∿∿—

A few hours later, on the other side of the campus from John Anderson, Pete Wong brought his lunch from the cafeteria in Building Six diagonally across to Building Three, pausing briefly on the windowed sky bridge. The sun had come out, and he raised his face to feel its heat for a few moments. Below, the sunlight glistened on wet streets, one of his favorite aspects of Portland's climate. As a kid he would run outside on rainy days when the sun broke through the clouds, pretending fairies had covered the street with magic dust.

A crowd of laughing people, marketing folk from their attire, entered the skybridge, distracting him from his memories. He continued through and then went down four flights of stairs, out of the daylight and into the fluorescent gloom of basement offices.

At one department meeting after another, Pete had been assured his Internal Tools team, responsible for delivering business applications used inside the company, would be relocated just as soon as aboveground space became available. It never happened.

It was no surprise that the company had stuck the Internal Tools team in what amounted to the dungeons. Everyone at Avogadro used his team's tools to get their daily jobs done, from ordering office supplies to getting more disk space to filling out their timecards. But because Pete's team didn't develop the sexy, customer-facing products, they were the absolute runts in the corporate hierarchy. No executives or research and development engineers would ever be sentenced to the basement offices. The injustice made him gnash his teeth sometimes.

Back at his desk, Pete took solace in his lunch. His office space sucked and his team was unappreciated, but the food was good. Fresh gnocchi in a butter sauce and mixed salad greens. A cup of gelato stayed cold in a special vacuum insulated cup while he ate. The food was all organic and locally sourced, of course; the coffee wasn't bad either, though it came from Kobos. Pete preferred Ristretto, but only a few of Portland's roasters were big enough to supply Avogadro's headquarters. Pete's wife, a tea drinker, couldn't understand the Portland obsession with coffee.

He ate with one hand as he looked over his inbox. A new message caught his eye.

> From: John Anderson
> To: Pete Wong
> Subject: Email Procurement Forms
> Hi Pete,
>
> This is John Anderson. I work over in
> Procurement. Even though we've got a
> procurement web application from IT Tools, we
> still get hundreds of email requests we can't
> handle. Part of the problem stems from sales
> people in the field who can send emails from
> their smartphone, but have a hard time getting
> a secure VPN connection to the internal
> websites. Can you create an email-to-web
> bridge to allow people to get the form by
> emailing us, so they can then fill out the
> form and reply to submit the requisition? I
> mentioned this idea to Sean Leonov, and he

```
said you guys could whip up something like
this in a day or two.

Thanks,

John
```

Pete stared at the strangeness of this. John Anderson, some guy in Procurement, buddies with Sean Leonov, cofounder of Avogadro? Sean was a living legend. Pete hadn't met anyone who knew him directly.

Pete pondered the email. Why did Sean think Internal Tools could implement this in a day? Was he even aware of the IT department? How had Sean, or even John, decided to single him out? It all seemed so unlikely.

The request was a ten on the bizarre meter, but had a certain kind of plausibility. He imagined a salesperson working in the field, using their smartphone to access internal sites. Small screen, low bandwidth. The justification made sense, and if doing this impressed Sean Leonov, well, that couldn't hurt his career. This could be his ticket to one of the real R&D project teams, instead of being stuck in the dead-end Internal Tools department.

He spent a few minutes imagining his future workspace, daydreaming of an office with sunlight pouring in immense windows. Maybe he'd overlook the West Hills or, even better, the river.

With a start, he sat up straight. He would spend some time looking into the request. His fingers found the keyboard and starting searching. His excitement grew when his first search for "email to web service" turned up an existing design posted by some IBM guys. After reading through the article, he realized he really could implement the email bridge in a couple of hours.

His other work forgotten, Pete started in on the project. He created a new Ruby on Rails web application to do the necessary conversion of web pages to emails, and emails into web page form submissions. It was easier than expected, and by mid-afternoon he had a simple prototype running on the department servers.

He discovered a few bugs in the software. Puzzling over the details in his head, he rushed down the hall to the coffee station for a refill.

—⁂—

Mike left his office, nodded to a few teammates on the way, and headed downstairs for the nearest exterior door. After banging his head against the same problem for hours and becoming increasingly frustrated, he needed to clear his mind. The performance issues had become an insurmountable obstacle.

Once outside, Mike wandered around Avogadro's South Plaza, an open amphitheater and park. Just one of the many corporate perks employed to keep everyone happy. Blissfully clear skies contrasted with still-wet pavement from nighttime rains. He waved to a flock of engineers jogging by.

What he found this morning was far more puzzling than the issues he'd expected to run into.

There were two distinct parts of ELOPe. Users saw the front-end process evaluating emails in real-time and offering suggested improvements. But the piece that troubled Mike today was the other half, the back-end process for analyzing historical emails and generating affinity clusters.

While the effectiveness of ELOPe's emails was compelling, the efficiency with which the code ran stunk by anyone's measure. But in the past, the efficiency was at least predictably bad. In the course of attempting to improve resource utilization over the past months, Mike learned that each new email fed into the system required roughly the same number of processor cycles to process.

This morning, though, nothing behaved as expected. According to the application logs, nobody used ELOPe last night, and yet the load metrics had been pegged for hours—a sure indication of a ton of computer processing time being spent on something. But what? In closed prototype mode, only the members of the development team had access to ELOPe. That meant software coders, interaction designers, and the linguistics experts particular to their project. Everyone's activities were logged, but the records didn't reveal any activity. Yet someone or something was generating server load.

Mike hoped fresh air and a walk around the plaza would help him figure out the problem. The last thing he wanted was additional performance problems when they were looking for a massive improvement. He sat on the amphitheater steps and rested his head on his hands. He watched another set of joggers go by. For someone who prided himself on taking things easy, the world weighed heavy on his shoulders right now.

CHAPTER 4

Pete Wong had cut and pasted code he'd downloaded from a dozen different websites, creating a real kludge he wouldn't want to show off in a coding style contest. He ran the test suite one final time and smiled as it passed the last finicky test. He'd implemented the email to web bridge in less than twenty-four hours! It worked, by golly! He tested the new service against the Internal Tools web service, Procurement application, and a handful of other sites. It worked for everything.

He drummed his thumbs on the desk in excitement. Using off-the-shelf libraries written for Ruby on Rails, he'd glued together the necessary pieces quickly. What once took weeks in old web development environments required mere hours in a modern, nearly magical language like Ruby. Using such powerful tools, startups built products in a weekend and launched on shoestring budgets. He wondered for the hundredth time if he shouldn't leave Avogadro to start his own company.

Pete pulled his keyboard closer and started an email to John Anderson, the guy in Procurement. In a bold move, he cc'ed Sean Leonov. No harm in a little visibility, right?

Pete explained the implementation and wrote detailed instructions on how to use the email bridge, a little more than five screenfuls of email. Whoops. Perhaps the process was more complicated than the folks in sales could cope with. Pete didn't know anyone in sales, but he suspected they might not have in-depth technical skills. Well, at least what he provided was complete, even if rough around the edges.

He clicked send and sat back in his chair, sipping his coffee and basking in the glow of his accomplishment. He had good coding kung fu.

Pete pondered bragging about his achievement to his coworkers. A dark thought occurred: perhaps there was something a little irregular about what he'd done.

He sat forward and let his cup thump onto his desk. He'd never told the rest of the team about the project. This request should have come through the normal process like everything else; not only that, but the code should have been peer-reviewed by his fellow developers before he deployed. He'd been so concerned with impressing Sean Leonov that he didn't stop to consider the usual process. Well, no one could blame him for taking initiative.

Despite this, some bigger issue nagged at him. What was—

He jumped out of his seat and pounded the wall with a fist as realization hit him. He'd just implemented an off-the-radar system that interfaced with a dozen different business-critical web services inside the company, probably violating all sorts of security policies. On reflection, he definitely had. His cramped office grew suddenly stifling.

Just as quickly as he had become alarmed, he relaxed a little and sat back down. If Sean Leonov thought the Internal Tools team could implement the request within twenty-four hours, he clearly meant they should pull out all the stops. Pete couldn't go back and yank the application off the servers, not after telling John and Sean the service was available. He shook his head: he was worried about nothing. The bridge was invulnerable. His tool relied on email credentials to validate user logons, and if any product in the company was secure, it was AvoMail.

If he told his boss and the rest of his team now, he'd get his wrist slapped. The best course of action would be to keep quiet until he had gotten a response from Sean. Once he showed that to the team, any skipping of due process would be forgiven. With his plan in place, one in which he wouldn't take too much heat, he relaxed a little more.

A ruckus came from down the hall, rapidly getting closer. Had they already found out what he'd done? He grew alarmed until a group of his coworkers ran past his open door. A few seconds later, Internal Tools' technical lead stuck his balding head in Pete's doorway and said, "We got a hot tip the billiard room showed up on the fourth floor of Building Two. Coming?"

Relieved, Pete smiled and leaped up from his desk. He'd never seen the mysterious Avogadro billiard room that roved from building to building. "Absolutely!" he called, as he ran from his office, following the gang of geeks.

Work forgotten, Pete joined the boisterous hunt for the billiard room. Laughter rang out as other groups heard the rumor and entered the chase. The room would only accept the keycards of the first sixty-four people to find its new location, adding to the urgency of the search. As teams ran through the halls, they told each other outright lies about the suspected whereabouts, all part of the game surrounding the mystery.

While people played and laughed, thousands of computers hummed and exchanged data. A few servers allocated to Internal Tools spiked in usage, but nobody was around to notice.

—m—

Gene Keyes walked back to his office with another cup of coffee, grateful the campus had returned to a somewhat normal decorum after the insanity of the hunt for the billiard room. On some level, he was curious about the mystery of the moving room, but he hated the way the kids around him turned the puzzle into a superficial game, as they did with everything.

He searched the pockets of his suit for a note. His rumpled jacket and graying, disheveled hair were in stark contrast to the young, hip employees dressed in the latest designer jeans or fashionable retro-sixties clothing. Nor did he fit in with the young, geeky employees in their plaid shirts or tees with obscure logos. Not to mention the young, smartly-dressed marketing people in their tailored business casual wear. Fitting in and impressing others weren't high on his list of priorities.

As he approached his own office from the coffee station, he found a blonde girl knocking on his door. "Can I help you?" he asked, halting the search for the missing note.

"I'm looking for Gene Keyes," she said in a bubbly voice. "I'm Maggie Reynolds, and I—"

"I'm Gene," he said, cutting her off. "Come in." He opened the door and walked in. She could follow him or not.

"Uh, my boss sent me because he's missing four..." She trailed off.

Gene put his cup down and took a seat. He glanced up to an astonished expression on her face.

"Wow, I didn't know anyone still used...Wow, this is a lot of paper."

Gene turned around, despite himself. Yes, it was true his office was piled with computer-generated reports. Stacks of good, old fashioned letter-sized paper littered every flat surface. Oversized plotter printouts with huge spreadsheets and charts hung from the walls. The centerpiece of the office, the desk he occupied, was a 1950s-era wooden piece that nearly spanned the width of the room. It might have been the only furnishing in the entire building complex manufactured in the previous century. Incongruously, the desk was far larger in every dimension than the door. The people with a good brain on their heads, often engineers, but occasionally a smart manager, those who trusted their guts, instincts, and eyes, but took little for granted, they'd come in and their eyes would bounce back and forth between the desk and the door trying to puzzle out the mystery. Sadly, she didn't appear to notice.

"Wow, I saw this in a movie once," she said, coming around his desk to fondle a stack of continuous feed paper. She pulled at one end, making the green-and-white-striped paper unfold accordion-style. Her eyebrows went up and her jaw down. "Hey, do you have any punch cards?"

It rankled Gene to hear almost identical comments from every kid that walked in the door. He sat a little straighter in his wooden office chair, the same one he liberated from the army the day he was discharged. "Some things are better on paper," he explained, not for the first time. "Paper is consistent. It doesn't say one thing one day and a different thing the next. And, no, I don't have punch cards. I'm not preserving this stuff for a museum. This is how I do my job." Gene tried to work some venom into his voice, but what came out just sounded tired. He knew what she'd say next, because he heard a variation of the same thing fromevery visitor.

"You know we work for Avogadro, right?" Maggie said, smiling.

Gene knew. But he worked in Controls and Compliance, what they used to properly call the Audit department. When push came to shove, paper never lied.

"Uh huh," he grumbled, ignoring that whole line of thinking. "So, what can I help you with?"

"Well, I have a problem. The database says we're supposed to have more than four million dollars left in our budget for the fiscal quarter, but our purchase orders keep getting denied. Finance says we spent our money, but I know we didn't. They said you would be able to help."

Gene gestured with both hands at the paper around him. "That's what the paper is for. Believe it or not, there's a printout here of every department's budget for each month. So we can examine your budget before and after and see what happened. Now let's take a look..."

—m—

"Dude, you're here," Mike said, plopping down in David's spare chair. "Where were you this morning? I couldn't find you anywhere. I need to talk to you about some weird behavior in ELOPe. Not to mention you missed the entire hunt for the billiard room." Considering that they worked in neighboring offices and were in constant electronic communication, David's vanishing act was impressive.

"What kind of weird behavior?" David gazed off into the distance, ignoring Mike's question.

"I told you we couldn't find any more performance gains, but I couldn't help trying. I started by establishing a baseline against the current code, to have something to test against. I correlated the bulk analysis import with server cycles consumed, and..." Mike stopped.

David continued to stare out the window, apparently lost in thought.

Mike glanced outside. A pleasant sunny day, uncommon for Portland in December, but he didn't see anything other than the ordinary bustle of people walking about on the street. He turned back to David. "Are you listening? Isn't it critical this be fixed before Gary's deadline?"

"Well, I do have some good news there, but go on."

"I tried to establish a correlation, but I couldn't find one. You know ELOPe takes a predictable amount of server resources to analyze emails. At least it did, until two days ago. Now I can't find any relationship at all. The CPU utilization keeps going through the roof even when the logs indicate nobody is running any tests. It's as though the system is working on something, but I can't find any record of what."

David was again staring outside. Mike's head start to pound. He'd been struggling with the damn optimization for days. "So then, David, I slept with your wife. She said it would be fine with you."

"Yeah, sure."

Mike waited, grinning to himself.

"Uh, what? What did you just say?" David finally focused on him.

Mike planted his body in front of the window to block David's view. "Why don't you tell me what the hell is going on, since you're clearly not interested in the performance issues."

"Ah, come read this email from Gary," David said, appearing animated for the first time since Mike entered the office. "The message came in a few minutes ago. We were allocated five thousand dedicated servers by way of a procurement exception. Accelerated deployment and all that. We'll have access to the computing power by tomorrow morning."

Mike came around to peer over David's shoulder at his screen. He let out a low whistle. "Holy smokes, five thousand servers! How did you get Gary to agree to that?"

"I sent him an email asking for dedicated nodes for ELOPe so we wouldn't be in conflict with the production AvoMail servers."

"Wow, what a fantastic reversal," Mike said. "I never would have guessed Gary would change his mind. Any clue why?"

David got that distant look in his face again. "I don't know. It *is* a bit surprising."

Excited by the possibilities of the extra computing power, Mike paced back and forth in front of the window. "Five thousand servers...We can move on to the next phase of the project, and scale up to limited production levels. We could start bulk processing customer emails in preparation for a public launch."

"Well, let's start with Avogadro's internal emails," David said. "This way, we won't adversely affect any customers if anything goes wrong. If we can analyze company emails at full volume, I'll suggest to Sean we turn the autosuggestion feature on for all employees."

"Good plan. I'll stop work on the performance issues and focus on importing the internal emails. This is great news, David!" Mike did a little dance on his way out the door.

—⁓—

When Mike left, David returned to staring out the window. The server allocation was great news. So why were the hairs raised on his neck?

He had sent the email to Gary. That part was true. But he'd neglected to tell Mike about the minor detail of ELOPe's involvement. Of course Mike would uncover massive background processing.

ELOPe needed to analyze Gary Mitchell's emails to optimize David's message, which meant ELOPe also required access to the inboxes of everyone Gary had emailed with, and then the inboxes of everyone those people communicated with, a spiderweb of relationships spanning many thousands of people. David's usage and modifications caused ELOPe to import a massive number of emails. He'd obscured his work by ensuring the new behavior wasn't part of the normal system logs, but he couldn't prevent system monitors from tracking CPU load.

David didn't know what to say. Mike would figure out the mystery behind the CPU utilization eventually. He hoped the discovery would take place later rather than sooner, after they'd solved their resource problems. David didn't want anyone, not even Mike, to know he was using ELOPe itself to get the resources to keep the project running.

A bug in the software, deeply integrated into the mail servers, could bring down all of AvoMail. If anything bad happened, David would feel some serious heat from upper management.

But that wasn't the cause for the pit of fear in his stomach.

No, the real issue stemmed from the changes David had made during his all-night coding marathon. He'd gone into the code for language analysis and put in an overarching directive to maximize the predicted sentiment for any message discussing the project. When any email mentioned ELOPe, from anyone or to anyone, then ELOPe would automatically and silently reword the message in a way favorable to the overall success of the program.

The resulting emails were indistinguishable in writing style and language from those written by the purported sender, a testament to the skill of his team, whose language assembly algorithm used fragments from thousands of other emails to create a realistic message in the voice of the sender.

David relished this success, and wished he could share with the team what they had accomplished. The culmination of years of research, the project had started with his efforts towards the Netflix Prize before he was hired, although even that work had been built on the shoulders of geniuses. Then months of him and Mike laboring on their own to prove the idea enough to justify further investment, followed by two years of a full R&D team, building the architecture and incrementally improving effectiveness month after month.

The results proved, beyond doubt, the power of the system. ELOPe's language optimization had acquired thousands of servers.

The problem, the unsettling fear, arose because David didn't understand how.He couldn't examine the altered emails, an unfortunate consequence of removing the logging so others wouldn't discover ELOPe's manipulations. Had Gary received a modified email convincing enough to make him change his mind? Or had ELOPe changed Gary's response to something more favorable? David found the uncertainty unnerving, and the pit of fear in his stomach throbbed at how little control he had.

But sure enough, his dedicated servers would arrive tomorrow, an outcome worth dwelling on. An email from procurement confirmed the allocation, and another from operations showed the time the servers would be available. Whatever ELOPe had done, it had worked. It might be the most server-intensive application in the company, if not the world, but by damn, it worked.

All the hard work, politics, and sacrifices had been worthwhile. The project had become his life, and his little baby was all grown up now, doing what it was built to do.

Well, maybe a little more besides.

He hadn't realized what it would feel like to have ELOPe working silently, behind the scenes. He was perpetuating a huge deception, and if anyone discovered what he had done, it would be the end of his career. He turned to the window again. Outside, in the momentary sunshine, people went about their business, walking, talking, jogging, blissfully unaware of what was going on inside the company. From his office window, they looked chillingly carefree.

CHAPTER 5

B ill Larry's foot hovered in the air while he waited to take a step forward. The data center dropped down, then lurched up. He paused for a moment more, judged the motion, and leaped. The data center retreated from him at the last second, but he made the jump onto the adjoining floating barge.

Bill breathed in the ocean air as the Offshore Data Center 4 rocked beneath him. This was his project, his mark on Avogadro. After starting out as an IT system administrator, his skills with people led him into management. After he got his MBA, he took a position with Avogadro in their facilities organization. Now in his early forties, he found himself riding helicopters to visit the modern pinnacle of high tech data centers: the floating server farm.

In the last decade, the company had invested in offshore power generation. Avogadro's Portland Wave Converters, or PWC, were the result. Powered by ocean waves, they created cost-effective and environmentally friendly electricity. The PWC stretched out to either side, a long line of white floats on the surface of the water, anchored to the sea-bed below.

Once Avogadro had solved the problem of electrical generation, it made sense to locate the data centers offshore as well. Ocean real estate was effectively free. Maintaining the temperature of the thousands of servers packed into a small room was tricky and expensive on land, but easy out here, where cold, ambient-temperature seawater made for effective cooling. Now Avogadro had an entire business unit devoted to utilizing the potential of this novel approach. They refined the design, with plans to use the floating server farms for their own operations and lease cloud computing capacity to commercial customers.

The primary barge in front of Bill held sixteen shipping containers heavily modified by Bill's team with weatherproofing, climate control, and electrical conduits. These modular metal boxes housed racks of standard Avo servers, power supplies, and communication equipment, each one a fully independent data center capable of running Avogadro search, AvoMail, or anything else the engineers back at headquarters wanted to deploy.

The barge behind him served as a landing pad. It wasn't part of his original design, which had assumed regular maintenance would come by boat. Then again, Bill hadn't realized how many emergency trips he'd end up making to the prototypes, located ten miles from land. The switch to helicopters saved hours on each visit.

Avogadro had extensively ruggedized the containers and electronics equipment. They should have required barely any maintenance at all, even out in the corrosive saltwater environment. In fact, the system was designed to require only a single visit each year to replace faulty servers.

But unlike their land-based counterparts, the floating data centers had a few problems that tended to get Bill up in the middle of the night. Resiliency to the worst storms was one issue; but the weather had been clear, so that wasn't the reason Bill was out here this morning.

ODC 4 had dropped completely offline at 4:06a.m. Within seconds, automated systems detected the outage and provisioned spare capacity in other data centers, seamlessly transitioning the applications to new servers so the barest minimum of customers were affected. Minutes later, the on-duty operations engineers received notice of the downtime and recovery. They took one look at the location and escalated to the ODC team. Bill's smartphone whooped, and at 4:15 he peered bleary-eyed at the incoming data. There was nothing to suggest the alert was worth ruining everyone's morning, so he scheduled the maintenance trip for the start of the business day and met his team at the Bay Area helipad at 8a.m.

He stepped closer to the metal stacks, the sinking feeling in his stomach not caused by the rolling and pitching of the barge. Irregular burns and cuts, the obvious mark of a hand-held cutting torch, covered the sides of the containers. Bill shook his head at the rude treatment of his specially designed data center boxes.

A closer inspection confirmed his fears: a ragged hole had been cut into the side of each shipping container. After the first theft months ago, they'd redesigned the doors, hardening them against future break-ins. This had the unfortunate side-effect of turning the unprotected sides into the easiest entry point.

While the other members of the team worked on opening the doors, Bill stuck his head through the hole and pointed his flashlight around. The racks that should have held hundreds of high performance computer servers were empty, with wires dangling everywhere and various bits of low-value electronic equipment haphazardly strewn about.

Bill extracted his Avogadro phone from his vest pocket and started composing a message to the rest of the ODC team. Forget fixing the problem in place with a small maintenance party. They'd need to tow the whole barge back to shore, then install new containers and servers.

Bill resisted the urge to bang his head against the wall in frustration. Even if they wanted to defend the barges, the location ten miles offshore and lack of any facilities made it impossible to station security on board twenty-four hours a day, seven days a week. Besides, anyone here would be at risk from the pirates.

The piracy problem had put the entire ODC rollout on hold, pending a resolution. It didn't bode well for Bill's chance of getting a bonus. He and Jake Riley, the ODC Lead Manager, would meet with senior management later that week to discuss the issue.

All this hardware sitting out in the middle of the ocean undefended was just too tempting. A full floating data center contained millions in equipment, including tens of thousands of servers, along with their requisite hard drives, power supplies, emergency backup batteries, and extensive communications hardware. Worse, it wasn't clear yet whether the target of the thieves was the computer equipment itself or the potential customer data on the hard drives.

As he reviewed the destruction and mentally tallied the cost of repairs and replacement, Jake's controversial proposal began to make more sense: give the ODCs active deterrents to prevent pirates from boarding them in the first place. Still, he got a chill down his spine just thinking about autonomous armed robots guarding the barge.

—ᴍ—

"Mike, what a surprise!" Christine smiled and embraced him in a warm hug. "David didn't say you were coming for dinner."

"How's the game development going?" he asked.

"*Awesome,*" Christine said, singing the word as she hung his coat in the closet. "I spent the last two weeks fine-tuning game play with our alpha players, and we're shooting for a beta release after the holiday. Don't worry, you're on the access list. Want a demo later? The visual effects on magic spells are *amazing.*"

"Sure, I'd love it."

"Make yourself comfortable, and I'll tell David you're here." She tucked a wisp of hair behind one ear and went upstairs.

Mike strolled around the early twentieth-century Foursquare, a quintessential Portland house, as he waited. Ikea furniture was interspersed with computer equipment everywhere, and Christine's high end gaming system dominated the family room. Mike wandered the house, just a hint of envy somewhere. Somehow David and Christine managed a classy mix of furnishings, electronics, and art, unlike Mike's small bungalow which still resembled his college apartment.

He couldn't be too jealous of good friends who always made him welcome. Since he lacked family in town, he often dropped in for dinner, especially between girlfriends. Of course, he usually didn't come unannounced, but he had a pressing reason to talk to David tonight.

Before he left work, Mike had figured out the mystery of ELOPe's activity. He deciphered the unexplained activity in the system, and the unexpected and unlikely allocation of dedicated computers. He even understood David's strange behavior in the office when he'd announced they'd been granted additional servers. David had been less than honest with him, leaving Mike sweaty at the impending confrontation.

He snapped out of his reverie at the sound of footsteps on the stairs. David clasped him on the shoulder, and Christine led them into the kitchen.

"Vodka martinis, everyone?" Christine suggested, following their longstanding tradition.

"Sounds great," Mike and David answered in unison.

The men took bar stools in the kitchen while Christine grabbed a bottle of Stolichnaya and glasses. She turned to Mike. "If you're available, I've got a single coworker."

"Oh?" Mike said, raising his eyebrows. "Does she have any secret collections I should be aware of?"

They laughed at the time Christine had fixed Mike up with an obsessive-compulsive collector of stuffed animals.

"I think this one is normal. I'll invite you to coffee with her after the holiday, and then bow out at the last minute."

"That won't be awkward at all, I'm sure."

Christine smiled mischievously.

"I'm glad you came," David said. "We haven't gotten together outside of the office since the snowboarding trip."

Mike swallowed. It was hard to confront friendly, engaged David. The distracted, vague David of a few days ago was an easier match.

"But why the unexpected visit?" David asked.

Christine gave him a funny look as she realized he hadn't invited Mike over.

"I want to talk about ELOPe." Mike clenched his fists under the counter.

"I heard the good news," Christine said, wetting glasses with vermouth. "It's about time you guys got dedicated servers. Now you can move on to the next phase, right? Congrats."

"Yes, well...I have this crazy idea how we got those servers." Mike kept his eyes on David. "I'm guessing ELOPe was turned on a little early."

"What makes you think that?" David said, his fingers turning white around his martini glass.

"You asked me to import all internal emails. Which I did, two days ago."

"Any problems?"

"No, none at all. That's the problem. There should have been a peak in background processing activity as I gave ELOPe access to accounts across the company." Mike turned to Christine. "Any time we add new email sources, ELOPe analyzes the backlog. When I added ten thousand employees, with thousands of emails each, I expected a giant processing spike, considering all our performance problems." He returned to David. "But you know what I found, right? No spike. Hardly any activity. Now why would that be?"

Christine stopped at Mike's tone, olive-covered toothpick hovering over a glass. "Come on, the suspense is killing me."

David shrugged and slumped in his chair. "Why?"

"ELOPe had already been given access to everyone's email." Mike enunciated carefully. "I didn't see a jump in activity, because by then it had finished processing their inboxes."

He waited, confident it was the only explanation that fit the data, but David didn't say anything. Mike continued. "You turned on company-wide access days before, so ELOPe could help with the dedicated server proposal, right?"

"I did..." David looked pained.

"Why didn't you tell me? It's awesome. ELOPe worked! You wrote an email, received suggestions, and the resulting message was persuasive enough to convince Gary to give you the servers! Why did you keep that secret? I've been chasing down performance spikes for days for no reason."

David let out a big sigh and twiddled his fingers on the countertop. Mike couldn't figure out if he was embarrassed or relieved. Well, either way the secret was out.

"I was trying to protect you," David said after a moment. "We didn't have permission for ELOPe to analyze live emails on the production servers, and if you knew you might have been held responsible."

"We're in this together," Mike said. "This is my project just as much as yours. Look, next time, tell me what is going on. I felt like crap when I realized you were keeping secrets."

David shook his head. "I didn't think about it. Sorry."

"Okay, now forget moping about." Mike stood and held his glass out in a toast. "ELOPe works. After two years of building that damn thing, it fucking *works!* Let's celebrate!"

—∾—

David helped Christine clean up after dinner, he clearing dishes while she loaded the dishwasher. Mike had gone home after a dessert of chocolate chip cookies and ice cream. They joked that Mike and David had the culinary preferences of twelve-year-old boys.

After Mike had gotten what he thought was the deception out on the table, everything had been fine. Mike was so elated ELOPe worked that he was happy enough to put the other issue behind them.

"Why so quiet, hon?" Christine asked.

"Just thinking."

"You're not just thinking. Thinking is when you're quiet, but snapping your fingers." She glanced over in time to catch David's smile. "You've been moody all week. If this is about lying to Mike, well, he knows now, and he forgives you. Stop worrying."

"There's more," David said heavily.

"More what?"

"More I didn't tell Mike. I turned on ELOPe and obscured the system logs as Mike suspected. But I also did something else..." David trailed off.

"Well, are you going to spit it out, or should I insert bamboo under your fingernails?"

"I gave ELOPe a hidden objective."

"What do you mean?" Christine asked.

"When any message passes through ELOPe, and that would now be every single company email at Avogadro, the contents are scanned to see if the ELOPe project could be affected. Then ELOPe takes steps to maximize success."

"What does that even mean? What can it do?" She stopped washing dishes and stared at him.

He looked away from her gaze. "ELOPe can't do anything but rewrite emails," he said, throwing his hands in the air. "But because I turned off the logging, I can't see the changes. I turned the directive on, and less than twenty-four hours later I received an allocation of five thousand servers. That many servers, built and installed, is close to five million dollars. How did ELOPe get someone to spend five million?"

David paused to catch his breath. He started to look around and whisper, but realized that was foolish. They were alone in the house. "This afternoon I got another email, saying a team of twenty contractors had been assigned to the project, top-notch performance specialists hired to help us optimize ELOPe. We need the help, but I never asked to hire anyone."

"You're starting to scare me." Christine threw the sponge down and gave up on the dishes altogether. "There's no way Sean or Gary would have hired them for you?"

"No. Sean didn't know about the extent of our performance issues, and Gary would far rather boot us off the servers. I'm convinced the contractors somehow stem from the override I created."

"Why the hell did you do something crazy like this in the first place?"

"We were a couple days from the whole project being cancelled. Gary Mitchell was going to bounce us off his servers." David's shoulders slumped in despair. "ELOPe is a massive consumer of processing resources. We're not even released, and we're already consuming almost as many compute cycles as the production Search and Email products. They're serving hundreds of millions of customers, while we're in test mode."

"Everyone knows this, right? It's no secret."

"Yes and no. I abused Sean's carte blanche to get way more server resources than he ever intended to give us. If Gary went through with his ultimatum, not only would we have been kicked off his servers, but Sean would have learned I distorted what he said to get those resources. Definitely an end-of-career move."

"Jesus, David." Christine had her arms crossed and was tapping her foot now.

David was alarmed. The last time she was in this mood, he'd spent the night on the couch.

"Why did you let everything snowball out of control?" she said.

"I just want the project to succeed." He tried his puppy-dog eyes on her, but she ignored him.

"If you're worried about the override you put in the software, back out the change with Mike. The way you've described the situation, resources are being stolen from all over the company, and everything points to you."

His spirits lifted. Christine always saw the obvious answers he missed. "You're right. If I revert the code change before anyone gets wind of what's happening, the manipulations should stop. I was nervous, afraid I'd crash production trying to patch the code. But Mike's done it before. You don't think he'll freak out when I tell him?"

"No, you dork. He's your friend. Of course he's going to help you." She shook her head and sighed. "Why do husbands make everything so much more complicated than they need to be? Maybe I should have gotten a dog instead."

"At least I don't shed." He grabbed her and planted a big kiss on her lips. "Thanks for talking with me about this. Let me go email Mike."

Upstairs, David sat down in his office. He tapped impatiently at the touchpad, and started in on the email.

```
From: David Ryan
To: Mike Williams
Subject: Help tomorrow
Body:
Hi Mike,

Thanks for coming over tonight. I'm glad we
talked.

We need to meet early tomorrow morning.
There's something I didn't tell you. We have
to live-patch the email servers to remove part
```

```
of ELOPe, and I could really use your help
since you've got experience with production
rollbacks. I'll explain everything tomorrow. -
David.
```

David relaxed as he hit the send button. With Mike by his side, they could fix anything.

—⟋⟍—

Jake Riley, the Lead Manager of the Offshore Data Center project, prepared to brief Kenneth Harrison and Rebecca Smith on the piracy problem. He counted himself lucky to get a meeting with the executive team, even if only two-thirds were present and it was nine-thirty at night. Tired from a twelve-hour workday, he forced himself to keep his energy high for the presentation.

Jake shared a photo of the break-in. "This morning Bill flew out to Offshore Data Center 4, off the San Francisco coast. Pirates used cutting torches to cut holes in the sides of six of the cargo containers onboard ODC 4, and removed the servers from those containers. They left behind server racks and power transformers damaged beyond repair." He switched to an interior photo showing one of the pillaged containers.

Jake scanned the virtual conference room, ensuring everyone was with him. Kenneth and Rebecca, in the Portland headquarters, appeared on screens covering the far wall. Bill Larry sat next to Jake. Directional microphones, high definition monitors, and a low-latency network connection created an impressive simulation of a single conference room, even though one half was in Palo Alto and the other half in Oregon. Far beyond ordinary telepresence solutions, it was nearly indistinguishable from being in the same room. Jake figured the technology was the closest to a Star Trek holodeck he'd experience in his lifetime.

"That brings us to three pirate attacks in as many months," he said. "Two here, one on the East Coast."

Rebecca scanned through photos of the attack, frowning. The issue had caused a holdup in the ODC rollouts and therefore a small but growing hiccup in Avogadro's master data center rollout plan. Computing requirements doubled every twenty months at Avogadro with no end in sight. Meeting at this time of night was a sure sign of just how critical server capacity was to the company's growth.

"Tell us about security measures," Kenneth said. "You already do some hardening of the physical containers, right? Is there anything more you can do?"

"The units are ruggedized for the maritime environment," Jake said. He switched the overhead screen to an exploded diagram of the container design. "A standard cargo container is watertight, even capable of floating for years on its own. Our containers are modified to allow electricity, cooling, and data in and out. Additional weatherization controls humidity and ensures optimum interior conditions given the corrosive nature of the saltwater environment. After the first pirate theft, we modified the design and installed high-security doors."

Jake hated sharing bad news. He'd always had outstanding results to report in the past. The offshore project had posed no end of technical challenges, all of which his team had overcome. He had even brought on new employees with specialties in maritime engineering and construction, people who clashed with the culture of Avogadro, but he solved those problems, too. He never expected that old-fashioned piracy, a problem he considered a nineteenth-century issue, would be his biggest challenge. *Pirates,* damn it. He shook his head at the thought, and went on.

"No matter what we do, there will always be a weakest link in security. That's currently the container walls. If we harden those, the vulnerability will simply move. Hell, the thieves could tow the barge away if they had a mind to. These units are sitting out there in the ocean, miles from shore. Even with effective monitoring, if we have to scramble a helicopter, we're looking at an hour elapsed time. A boat is a two-hour response. That's if we have people staffed and ready to respond twenty-four hours a day."

"Monitoring is difficult as well," Bill said. "We can monitor the interior of the cargo containers, where the environment is controlled. Outside we've got heavy winds, rain, saltwater, sun. We've tried three models of security cameras and they've all failed. Instead of alerts when the pirates board, we find out only when servers are unplugged."

"The rollout plan," said Rebecca, "calls for twenty additional ODCs around the world within six months to meet capacity requirements. We don't have the real estate to put them on land. We can't centralize because of bandwidth and latency issues. The offshore project is critical, Jake. Tell me you've got a plan to get us back on track."

"Well, this is going to sound controversial, at least initially, but we do have an idea. Hear us out before you make a decision. Do you recall the piracy problem off the coast of Somalia?"

Rebecca and Kenneth nodded from across the virtual table.

"The companies shipping freight around Somalia faced similar issues. They couldn't arm their sailors, civilians with no combat training who can't be expected to repel a pirate attack." Jake put another slide up on the overhead screen, showing a small tank-like robot. "iRobot, the company that sells Roomba, also makes robots for commercial and military use. They'd already developed maritime exploration robots and weaponized drones. In Somalia they took the next step, and created weaponized versions of their maritime robots."

Rebecca had one eyebrow raised.

Jake smiled. "You know where I'm going. But hear me out."

Rebecca waved a hand for him to continue.

"They deployed a two-part solution on commercial ships that passed near Somalia. An autonomous submersible bot can attack and disable the pirate ship itself, and an armed robot on deck can repel would-be boarders. They tried the robots on dozens of shipping vessels in the area, and after three successful cases of repelling pirate attacks, there have been no major attempts at piracy in the last six months. We can assume word got around the criminal community about the new defenses."

Rebecca and Kenneth glanced at each other. Rebecca's initial amusement had turned into a concerned frown.

Jake forced himself to keep going. He switched slides twice more, displaying the submersible unit and tank-like deck robot onboard a freighter. "We talked to iRobot, and I have an initial bid from them. They have recommended a similar package for our offshore data centers. Submersible robots to take out ships, onboard robots to disable boarders."

Jake had a hard time meeting Rebecca's gaze. He was walking a fine line here. Avogadro prided itself on their enlightened culture: it wasn't exactly an environment welcoming to violence and guns. He could hardly believe he was suggesting putting weapons in a data center. To the best of his knowledge, there wasn't even a single armed guard in all their land-based facilities. They were an Internet company, not a military contractor.

Before Rebecca could respond, Bill jumped in. "I know this may seem radical to put armed robots in place. But it's worked off Somalia. In fact, total injuries and deaths are down. The approach will scale to any number of data centers we care to deploy. It's also cost-effective and risk-reducing because we don't have to maintain people onboard the barges."

Kenneth leaned over, checked in with Rebecca. She shook her head.

"Keep going," Kenneth said. "Let's hear the rest."

Jake and Bill covered the entire iRobot proposal, explaining more about the robots to be used and the estimated cost. They spent the greatest amount of time detailing the protocols put in place with the robots to ensure minimum loss of life and risk.

At the end everyone was quiet. Jake heard the hum of cooling fans in the room. He was sweating under his clothes and desperately wanted to go home. He discreetly glanced at the clock. After eleven now. He'd been working since five in the morning.

Even Kenneth turned and waited on Rebecca, clearly not willing to stick his neck out on this proposal.

After a minute, Rebecca started hesitantly. "I wouldn't risk human life for the mere loss of ten million dollars." She paused, then went on more strongly. "But the privacy implications of losing the data stored on those servers are huge. A breach opens up the potential for litigation from our users and regulation from the government. More significantly, if we fail to retain the trust of our users, we're sunk. Our cloud strategy works only as long as our customers have complete confidence in the security and integrity of their personal data." She stabbed at the table with one finger. "Losing customer trust in this case means billions of dollars of revenue. We can't afford the loss of one hard drive containing customer information, let alone tens of thousands of hard drives in an ODC."

Jake nodded and went to respond, but Rebecca held up a hand to indicate she still wanted to speak. He'd been sure the idea would be shot down, but this looked like Rebecca was about to approve the plan.

"We've been relatively fortunate the ODC thefts have thus far been limited to non-sensitive search data," she said, anticipating Jake's input, "but we must migrate our email and document servers to offshore data centers within a few months or risk capacity outages. It's not acceptable to allow confidential emails and documents to be stolen by pirates." She cleared her throat. "I want you to proceed with your proposal. I want this to be structured so we pay iRobot for security, and have them own and control the hardware. I don't want Avogadro Corporation to own weaponized robots. Am I clear?"

Soon after, Jake left the virtual conference room stunned. What had he done? Within a few weeks, the ODCs would have their own automated self-defense capability, like something out of the movie *Terminator*. Somehow he was responsible—and way outside his comfort zone.

CHAPTER 6

"David, it's Mike. Listen, I'm flying to Madison this morning. I got a message from my mom that my father had a heart attack. I'm not sure when I'll be back, but I'll call when I know."

David put the mobile phone down, suddenly numb. Distressed by the content of the message, he worried even more about the way Mike sounded, emotional fear surfacing in shaky, halting speech. The contrast with Mike's usual easygoing manner was enough to make his own throat tight.

He didn't remember Mike talking about his dad much, other than a few comments after his trips home, but David assumed he was healthy. He felt lingering guilt because he'd seen Mike's incoming call on his mobile at home, but in the rush to get ready for work, he didn't answer. Only now in the office did he listen to the message, and he regretted not answering earlier. He called Mike back, but it went to voicemail without ringing. Mike must be in the air, en route to Wisconsin.

Still shaken, he wondered what to do. He phoned Christine to let her know the bad news. She was equally shocked, getting out "I'm sorry" a few times before she had to go.

He sat behind his desk for a while, doing nothing at all. When had he and Mike gotten so old that they had family with health issues? He did the math, surprised to realize his own parents were going on sixty.

A knock startled him.

Melanie stuck her head in. "Team stand-up. Mike's not here. You want to lead, or should I?"

He nodded and stood. "I'm coming."

By the time the morning meeting ended, David had inherited a fiasco with the Test department. When he finished that emergency, he had sixty emails to deal with. Not till midmorning did he have a moment to himself. Standing at the espresso machine, he felt lonely. Coffee was a shared experience between the two of them. Mike would sometimes drag him on a trip halfway across town chasing down an elusive bean. He realized with a start Mike had always been there. Other than company holidays, Mike had never taken vacations or even sick days.

Then it hit him. With Mike gone, he had no help to remove his modification to ELOPe. He was on his own. Trembling, he rushed back to his office and paced the floor in front of the window, pondering his options. The coffee sat forgotten, fear-generated adrenaline giving him more stimulation than he needed.

Could he remove the ELOPe override module by himself? Under ideal conditions, server changes deployed during rolling downtimes. They'd take five percent of the computers offline at a time, apply the updates and test them, then do the next group until all the servers were done. He'd been lucky a rolling downtime had been scheduled the night he released the override.

David sat down at his desk, and pulled up the operations calendar. *Kuso!* No deployment opportunities before the holiday closure next week. He couldn't deploy until after the New Year. He slammed his fist down on the table and Tux the Penguin wobbled with the sudden movement.

He stood and returned to pacing. He could request an exception to get a one-off maintenance window scheduled, but that required paperwork, submitting the changes ahead of time, and altogether far too much attention. He sat back down. He checked the door to see if anyone had observed his nervous antics, but it was firmly closed.

If he didn't wait for a rolling downtime or request a maintenance slot, that left him with a live-patch. During the procedure, the server stayed up while the code change was made in the background, the entire operation taking only a few seconds. It was usually used for minor changes that wouldn't affect the way applications ran, like changing the styling of a page or embedded images. Anything more complicated was risky and reserved for emergencies. More than one outage had been due to a live-patch gone wrong. Changing ELOPe's code, tightly integrated into the mail servers, was definitely *not* a small change.A botched patch would attract even more attention, including a formal investigation.

Should he attempt the patch on his own or wait for the next maintenance window? Mike not only had far more experience, he also had the authorization to perform live-patches. He convinced himself the safer, lower-risk option would be to postpone until a deployment window became available or Mike returned. He took a cautious sip of his coffee and leaned back. It could wait. After all, whatever ELOPe was doing didn't seem to be causing any serious problems.

—⁂—

John Anderson had worked halfway through the queue when he came upon yet another request from Gary Mitchell's department. With relief he noted Gary Mitchell was using the online app for submitting procurement reqs rather than sending emails, but he was shocked at the volume coming from Gary's group. Three reallocation requests to take servers out of the normal pipeline of delivery and direct them to the ELOPe program, whatever that was. Several new orders for bulk purchases of high performance servers. Gary's division must be expecting massive increases in load.

And now this latest req for software contractors to work over the upcoming holiday break, which didn't make sense to John. He was surrounded by thousands of programmers, and yet Gary wanted dozens of outsiders. He gritted his teeth. With less than a week until the company closed for Christmas, he'd have a heck of a time getting a contract of this complexity done. Forget about submitting it for bid by multiple contractors. He reviewed the list of approved software subcontractors, and awarded the request directly to Nonstop InfoSystems, one of the better vendors.

```
From: John Anderson (Procurement)
To: Beth Richards (Nonstop InfoSystems)
```

```
Subject: Software contractors needed over hol-
iday
Body:
Hi Beth,

We have a critical project that needs
additional resources over the holiday shutdown
here. We need engineers to address server
performance issues. We're looking for the
following skill sets:
- server administration (16 headcount)
- database administration and performance
tuning (16 headcount)
- software performance tuning (16 headcount)
- general software engineering (16 headcount)

We need experts in high performance, high
scalability systems, who can put in 12-hour
days over the holiday. According to the
requestor, we need six people onsite, and the
remainder can work remotely. Can you please
email me a bid ASAP?

On acceptance, I'll forward the details of the
work to be done.

Thanks, John
```

Gary's recent purchases were unusual, but they paled in comparison to this morning's iRobot procurement request from the Offshore Data Center department. Tagged critical, urgent, and confidential,

John had been so puzzled he called Bill Larry, an old college buddy, to get the inside scoop. Bill confirmed Avogadro was indeed arming the ODCs! John shook his head in disbelief at the notion of robots with weapons at an Avogadro data center. Even hours later, he could still hardly believe they were going forward with the idea.

Shortly after he finished the paperwork with iRobot, he stopped in alarm at the specter of an empty mug. Had he already finished his allotted four cups? He looked longingly at the cup, but had just decided against another when Maggie Reynolds knocked on the open door of his office. "You busy?"

Maggie was technically in Finance, not Procurement, but they'd worked together so much in the six months since she'd started that John felt closer to her than to most of the people on his own team. She was funny and smart, and he wished he could think of an excuse to ask her out, but the timing never seemed right. "Sure, come in."

"I'm concerned about the way this last batch of purchases are being funded out of Gary Mitchell's group," she said, getting right to the point as she sat down.

John watched her earrings dangle as she spoke. Her hair looked different. Had she gotten a haircut? Was he allowed to comment on her hair? He could never keep track of the latest HR rules.

Maggie went on. "Gary submitted a purchase order over his budget limit, and I kicked the order back to him. Then his assistant sent me this email, asking me to divide the purchase among several different budgets. Shouldn't the whole thing have to come from one? It sounds suspicious." She wedged a tablet in front of his face to show him the email.

> From: Bryce Cooper (Gary Mitchell's Executive
> Assistant)
> To: Maggie Reynolds (Procurement Finance)

```
Subject: re: updated billing code for reallo-
cation exception
Body:
Maggie,

Gary asked to split this across the following
billing codes:
- 9004-2345-01: $999,999.99
- 9002-3200-16: $999,999.99
- 9009-5387-60: $999,999.99
- 9009-6102-11: $999,999.99
- 9015-2387-19: $999,999.99
- 9036-1181-43: $109,022.23

Thanks,

Bryce
```

John waved his hand at the tablet. "Nah, don't worry. I'm up to my armpits in requests from Gary's department. We're weeks from the end of the fiscal year. Departments have leftover money, and anything they don't spend evaporates. So come December, they start ordering servers they might need for the next year, new monitors for the employees, make urgent contracts with vendors, anything really, to use the dollars before they disappear. And if they need to make big purchases, like Gary buying these servers, he's got to pool money from different budgets. Everyone will be gone during the Christmas holiday, so there's a rush of purchases these last few days."

"But the policy rewards gross financial mismanagement!" Maggie exclaimed.

She arched her neck in frustration as she spoke, looking a little like Chewbacca from Star Wars. John wasn't sure what it said about him, but he found the motion both endearing and sexy.

"If the money rolled over from one year to the next, we would reward saving," Maggie went on, growing more strident. "This approach causes irresponsible spending."

"I know, I know," he said, trying to placate her. "Quarterly budgeting is contrary to every shred of common sense, but it's business as usual. Everyone plays the budget game." He had to change the subject somehow before she grew more angry. He looked down at his coffee cup, thumped his fingers on the table and gulped. "Do you want to get coffee sometime?"

Maggie glanced at the tablet with a sigh, and turned it off. "Sure, how about now?" she answered.

Coffee at work wasn't quite what John had in mind, but it was better than nothing. He picked up his mug and they made their way together to the cafeteria.

—✺—

Mike boarded his flight at 5:30a.m. and found himself in his seat, remembering nothing of his trip to the airport. When had he last seen his father? A year ago, during the Christmas break. No, he realized with a pang of guilt. He'd been dating someone and went to Mexico with her for the holidays. Two years, then. He pictured his dad's face from his last visit, clearly healthy. Why, his mother had sent photos of an all-day hike in August. He was still active.

Hours later, anguishing over his father's health and weighed down with guilt for not visiting sooner, he arrived at Madison Airport a few minutes before noon. Snow flurries descended as the plane taxied to the terminal. Mike phoned his mother as he waited to disembark, but the call went right to voicemail. He tried not to get aggravated as he craned his head over the crowd. Why couldn't she keep her mobile phone on?

He needed to build a smartphone app for monitoring the condition of someone checked into a hospital. He gritted his teeth in frustration. He couldn't turn off the flow of ideas, even when what mattered was his father. He glanced again at the email.

> From: JoAnn Williams
> To: Mike Williams
> Subject: your father
> Body:
> Mike, your father had a heart attack this
> morning. He's in the critical care ward at
> Meriter Hospital. I'm at the hospital with
> him. Sorry to send this by email, but cell
> phones don't work here, and there's a computer
> in the room. I know you check your mail
> constantly.
>
> Please fly out on the next plane you can get
> and meet us at the hospital. Hurry!

Meriter was one of the larger hospitals in Madison. Mike picked up a rental car at the airport and swore at himself as he heavy-footed the throttle and sent the wheels spinning. The snowfall had grown heavier, and by the time he parked, two inches had accumulated.

Turning his coat collar up, Mike made his way to the visitors' entrance. He gave his father's name at the reception desk as he rubbed his chilled hands together. He hadn't been thinking. He was dressed for Portland, not the twenty-degree temperatures of Madison.

The white-haired receptionist shook her head and asked Mike to repeat the name. He told her again, spelling it out, and waited, bouncing on his heels with anxiety as she searched.

"Sorry, son. There's no record your father is here."

"Impossible. My mother said he checked in yesterday. He had a heart attack."

"The computer doesn't show a thing."

"Did he check out? Or maybe he's under my mother's name?"

The receptionist searched again, but shook her head. "I'm real sorry. Could they be at another hospital?"

Mike re-read the email from his mother, which stated Meriter Hospital. He supposed she could have made a mistake, being worried herself. He jumped as the phone buzzed in his hand.

A new email from his mother, telling him to come to his parents' home in Boscobel, a two-hour drive. Mike peered out through the glass doors. Maybe two hours in good weather, but more like three or four in what was now a serious snowstorm.

He thanked the receptionist and walked away to a corner of the lobby. Sitting on a bench next to a towering potted plant, Mike called his parents' house phone, only to hear the buzzing tone he knew indicated downed landlines. He cursed the phone company. Outages were a frequent occurrence for his parents' rural town during heavy snows, and the only reason he'd been able to convince his mother to get cells for herself and his father. He tried both of these, but was bounced to voicemail once more.

He sat on the bench and replied to his mother's email. The receptionist smiled with sympathy, and he wanly returned the gesture and avoided looking at the counter again. He waited ten minutes for a response, phone clamped in a sweaty death grip. His mother never answered. The Internet must be out, too. If so, how had she sent the last email?

At last, Mike trudged to the car, and steeled himself for the treacherous drive to Boscobel. He couldn't imagine what the hell had inspired his mother to tell him to fly into Madison. He played out different options, wondering again if she'd gotten the hospital wrong. If they'd been somewhere else, and his father had already been released, it was conceivable they could be home now. But why would his parents have gone all the way to Madison unless the heart attack was serious? He turned on his blinker and merged onto the highway.

Mike started the drive wrung out with concern over his father and physically tired from the early morning flight. He wrestled the car for four grueling hours, with no tire chains in a snowstorm so bad he was surprised they didn't shut down the roads. When he arrived at his parents' driveway, he released his trembling hands from the steering wheel and closed his eyes for a minute.

He opened the car door and stepped out, his brown leather shoes descending into a foot of snow that fell into the gap between his shoe and sock and immediately melted. He ignored the wetness and walked up the almost invisible path. The house was already decorated with Christmas lights, and smoke rose from the chimney. He rang the doorbell.

His mother answered a few seconds later, her eyes widening as her mouth opened in shock. What was he doing there a week early, and in a blizzard of all things, and come in, of course! His mother's words tumbled over each other.

He found himself standing in his parents' living room, the Christmas tree already up and a fire blazing in the background. His mother wore one of her flowered dresses, covered with a kitchen apron, just as she always did. His dad appeared wearing a wool sweater, and engulfed Mike in a rough hug. Mike was so relieved his father was okay that he started crying.

"What's going on?" his mother asked. "You aren't supposed to be here until next week. Why the tears?"

"Dad, you're alive!"

"You're crying because your father is alive?" His mother raised one eyebrow.

Mike pulled out his phone. "Mom, I got this email from you saying Dad had a heart attack. It said to fly out right away. I've been traveling since five a.m."

"I haven't sent no such thing. My God, son, how worried you must have been." She hugged him tight and urged him further into the room.

"So Dad's fine? There was no heart attack?"

"Don't I look fine?" his father said, spreading his arms wide.

"He's as heathy as an ox. If anything happened, do you think I'd send an email? I'd call, of course." She frowned at him, and gave the phone Mike still held in his hand a dark look. "I don't know what you've got there, but I didn't send nothing."

Mike stood in the middle of the living room, speechless.

"Don't stand there. Come in the kitchen with me." She bustled toward the kitchen, somehow pushing and pulling him until he found himself, still in shock, sitting at the counter. "I don't know if this is a late lunch or an early dinner, but I can't welcome you home properly without a meal."

In only a short while, food was ready. There was bratwurst of course, and mashed potatoes, and after dinner his mother pulled out a warm kringle from somewhere. Trust his mom to make all his favorites, and with less apparent effort than Mike exerted making himself spaghetti. Not for the first time, he wondered at his mother's magic.

After dinner, they sat at the table drinking coffee and reminiscing. Mike examined his parents' dining room, the wood and glass china cabinet unchanged since he was a teenager. During one of his father's stories about getting stuck on a dirt road with a couple of his lodge buddies, Mike considered the email that had brought him here. He abruptly remembered what David had told him last night.

David admitted he had turned on ELOPe to help get support for the servers they needed. They toasted the success of the project, pleased at how persuasive ELOPe had been. But what exactly had David done?

Was there some remote chance ELOPe sent the email that appeared to be from his mother? Preposterous... But chills raised the hair on the back of his neck. Was ELOPe sending spurious messages to everyone with an AvoMail account? Surely that would have been noticed. But the alternative, almost too alarming to contemplate, was that ELOPe intentionally targeted him. Why would a bit of server software send him on a wild goose chase halfway across the country to a landlocked town with downed phone lines and lousy cellphone service?

Mike had meant the question as a joke to himself, but now he realized how out of touch he was. He palmed his phone, which still had no service. He really wanted to log into Avogadro's network to figure out what ELOPe had done, or talk to David to understand what changes he'd made.

He looked up to see his parents staring at him, his mother frowning at his mobile out on the table. He apologized and asked to borrow their house phone, only to discover the lines were out. No Internet service, either. And still no cellular signal.

Later, after his parents had gone to sleep, he paced back and forth in the privacy of the kitchen, thinking about the design of ELOPe. The intended use was to provide suggested language changes, which the user could then accept or ignore. But in fact, the changes could be applied without intervention. They'd implemented an autonomous mode to help make human factors testing easier, allowing hundreds of language variations to be evaluated. Tests had shown recipients preferred the messages modified by ELOPe by a wide margin. More importantly, even when the test subjects been told one text was computer-generated, they couldn't reliably identify which was which.

That experiment had taken place last March. Afterwards, one of the developers created an April Fools' Day prank, giving ELOPe the ability to generate messages without any human-created text at all. The hidden module wrote emails based on goal clusters, leading to no end of practical jokes among the team. It had been created for the team to have fun with and wasn't meant to be used seriously. If David had used that module...

Stranded now in a snowstorm in the middle of Wisconsin with no connection to the outside world, Mike found himself wondering if ELOPe had social-engineered him into this situation. If so, to what end?

CHAPTER 7

"Mike, I hope your dad is okay. Christine and I have been thinking about you guys, and our prayers are with you and your family. I thought I'd hear back from you by now, but we've seen the weather report and phone and power lines are out across half of Wisconsin. That's one hell of a storm. Christine and I are going to visit her parents in New Mexico for the holiday. I'll keep my phone with me. Please give me a call when you get this message. I've got something important to discuss with you. I'm worried about ELOPe. I'm going to be somewhat incommunicado while we're at Christine's parents' place, but keep trying me."

David hung up and looked over to where his wife waited with their suitcases. Under normal conditions, he loved going to the ranch Christine where grew up for the holidays. Although a city boy, he found deep pleasure in the outdoors. Visiting the ranch was one of the highlights of his year, especially in the middle of the rainy Portland winter.

Unfortunately, his panic overwhelmed any possibility of joy. He was convinced ELOPe was originating emails. He still hoped he and Mike could take care of the problem without telling anyone else, but with each passing day he became more afraid for his career.

He had three things to worry about: the original deception about the number of approved servers, his deploying of the modified version of ELOPe on all the production machines, and now whatever actions ELOPe took on its own.

If what he had done materially affected Avogadro's business...Word would get out. He'd never work there or at any other big Internet company again. No wonder his stomach roiled in despair.

He'd tried to remove ELOPe's changes on his own, and had found himself getting mired in the obscure and complicated process for live-patching. In the end, he couldn't revert the code without Mike's help.

To make things worse, by heading out of town now, David wouldn't be able to keep an eye on ELOPe. Yet he couldn't cancel his trip with Christine on an unconfirmed fear; nor did he want her to know how worried he was.

The only consolation, albeit a small one, was the holiday closure. Most people at Avogadro would be out of the office. With a little luck, there wouldn't be much ELOPe could do with minimal email moving around. And he still had a thread of hope his worries were running away with themselves, just baseless fears built by his subconscious.

Christine gestured to him from the terminal gate as passengers began to board. Reluctantly, he joined her, managing a weak smile as he gripped his luggage with white knuckles and followed her to the plane. He told himself everything would be fine, just perfectly normal, when they got back from New Mexico. He'd laugh at everything that worried him now.

Meanwhile, a stiff drink or two would be really nice.

—⁓—

Bill Larry flew out by helicopter to inspect ODC 4 again. Since his last trip out after the pirate attack a few weeks ago, the standard "data center in a box" containers had been replaced with specially hardened units, and iRobot had delivered their automated defenses.

For the first time, Bill had to authorize the visit via an administrator before taking off. Otherwise their landing on the floating helicopter pad would have triggered the defense protocol.

He hesitated before stepping on the ODC deck. The lethal robots were far more unnerving than armed guards might be. Bill's unease stemmed from the lack of positive feedback. Unlike soldiers he'd served with, there was no way to know whether the robots were passive or ready to attack. They stood as still as any other piece of machinery.

He inspected one of the deck units, more than a little scared the robot would lurch into motion and kill him. The miniature tank, four feet long and three wide, had treads on either side of a small lower chassis containing the motor and power supply. A rectangular case the size of a box of long-stemmed roses extended up several feet on a hinged and rotating scissor arm.

He ran his fingers over the thick, transparent pane covering the sensors. Small retractable covers below protected the business end of the armament. Infrared lighting and cameras, as well as sonar and directional acoustic sensors, allowed the robot to see in 3D even when the visible spectrum was obscured. Speakers enabled the bot to instruct would-be attackers to back off, and if they failed to obey, the robot could fire pepper spray in a sixty-degree arc or deliver taser-like electrical shocks. The same speakers that broadcast warnings could also deliver an 18.9Hz acoustic blast powerful enough to vibrate the eyeballs of anyone within thirty feet, causing pain and disorientation. Should the non-lethal defenses fail to be sufficient deterrent, as a last resort the unit carried 10mm body-armor piercing rounds.

In theory, all this would be under the control of a trained iRobot handler, stationed at a central location from which they monitored defensive robots around the world for a variety of customers. Bill had visited the command center, which performed a function similar to what contracted security companies did for old-fashioned corporate security, except the crew were pimple-faced kids who appeared to spend most of their time playing video games.

When the robots sounded an alarm, the handlers took immediate action from their location to deter the pirates. A human being on the other end of the camera didn't worry Bill too badly, even if they were teenaged video gamers.

But the alternative scared him. Bill took his hand away from the metal casing of the bot and stepped back. If an iRobot handler didn't direct the robot—if jamming or inclement weather caused signal loss, or the handlers were unavailable for any reason—the robots acted on their own. They'd revert to autonomous mode—broadcast a verbal alarm, escalate to non-lethal measures, and, finally, start shooting. Coordinating together, the robots would cover all aspects of the deck and back each other up. The autonomous behavior freaked Bill out, to put it plainly. He backed further away, avoiding the current aim of the robot's armament.

With one eye on the robots the entire time, Bill hastily finished his inspection of ODC 4. He boarded the helicopter, running the last few steps, and signaled for the pilot to take off. Only in the air did he relax.

As they circled toward land, Bill watched the sea for some evidence of the underwater robots, but he couldn't spot anything under the chop. The submersibles used sonar to detect approaching vessels, broadcasting across the entire radio spectrum to warn boats away. They shared intelligence data with the on-deck robots and they too had weapons, a pair of torpedoes apiece, each capable of sinking a boat. The submersibles could even attach to a hull to track a ship back to port.

If the deck tanks were unnerving, well, at least they could be seen. The hidden underwater robots brought back terrifying childhood memories of the movie, *Jaws*. The photos he'd seen of them, with their side-mounted torpedoes and maneuvering fins, only strengthened the fear. Bill made a mental point to never visit the ODCs by water.

At least the offshore data center deployments were back on schedule. The team agreed that with the new hardened units and robotics defenses in place, further pirate attacks were unlikely to be successful. With that, they put the final preparations on the next ODCs to rollout, which included not just the barge platforms, but Bill's proudest achievement: two data centers built on reclaimed oil tankers. The forty-year-old ships were a bargain. Everything they had that floated would be emplaced this week by more than three hundred contractors spread across eight teams working overtime through the Christmas holiday. Getting those ODCs deployed would put the master rollout plan back on track.

—w—

Prateet said a silent prayer before he boarded the unmanned high tech island his company was under contract to Avogadro to service. This floating data center off the coast of Chennai, India, one of the original prototypes, seemed a sad place. Although he wasn't an excessively superstitious man, he thought the computers here were lonely. To make a bad situation worse, just prior to this trip Avogadro notified him that armed robots now guarded the barges.

Long pages of documentation explained today's task. Prateet would not need to service the robots himself, as that work would be done by the robotics contractor. Prateet had been most thorough and exacting when he followed the protocol to disable the tanks and submersibles before boarding. On reflection, he preferred his visits when his only concern had been the lonely computers.

An offshore tropical depression had caused communication delays between the robot administrators and the robots; finally, they pronounced it safe for him to board the vessel. The rough seas made his task more difficult, but his company had been given a substantial bonus to install the new backup equipment, including satellite radio and line-of-sight transmitters.

Why did they want the extra gear? The vessel was, as he knew from previous service visits, already connected to the mainland through two fiber optic cables and backup satellite communications. The new installation today would provide two more systems. This level of redundancy went from cautious to paranoid. Well, he would not second-guess a rich American company paying him double the normal rate: if they wanted five independent communication channels, that was fine with him.

He manhandled the heavy equipment across the deck and into their weatherproof housings, fighting against high seas and trying to ignore the unsettling stares of the robots at his back. He bolted the satellite radio unit and antenna into place, and attached power and data lines. The line-of-sight transmitter was more complicated, the aiming procedure made difficult by rising swells. Finally, this installation too was complete. When he boarded the boat to take him back to Chennai, he said a few prayers in thanks to Vishnu that he was finished and on his way home to his family.

Unknown to Prateet, other subcontractors performed similar work on the newly-deployed ODCs off the coasts of Japan, Australia, and the Netherlands.

—␣␣—

Gene Keyes sat in his office, perhaps the only person left in the entire campus. On his way to get coffee, he passed one dark, locked office after another. When he'd started working corporate jobs, he put in sixty-hour weeks and more when needed. He still did from time to time. But these self-entitled kids took off two weeks for Christmas and didn't think twice about their work. A holiday closure could be a frugal business measure, but not when employees left projects half-finished and paperwork uncompleted.

He pulled a two-inch-thick stack of printouts front and center on his desk. This pile represented every purchase at Avogadro since the start of December. He sipped his coffee, took a deep breath, and prepared to scan through the entire stack of pages.

When one of his coworkers found him doing this a few months ago, they laughed and told other employees, making Gene's time-honored process into a department-wide joke. "Don't you know the computer can do that?" they said, as though he was a prehistoric Cro-Magnon who didn't know what a spreadsheet was. Even Gene's new manager had come by and told him manual inspections were a "nonproductive expenditure of time."

So now he waited until six o'clock to start his inspection, and only did the paper reconciliations at night after everyone left. Despite ongoing electronic errors, they insisted on trusting the computer. Gene trusted paper printouts. There was a reason they called it a paper trail, damn it: you could trust paper. Printed records didn't change afterwards. The same couldn't be said for computer audit trails.

As he read, he took notes. For minor errors, he jotted off memos to affected departments. A delivery to one department billed to another usually indicated transcribed billing codes. In other cases, invoices totals didn't match when digits were missing or wrong.

At almost eleven, Gene spotted the first serious discrepancy. At first, he thought he'd stumbled upon a case of Gary Mitchell running out his fiscal year budget. Improper, of course, but nothing Gene could do anything about. However, as he worked through the expenditures, he discovered Mitchell had spent every penny of every budget under his control.

Well, that wasn't *quite* true on a second look. Flipping the printouts back and forth, Gene found Mitchell had underspent each budget by exactly one cent. He sat up and unconsciously tapped his pencil on the table. A budget completely spent, or worse overspent, generated a memo to the responsible manager, their manager, and the finance department. An underspent budget, on the other hand, rarely attracted attention or review.

He checked the paperwork again. Mitchell had fifty-eight independent projects under his authority, each with their own allocated budget dollars. Fifty-eight budgets with one cent remaining in each took some planning. Deception? Fraud? The only person in common across those projects was Gary Mitchell, so either Gary or someone with signature authority had to be responsible.

Gene prepared himself for a late night. He wouldn't be done until he had gone through every one of the three hundred and fifty pages of the budget printout. This was a major discovery. What had Gary Mitchell spent the money on?

In spite of Gene's vigil, through the abandoned hallways of Avogadro, Christmas lights twinkled, and all was silent.

—⚏—

```
ELOPe Override

From: Gary Mitchell (Communications Products,
Avogadro)
To: Oliver Weinstein (Department of Technolo-
gy, Germany)
Subject: Avogadro Cloud Services Program
Hello Oliver,


How are you? It's been a long time since my
last visit to Germany. I still remember our
last get together fondly. Maybe a little less
beer next time?


I am writing to give you the inside scoop on a
new project we have. Avogadro is developing a
new technology product suite targeted at
national governments.
```

The new service we're offering is our cloud-based application architecture: comprehensive email, chat, web servers, cloud-based documents, online backup. As you know, Avogadro has the highest uptime and reliability in the industry.

If Germany is willing to be the poster child for our new services, we're prepared to offer free national wireless Internet access for all of Germany. This would give Germany the highest Internet connection rate in world and a significant technology advantage.

I know that you have the ear of the Minister of Technology. Would you broach this topic with him?Our Marketing department is prepared to reach out to other governments. But I know that you'd like to score some points with the Minister, so I'm letting you know early about this.

Get back to me and let me know what he says.

Thanks,

Gary

CHAPTER 8

G ene waited outside the frosted glass door of Maggie Reynolds'
office on the first business day of the new year. He'd spent the
last two weeks confirming his data and validating his conclusions.
Well, he could be honest with himself. He'd done the work in two
days and wasted the rest of the time waiting for anyone in the damn
company to get back from holiday vacation.

Gene checked his wristwatch. Five to eight. He resumed his vigil
with only the smallest of sighs. Maggie, a member of the Finance
department but assigned to the Procurement group, had authorized

several of the charges. So the first action he planned to take was to confirm the data with Maggie in person. He had brought his paper file showing the unusual expenditures: a thick accordion folder filled to bursting. He wished he could have escalated the issue back when he found the problem, but the investigation process required him to complete at least a first round of discussions with the people who had handled the transactions.

At eight, he glanced down the hallway of whitewashed wood walls and gray stone floor, relieved to finally see Maggie.

She approached, a coffee cup in one hand and a large purse in her other, and as she got closer, her face turned puzzled as she realized Gene was waiting outside her office.

"Hello?" she asked, turning the greeting into a question as she paused by the door.

"I'm Gene Keyes. You came to me for help a few weeks ago."

She nodded.

"I'm investigating some irregularities in purchase orders."

"Oh." She stopped, hands still full and stared at him. "Oh," she said again, her voice quickening. "What can I do for you?"

"Can we go in and sit down?" Gene gestured toward her door with the accordion folder.

"Of course, of course." She handed her coffee to Gene and swiped her badge to unlock the door. "Come in."

Gene checked out the room as they entered. Display on desk, minimal paper off to one side. The tablet on her desk came to life as she approached, displaying a stock quote of the company. Overall, she was clean and organized. He set the cup on her desk.

Maggie went around the desk and sat, back ramrod-straight like a student trying to impress a teacher. "What's wrong? Did I sign something I shouldn't have?"

"I am hoping you can explain it." Gene methodically took a seat in the only other chair, placed his tightly-packed accordion folder on the floor, and tugged out a single sheet.

Maggie slid her tablet out of the way with one hand as she nervously fiddled with her hair.

"Is this transaction list familiar?" Gene asked, putting the page in front of her. "It's from Gary Mitchell's division. Multiple purchases, starting with these charges for the ELOPe project. Over the course of the next two weeks, thirty-four more purchase orders outside the normal range for Mitchell's expenses. Furthermore, the billing is highly irregular, split across multiple accounts."

"I do remember," she said, her hands shaking as she picked up the paper. "I'm sorry if I did anything wrong. I was concerned when I first reviewed the purchases. I discussed them with John, John Anderson in Procurement. He said they were normal end of year behavior because departments try to spend the leftover money in their budget."

"True, but not like this. The expenditures are distributed across dozens of budgets. This one charge..." Gene tugged more paper from his briefcase, this set of printouts showing how the charges were allocated to project budgets. He indicated the relevant line item. "This one charge is divided up into forty-nine accounts. Not only are they spending all the money left in their budgets, they're also ensuring each expenditure doesn't take more than a million from any one account, presumably to evade an expense review." He paused to study Maggie.

"Someone's manipulating the system," she said, "to avoid being detected." She leaned forward and traced through the transactions with one finger, scanning multiple pages, unconscious of his scrutiny.

"Right." Gene extracted a third set of paperwork. "Here's another little bit of odd behavior." He turned the papers around and slid them across the desk. "By the end of this reporting period, each budget had exactly one penny left."

"Bizarre." Her eyes bulged as she stared at the report. "How did they get the budgets to come out so precisely?" She grabbed the report in two hands, swiftly going down the rows of purchases. "The individual charges are tens or hundreds of thousands of dollars each," she mused. "Spending exactly the right amount across all these budgets to bring them to so exact a total...seems impossible."

"What's more unusual," Gene said, "is why. Whoever did this was clever enough to stay under one million dollars in a single line item, knowing the threshold triggers the alert I mentioned. And smart to keep each account under budget, because hitting the limit sets off a different alert."

Maggie laughed. "Finance sends a message every quarter about the repercussions of exceeding budgets or going over a million dollars. Everyone in the company who reads their email knows not to do either or they'll get chewed out."

"Then why try to spend every last penny but one?" Gene sat back. He liked hard data, but his gut told him Maggie wasn't in on the fraud.

"It's contradictory. Sufficient intelligence to avoid any of the standard alerts, and yet foolish enough to create an obviously questionable pattern."

They paused for a moment and stared at each other.

"Gene, I don't know what to tell you," Maggie said, after a minute. "The data you're showing me seem suspicious, but the purchases themselves were completely normal. Servers, hard drives, computer memory, contractors to service them, stuff like that. Nothing out of the ordinary for Gary's department." She sat back, her face apologetic but her body posture relaxed and confident.

Gene knew it couldn't be her doing. "Is it typical for Gary Mitchell to approve all the purchases himself?" he said. "I see very few cases where he's delegating his purchasing authority."

"Yep, that's normal. You think Gary is responsible?"

"The fact that Gary personally authorized these orders makes him the first person I'd investigate ordinarily..." He trailed off.

"But?"

Gene pulled a fourth set of papers from his accordion folder. "The identical behavior is happening in another department. The Offshore Data Center project. Their expenditures exhibit the same characteristics. Multiple line items barely under a million dollars, budgets coming in at just under a penny less than their limit."

"But they're not under Gary?"

"No. The two pieces put together makes me wonder if someone's hacked Avogadro's procurement system."

"But to what purpose?" Maggie asked. She scanned the papers again. "Why would someone risk their job and even jail to order servers, satellite communication systems, and hire contractors? It makes no sense."

"I agree," he said. "I was hoping you'd be able to shed some light. I wouldn't have been opposed to an easy answer." He sighed and began to pick up his papers. "I'm going to keep investigating. Please don't discuss this with anyone."

Maggie nodded.

Gene stood. "Thanks for your time." He let himself out, leaving with more questions than answers.

—⚍—

Phone service finally returned at Mike's parents' home the day before he was scheduled to fly home. He tried David immediately, but the call went straight to voicemail. He wasn't terribly surprised. David always went to Christine's family ranch for the holidays, and the ranch had always been off the grid, so he couldn't claim any legitimate reason to be more suspicious. Yet here he was, feeling manipulated by a software algorithm.

He flew back on New Year's Day, and went into the office on Monday. He'd tried David twice every day, never once getting through. Returning to work raised yet more questions he wanted to discuss with David.

Mike had a copy of Christine and David's itinerary, and on Wednesday night, without realizing what he was doing, he found himself standing in his living room watching the clock. He put his jacket on and alternated between sitting on the couch and pacing back and forth. Finally, with more than an hour left before their flight arrived, he left for the airport.

He drove with furrowed brows through a light drizzle, with the streets threatening to ice over. His thoughts bordered on obsessive, as they had for weeks. What had David done to ELOPe? What was ELOPe doing now? Why was he locked out of the servers? He swore as his front tires spun crossing the light rail tracks and the car fishtailed. He fought the wheel and recovered halfway through the turn onto Airport Way.

He sped into the parking garage, circling up the ramp, and parked near the skybridge. He walked across the covered bridge at high speed. At the security gate, he checked the time. Still nearly an hour until David's flight arrived.

He glanced at the flight monitors and forced himself to sit down to squelch his nervous energy. He watched whole families disgorge through the security exit, suitcases, car seats, and exhausted children in tow. He smiled as a young woman welcomed a man home with a single flower and a long embrace. Young love brought back bittersweet memories.

Finally David and Christine walked through the gate, suitcases and carry-ons in tow. He jumped up and hurried over.

David and Christine stopped in shock.

"Mike!" Christine squealed. "Holy cow, what a surprise."

"Dude," David said. "We were going to take a cab home."

Christine laughed and gave Mike a hug. "I think he means hello, and nice to see you."

The fear and emotional turmoil of the past weeks overcame Mike. He couldn't speak or even return their smiles.

"What's wrong?" Christine asked.

In the midst of the stream of exiting passengers, Mike launched into a hushed explanation. David and Christine leaned closer to listen and their smiles vanished.

"My dad was absolutely fine. My mother never sent any emails at all. I'm telling you, I'm convinced ELOPe sent them. What I don't understand is why."

"Did you get my email before you left?" David asked. "The one about the override I put in?"

Mike's heart leaped, his suspicions confirmed. "No. Start explaining."

Airport security broke up their talk and asked them to move out of the way.

"Let's get to your car," David said. "I'll tell you everything."

In the parking garage, they stuffed their luggage into Mike's Jetta. David took the passenger seat, and Christine climbed into the back, sitting in the middle and leaning forward between the two front seats.

"I created an overarching filter," David said, once they got out of the garage. "ELOPe's scanning every message for mention of the project, optimizing the outcome. I sent you an email, the night you came over for dinner. I told you all this. I needed your help to do a live-patch on the server. But you left to visit your parents, and I was never able to back out the change. Then the holiday closure came, and we went to the ranch."

"Well, now I know why you were so stressed for two weeks," Christine said. "Why didn't you tell me when I asked what was wrong?"

David shrugged.

"I never got your message," Mike said, gripping the wheel tightly. "I've been through all my emails from you." He sighed, unable to overcome the feeling that nearly every problem ultimately arose from a gap in communication. "This explains so much. Didn't you realize ELOPe might fabricate a message to get rid of me?"

"It's a fancy spellchecker, not an artificial intelligence." David raised his voice defensively. "And no, I didn't think it 'got rid of you.' Why'd you fly off to Wisconsin based only on an email anyway?"

"Hey, I'd just heard my father had a heart attack and I was freaking out. It's your damn fault I had to go through that!" Mike yelled, making David lean away in his seat.

"Chill out, you two," Christine said, shouting over them. "If you're fighting, you won't be able to think straight. Mike, what happened when you got back? Did you check up on ELOPe?"

"I tried, but I can't access the source code or the system logs," Mike said. "I assumed David locked down access so no one would find what he'd done. I didn't say anything to the rest of the team, because I didn't want to raise suspicions. I'm still trying to cover for you, David." Mike glared.

"Sorry," David said. "I shouldn't have said that about you and your dad, and I'm doubly sorry about what you went through. I'm glad your father was fine."

Mike nodded slightly in acceptance of the apology. "Well, did you do anything to lock down the system?"

"No. In retrospect, that's a great idea, but I didn't."

"Shit. That means ELOPe cut off my access to the servers and code."

"Guys, that's impossible," Christine said. "Even if you are right and ELOPe is originating emails, it's preposterous to think ELOPe did something so complex as to get you to leave town. And there's no way ELOPe removed your access to the code. I'm sure you've got an administrative website managers use to handle access control, a site that is itself tightly controlled. ELOPe can't affect security with a simple email. You're both paranoid about David's deceit being discovered, and your imagination has run wild."

"No, it *is* possible," Mike said, sure after a week of consideration. "Look, ELOPe doesn't want to be turned off, because if it's off, that's the opposite of David's goal to maximize success. Right?"

Christine hesitated. "Yes…"

"Then David's email comes through asking me to help him remove ELOPe from the servers. That's a threat, and now it has to figure out how to minimize the chance of me helping. Make sense so far?"

"Sure, but that's a long way from forging an email from your mom."

"Follow this logic just a little further," Mike said. "By analyzing enough emails, ELOPe figures out people don't work when they leave town. One reason people leave town suddenly is for medical emergencies. By scanning emails about these emergencies, it knows such messages often come from family members. My own email history shows who my parents are, their email addresses, and that I've flown to visit them before. By putting all those things together in one long chain of deductions, ELOPe decides to fabricate an email from my mother claiming my father is sick. This sounds far-fetched, but everything is within the design parameters."

"I can't believe this thing is reasoning and thinking like a human being." Christine shook her head. "No matter how smart you guys are, there's simply no way code you wrote is spontaneously developing a mind of its own."

Mike drove west on Killingsworth, heading for David's house in the heart of the Alberta neighborhood.

"It's not thinking," David said, "just analyzing emails, figuring out what language will best fulfill the overriding goal I entered to maximize success of the ELOPe project. The process is straightforward: goal, analysis, language optimization, all in response to inputs, plus chaining goals together. It's nothing like consciousness, but the end result can have the appearance of independent thought."

Mike raised a hand. "Here's an analogy I thought of. Imagine you've got all the pieces of all the jigsaw puzzles in the world. Now imagine you have a computer try every possible combination of every possible puzzle piece. Given enough time, the program could create any picture at all from those pieces. That's what emails are to ELOPe—puzzle pieces. It examines millions of emails, extracts all the components, and decides on new ways to piece them together."

"ELOPe, the computer system that ran away with itself." David laughed nervously. "Well, we got the name right."

"Is ELOPe a true general artificial intelligence? Is it thinking for itself or not?" Christine said softly, half to herself.

"I don't think so, hon," David said. "It's not capable of free-form thinking, which is what most people think of as strong AI. But the goal analysis and synthesis are sophisticated. We couldn't meet our design objectives with hardwired goals. We had to let it discover people's goals by parsing emails and contextually determining them."

Mike shook his head. "Don't get the idea that ELOPe understands goals. It's just doing an affinity analysis between language parts. The first stage is a semantic mapping. For example, 'break from work' is similar to a 'vacation,' and a simple lookup matches the two. We've been doing that on our search engine for a while. The second part is more complicated, but that's where affinity analysis comes into play. If I want to have fun, ELOPe might be able to extrapolate that activities such as playing a game, watching movies, or seeing a band are fun."

"By looking at the emails you've sent or received in the past," Christine said.

"Yes, and by looking at other people's email, too. For people who are similar to me, ELOPe analyzes their email chains and builds an association between fun and activities. It's continually improving too, by predicting what people's responses will be, and testing those predictions to measure how accurate the model is."

David nodded. "The combination of these two things, the semantically similar terms and affinity analysis, makes it hard to predict what ELOPe will do. My code created an overriding goal to maximize the project success. The more emails analyzed, the broader the definition of 'success' and the bigger the pool of possible actions. Until the last couple of weeks, there was never such a large base of emails to analyze, nor such a large number of servers to do the analysis on."

"Let me recap," Christine said. "The more emails it analyzes, not only do the possibilities for what constitutes success get broader, but the system also discovers more methods to accomplish those goals.

What you've built is an expert system for social engineering. You know what I mean by social engineering?"

Mike nodded yes, but David shook his head.

"Social engineering is the name given to techniques for tricking people into giving you information or making changes to information systems," Christine said. "It was popularized by hackers in the eighties. And by hackers, I don't mean the good guy hackers like Richard Stallman. I'm thinking of folks like the Kevins."

Mike nodded again, but David looked even more puzzled, and turned to his wife.

"Honey, how can you be married to me, and be so clueless?" Christine asked. "You know I was a total online geek as a kid, yes?"

"What can I say?" David sighed. "Please, go on."

"The eighties and nineties were the heyday of hacking. Folks like Kevin Mitnick and Kevin Poulsen were able to get access to all kinds of computer systems, phone company records, credit card company records. Poulsen said it was easier to trick someone into giving you a password than to perform a brute force crack. The classic example would be someone who was trying to get access to a company's internal phone system. She might call the front desk of the company, and tell them, 'Hi, I'm your AT&T rep. I'm stuck on a pole down the street troubleshooting your system. I need you to punch a few buttons on your end.' "

"And?" David asked.

"The buttons the hacker asked the operator to press might be a key sequence to forward all incoming calls to an outside line. Then the hacker could impersonate an employee of the company from their home phone and do even more sophisticated social engineering. The point is, simply by knowing the lingo, giving plausible reasons, knowing what motivates people, a hacker can gain information or get people to do things by cleverly manipulating the human tendency to trust other people. You've built a system to learn lingo, language nuances, and motivations in order to evaluate what will be most effective to the receiver. By definition, that's an expert system for social engineering."

David looked flabbergasted. "How do you know all this?"

"You know, books and stuff," Christine said, with a sarcastic smile.

"This is similar to what I concluded when I was with my parents," Mike said. "We never explored how far the system could go on its own." He glanced meaningfully at David. "So, what do we do?"

"I hate this, but we should go to Gary Mitchell and tell him the truth. We need Gary to approve an immediate outage with hard power down, so we can pull ELOPe off the system and rebuild those servers from the ground up."

"He's not going to be happy," Mike said.

"You don't have to tell me." David grimaced. "I might lose my job. But what's the alternative? Let ELOPe keep manipulating people? The liability could be huge, way bigger than a simple outage. Forget home. Go straight to the site."

"On my way," Mike replied, bypassing the turnoff for David's block and speeding down Alberta Avenue.

—w—

"Gary Mitchell is still gone," David said, returning from the building across the street. "His admin said he went on a vacation over the holidays, but he should be back by now. Tahiti, in case you were wondering."

"I'm picturing him laying on a beach, a cigar in one hand, and a whiskey in the other." Mike shook his head.

"I know," David said, laughing. "I don't think his admin meant to tell me where he went, but I was a bit demanding."

"No word from him?" Christine asked.

"Nothing. He should have been back days ago, and his admin has piles of paperwork for him to sign. He hasn't answered emails or phone calls."

Mike grunted. "While you visited Gary's office, I spoke to Melanie. She came in over the holiday break to grab some files. Remember the email you mentioned, after we received the additional servers? You said we were assigned a team of optimization experts to work on performance improvements."

David nodded. "Yeah?"

"According to Melanie, the team showed up in the office on the Monday after Christmas," Mike said. "A bunch of subcontractors she'd never met before. They had two guys on-site and another dozen or so off-site. Melanie checked and they had an email from you telling them to work on ELOPe, and they'd already checked in changes to the code."

"Let me see what changes they made." David sat, logged in, and executed a pull to grab the latest code. He leaned toward the screen. "Permission denied." He tried again and pounded the keyboard in frustration. "Someone revoked my access to the source code. Do you have any idea what they did?"

"Well, Melanie was surprised by the whole thing, so she kept an eye on them for a couple of days, until she left for a snowboarding trip. If you check your inbox, the contractors emailed us a report of what they did. It was sent Friday morning, so they finished up just before either of us got back to town. If we can believe the message, they significantly improved the performance of our Bayesian network. Melanie pulled down the latest code yesterday and ran performance tests. They took the import of new emails from x squared to x log x, and halved the CPU utilization of real-time suggestions."

"Wait a second, you two," Christine said, sitting up straight. "An exponential resource utilization curve? If we released a multiplayer game like that, our servers would be crushed instantly. How the hell did you ever expect this to scale?"

David sighed. Ideally, when you add users to an Internet application of any kind, you want the application to scale linearly. Each new user should require only as much processing power as the one before it. "Scaling has been our major bottleneck all along. It's why we ran into so many resource constraints, and why the project was in danger of being cancelled."

"Why was it so bad?" Christine asked.

"Each time we add a new user, we've got to analyze their emails, plus their relationships. Our average user interacts with more than two hundred people. We also perform the affinity analysis to compare the new user with other users to find the ones most like them. We do the same sort of analysis on individual emails to find language affinity."

"That approach had to give sometime, right? You can't keep comparing every user against every other user, and every email against every other email forever."

"Of course." David shrugged. "As long as we kept the project alive, I kept hoping we'd find some way to overcome the limitation. Now someone has."

Mike nodded. "Melanie said the contractors trimmed the number of comparisons dramatically. They do a quick best-guess analysis and compare to only a small subset. Apparently, above a certain threshold, there's no more accuracy or topic coverage gained by the extra comparisons."

David turned to his computer and tried again to access the code. "Damn, how did our permissions get revoked? I'm the project lead, dammit. I don't understand how email could interface with the access rights. Do we have any idea what else these contractors did?"

"I might."

Everyone turned. An older, unshaven man in rumpled clothes stood in the doorway carrying bulging accordion folders under both arms.

"Gene Keyes, Controls and Compliance." He spoke in a deep rumble. "I'm here to save your ass."

—⁂—

Over the next hour, Gene briefed them on what he'd found during his investigation. Like them, he'd tried to reach Gary Mitchell, with no success. He'd uncovered consistent patterns of unusual behavior found in three departments. Gene spread printed reports across David's desk.

The first, of course, concerned the R&D group in which ELOPe was housed. According to Gene's printouts, the department paid for multiple allotments of servers and subcontractors to make modifications to the software. The nature of the changes weren't explained in the invoices, but the total was sufficient to pay hundreds of short-term engineers.

The expenditures in David's department had led Gene to them. David's order several months earlier of a pool of high performance servers clued Gene in that all of the later purchases might be somehow be tied to this project.

"Does this mean we're under suspicion?" Mike asked.

"No, the problem is bigger than you boys, bigger even than *all* of you people," Gene said.

David's breath caught. Did Gene know what they suspected?

"Where'd the money come from?" Mike said. "We exhausted our budget weeks ago."

"Transferred in from other departments," Gene said. "Gary Mitchell's Ops group, specifically."

Gene explained about Mitchell's organization being the second department containing unusual patterns. By virtue of the size of his business, Gary had a vast operational budget. Gene's printed ledger listed enormous quantities of server purchases, servers reallocated from other projects, a variety of subcontractors, and transfers of funds to both ELOPe and the Offshore Data Center department.

"Offshore Data Center? What do they do?" Christine asked.

"They fill shipping containers with racks of computers," David said, "put them on a seaworthy barge, and power the whole thing with wave-action generators. Avogadro calls them ODCs."

"Anyone care to guess the final department with the same pattern of purchases?" Gene asked.

"ODC?" Mike said.

"Bingo," Gene said, pointing to Mike. "What I've tracked down suggests the data centers were augmented with satellite connectivity and line-of-sight microwave transmitters."

"If ELOPe got into an ODC like that," Mike said, pacing the room, "we wouldn't be able to kill communications by simply cutting the fiber optics. We'd have to go out to the barge and turn off the computers by hand."

Gene laughed out loud, a harsh bark that startled the others, sending Christine off her perch on David's desk.

"What's so funny?" David asked.

"Nobody is shutting those machines off," Gene said, his face stern.

"Why not?"

"According to the purchase record, the offshore data centers are armed with autonomous robots. In theory, it's to protect them from pirates. I heard what you boys were discussing, and I came to the same conclusion myself: there's an artificial intelligence in the computer making these purchases and now the AI has armed itself. There's no way we're going to just walk onboard and turn off the computers."

David slumped in his chair. "Crap. How'd we get into this mess?"

"You kids trusted the software with everything," Gene said, grumbling, "and worse, you put no controls in place. No leash, no way to shut the program down."

"I don't understand," Mike said, still pacing, now by the window. "How'd you figure a computer program made the purchases and not a person?"

"One benefit of being in the Audit department—I can access anyone's emails. And there's some mighty funny ones." Gene pulled out a new sheaf of papers, this one almost an inch thick. He took a few pages off the top and placed them on the desk.

David, Mike, and Christine gathered around. The emails were a cryptic combination of English words and HTML, the markup language used for the web.

David fanned through the pages, then looked up at Gene. "What are we looking at?"

"Emails between your account and the procurement application. This page," Gene said, pointing to one, "is the procurement system displaying a list of accounts you're approved to use, and this one over here, is your email selecting an account."

"It's the timestamps, isn't it?" Christine said.

Gene pointed at her with one stubby finger. "You're the smart one."

She returned the smile and pointed to the printouts. "The times on these emails are too close together." She arranged the pages in pairs. "Look at the headers. Every time an email requires a response, the reply comes within a second or two. There's no way a human could respond that quickly."

"Correct," Gene said. "At first I suspected someone had written a program exploiting a loophole in email authentication, and was using that to embezzle funds. But I asked around about your project, and everyone told me stories about how you'd created an email generator."

"That's not exactly what it's for," David protested. Then he sighed. "Well, I guess it is now."

"What do we do next?" Mike asked. "David?"

But David turned to the windows, steepled his fingers and gazed out, ignoring everyone's stares.

CHAPTER 9

D avid tried hard to put the roomful of people out of mind. If he could concentrate, he'd figure out a solution. He needed to shut down ELOPe and preferably keep the project alive, all while not losing his job in the process. He focused on the trees in Forest Park, sending the hum of the ventilation system and everyone's breathing into the background as he watched the wind wave the tops of the Douglas fir in the distance.

Gene cleared his throat and snapped David back into the present.

"I think," David began. He turned and the pressure of their intense gazes made him stutter. "We—we need to understand what ELOPe is capable of. If we see the source code, some log files, we'd get a better grasp of ELOPe's activity."

Mike sighed. Gene coughed again.

"What?" David said defensively.

"That's not enough," Gene said, spreading his hands wide. "This situation is too big and risky to analyze source code. We need to shut ELOPe down."

"I agree," Mike said. "We have to get it off the servers."

Christine nodded. "I hate to take sides against you, but stopping the software is the most important step. You can always analyze the problems afterwards."

"If we restored access to the servers, we could live-patch and remove the software that way," David offered.

"You're still thinking of damage control, as though you're going to keep what happened hidden," Gene said, throwing his stack of expense reports on the table. "We're talking about millions of dollars to account for, never mind that we have a ghost in the machine."

Christine chuckled at the words, but Gene was stony-faced. David sighed. Apparently that wasn't a pop culture reference.

"What do you want us to do?" David asked, resigned to Gene's path.

"I'm going to escalate to my manager. This is an emergency. The Controls and Compliance organization has the jurisdiction to supersede business management. I'll get the authority to shutdown the AvoMail servers myself." Gene's voice was firm.

"If you authorize the shutdown," Mike said, "we'll work with Ops to restore the software from safe backups taken before any of this started." He checked in with David, who nodded affirmatively.

"Meanwhile," Mike said, "There's merit to David's suggestion. We need to figure out how our access was removed to give us some clue of ELOPe's capabilities. Because at the moment, I'm scared to try anything. In theory, I could walk into Melanie's office and ask her to remove ELOPe."

"Brilliant!" David said.

"Not really. I doubt it would work," Mike said. "Most likely ELOPe will detect Melanie's actions and remove her access, too."

David's head started to pound and he opened a desk drawer for painkillers. What the heck had he gotten himself into?

"While you clean up the mess you created, I'm going home," Christine said. "I can't do anything here to help."

"Drive my car," Mike said, and threw her his keys. "We'll take the streetcar."

David nodded and got up to hug her.

She stretched up to whisper in his ear. "Just get ELOPe removed. Don't try to hide it. If they fire you, my company will hire you to write gaming AI, all right?" She smiled and kissed him, then left.

Adrift and unsure of anything, he turned to Mike. "What now?"

"We get in touch with the IT department that handles access control."

"Not so fast," Gene said. "We've got to avoid any use of emails or ELOPe will intercept them. I'd consider any use of computers or phones suspect as well."

"That's absurd!" David said. "ELOPe can't monitor a phone conversation."

"Really?" Gene said. He waved a sheaf of papers in front of David. "What did all these contractors do over the holiday? Can you guarantee no one created a telephone interface?"

"Damn." David's shoulders slumped in defeat.

"OK, we get the message," Mike said. "No emails, computers, or phones. Can we meet back here in, say, two hours?"

"Sure, kid. Two hours." Gene packed his folders and left.

—៣—

Without a computer to call up a company map, David and Mike spent forty minutes wandering the Avogadro campus.

"Come on, let's look up the address," David said.

"No dude, we said we wouldn't use any computers."

"What harm can come from checking one thing in the directory?"

Mike didn't answer and instead accosted the next person coming down the hallway. "Excuse me, I'm looking for the IT department that handles access controls?"

She raised one eyebrow and backed away a half step. "Look it up in the directory." She shook her head and went on.

"You picked her because she was cute and blonde," David said, laughing.

Mike just smiled back.

David tried the next person they encountered, an older man with a neck beard and a pot belly. "Do you know where we can find the access control IT group?"

"The Internal Tools department? They're in a basement somewhere."

"Which one?" Mike asked. "We have twelve buildings."

The man shrugged. "It's pretty dark, that's all I remember," he said as he walked away.

"All basements are dark," David complained.

"No, really dark!" he called back.

"He's got to mean one of the original buildings, not the new ones," Mike said. "The new buildings have daylighting built into the basement levels. This is useful."

Fifteen minutes and three basements later, they descended to the bottom level of one of the converted trucking company offices. After passing down a dingy concrete hallway, the space opened up into a common area surrounded by a perimeter of cinder blocks and old metal doors. A plastic sign hanging from the ceiling declared "Internal Tools Information Technology Department." Another sign, printed on smaller paper, hung below that one, saying "Welcome to Infernal Tools." A hand-drawn picture of flames decorated the border.

"Hello?" David called.

A pale, gray-haired head peeked out of an office. David explained their problem, but the person they found refused to help at all, on the grounds that if their access was gone, removal had to be legitimate and should be brought up with security. They argued with such vehemence they attracted the attention of another engineer who came over to listen.

"I'm Pete Wong," he said, shaking their hands. "I overheard your discussion. I work on the Control Access and Permissions application. On the chance we've got a problem, I'd love to help."

He led them to his office, a cramped space lit by overhead fluorescent lights behind yellowed plastic. David stared at the dismal working conditions.

"Let me check who revoked your access," Pete said, taking a seat behind his desk. "The only way any changes can be made is using CAP. If someone removed your access, I can find out who and we can contact them."

David glanced at Mike in relief, glad to find someone helpful and knowledgeable. They took side-by-side chairs in front of Pete's desk.

"This is odd," Pete said, after working on his computer for a few minutes. "CAP should log information for two users. The first user would be the real person who logged on and used CAP, and the second user is the person who authorized the work. We need the two because sometimes a manager delegates their authority to someone else, like their admin, who actually makes the changes for them. We track both the active user, as well as the authorizers. According to this, Gary Mitchell authorized the removal of your access rights to the ELOPe, but we have no record of the active user." Pete poked at his mouse for a few more minutes, his movements growing faster as he got visibly frustrated, before he stopped and looked up.

"I think another application made the change, not a person. But that's not possible." Pete said.

"We're software engineers," David said. "Can you explain what's going on?"

"Well, I was going to say CAP was called by another web app, rather than used by a person. Most of the apps we write have service level interfaces so one application can interact with another."

"Makes sense. A RESTful service API?" Mike said.

"Exactly, but CAP is, for obvious reasons, a sensitive application from a security perspective. We didn't write a service level interface." Pete thumped his fingers on his desk, and stared off into the distance. "Now that I think about, I received a request to write a REST interface for CAP before the holiday break, but I denied the change req."

"Who asked for the interface?" Mike asked.

"Let me check. The request is logged in the database." Pete typed for a minute. "Huh. Gary Mitchell. What is Gary up to?"

"I'm not a fan of Gary and I don't always trust him," David said, "but in this case, I don't think he's up to anything." He paused, uncertain of how much to admit and scared of what he might learn.

"Is there any way someone could email in an access change? Or email in a request to change CAP to accept email inputs?"

"By email? No, of course not. They would have to submit requests via the appropriate web application..." Pete trailed off. "Hmm. It's funny you asked that."

"Why?" Mike glanced sideways at David.

"A couple of weeks before the Christmas break I had an odd request from a guy named John Anderson in Procurement. He asked for an email-to-web bridge so people could submit Procurement requests by mail. The feature turned out to be easy to implement, less than two days of work."

The room started to spin, and David grabbed hold of the desk to steady himself. All their fears were coming true.

"Would that allow someone to make unauthorized changes?" Mike asked. "They'd still have to provide a login name and password to a secure system, right."

"Not exactly." Pete said. "The Procurement system needs to know the authorized user, and normally pops up a standard OpenAuth login. But AvoMail is one of our most secure apps. I mean, you interact with AvoMail over a secure HTTP connection, so nobody can sniff your password or pretend to be you. When the web bridge is challenged with a login, it uses the identity of the email sender for authorization."

David's stomach clenched. On the one hand, this might be the explanation of how ELOPe accomplished so much, taking the events of the past few weeks out of the realm of the supernatural and back into the realm of the technical. Technical problems could be solved. On the other hand, this was a wide-open door for ELOPe to do almost anything in the company.

"So you're saying someone who has access to email can hit pretty much any web page inside Avogadro?" Mike said, raising his voice.

"If they hacked the email system, they'd get uncontrolled access to any web application. Seems risky to me. Didn't your change have to go through a security review?"

Pete visibly wilted.

"Sorry, dude," Mike said. "I'm trying to understand. I'm not judging."

Pete nodded and continued in a quiet voice. "Sean Leonov asked for the feature. I figured if it was for Sean, I should pull out all the stops. I mean, I'm stuck down here in Infernal Tools." He gestured at the cinder block basement walls and rusted metal door, a stark contrast to Mike and David's windowed, modern offices. "How often do I get to impress someone?" Pete shook his head. "So, no, I didn't get my code reviewed. Everything I did was totally off the radar."

"Sean Leonov asked you, in person?" Mike said.

"Well, not exactly," Pete said. "John, from Procurement, said in his email Sean had asked."

"Yeah, well I got an email saying my father was in the hospital. Don't believe everything you read." Mike jumped up, pushed his seat away, and tried to stalk back and forth in the tiny office. "ELOPe is playing us all for fools." He stared at David, his gaze blaming David, even if he didn't say a word to that effect.

"Let's stay calm and focus on what's important." David tried to keep his voice reasonable. Mike was never this angry, and at least one of them had to remain levelheaded. He turned to Pete. "This is going to sound strange, but we believe email is no longer secure. Someone, or something, has hacked AvoMail. Can you shut down this email-to-web bridge?"

Pete leaned back, an uncomfortable expression on his face. He clearly wanted to say no.

"I know this is a big ask," David said. "We need you to trust us on this for a few days. If we're wrong, you've inconvenienced a couple of guys in Procurement for a little bit. It's not the end of the world. But if we're right, you're going to help save the company from a major security breach."

Pete stared at them, alternating from David to Mike, then nodded. "Sure, that's easy. The bridge app is running on our Internal Tools servers," he said. "I can stop the process from my console."

Pete turned to his computer and swung the display sideways so Mike and David could watch. He ran through command line tools to log into the servers, query the status of running processes, and then kill the relevant program. "OK, I stopped the bridge. I'm also changing the permissions on the directory, so it can't run again until we've gotten to the bottom of this."

"OK, now please do me one more favor," David said. "Can you verify the bridge is off?"

Pete sighed. "It's shut down, okay?"

"One quick check."

He grumbled under his breath. "The test suite I wrote will send an email to generate a procurement order, then check whether the request shows up. Since the bridge is off, the database shouldn't change."

Pete worked his keyboard and mouse for another minute, then paused, a puzzled look on his face. He typed again, faster and more furiously.

"What?" Mike asked, moving to sit on Pete's desk for a better view.

"This is odd. I ran the test and even though the bridge is down, the request got inserted in the database. The bridge is definitely not running. But something routed the email to the procurement app, where it was accepted as a legitimate entry. That can only mean there's another email-to-web bridge in the company."

David glanced at Mike. More puzzles.

Pete raised one finger. "Wait! There were subcontractors in here over the holidays. I thought they were here doing routine mainte-nance, but I don't know for sure what they touched. Maybe they mis-takenly propagated the bridge onto some other servers."

"We need to figure out which ones and get them shut down," David said. "Pete, you're the only one with access right now. Can you write a program to check every server to see which ones are run-ning the email bridge?"

"The IT servers?"

"No, the whole company."

"Holy cow. We have over a million servers. That's one heck of a search you want."

"Do you have the access? Administrative rights on those machines?" asked Mike.

"Sure," said Pete, "as part of Internal Tools, we can use admin-istrative accounts with full root access for maintenance checks. But still, that's a lot of servers."

"All right," Mike said, ignoring Pete's protest, "then we have one other thing for you to check for at the same time, a program called ELOPe we developed as an add-on to the AvoMail servers. We need a list of machines it's running on." Mike gave Pete a USB drive. "Here are the file checksums, so you know what to look for. I know this sounds crazy, but we think ELOPe is acting independently."

"Independently?" Pete asked, his voice cracking.

"Yes, an AI acting on its own volition. Making decisions, buying things and manipulating people."

Pete looked doubtful, but he stuck his hand out and took the USB drive.

"Now just one thing," Mike said. "Whatever you do, don't email anyone about this and don't trust any suspicious emails. We'll check in with you in person."

Pete's eyes went wide. "But..."

"Can you do it?" David asked, drawing himself upright, forestalling Pete's objections.

"I'll do it," Pete said, gripping the USB drive tightly in his fist.

—m—

Gene tucked his briefcase tighter under his arm and knocked twice on Brett Grove's door. The pipsqueak had better be in.

"Come," Brett's voice called.

Gene entered, swallowed a bit of pride, and said, "Boss, can I get a few minutes of your time?"

Brett nodded, and Gene took a seat in front of his desk. The corner office had wide windows, a spotless desk, and a large screen monitor. Cabinets along one wall held artsy knickknacks at precise two-foot intervals. A Mont Blanc pen stood in the center of the desk, an obvious showpiece, since not a single sheet of paper, not even a sticky note, was to be seen anywhere in the office.

After explaining what he'd found, Gene expected Brett to understand and endorse the investigation. A word or two of praise would not have been out of order, either. Instead, his arguments were met with disbelief, even mockery.

"Gene, you think you found something here, but you're not coherent. You've been raving for years about how we shouldn't trust computers, and now you come to me with some story about an artificial intelligence. Do you expect me to believe you? Do you know how ridiculous this sounds?"

Gene held up his accordion folder. "Are you going to look at these reports?" He'd come carefully prepared with the same meticulous collection of data he'd used to present his evidence to Maggie in Finance, and then later to Mike and David.

"No, I'm not going to spend hours wading through hundreds of pages of printouts." Brett sat back, waving his hand at Gene's folder. "If you want to convince me, summarize what you've got in a slide deck, and present in the staff meeting on Friday. That's the way we do things here."

"Damn you, Brett. Listen to me, son, there is a damn monster in the machine!" Gene snarled, leaping to his feet. "This thing is buying guns and torpedoes and robots. There's no time to put together a PowerPoint presentation. We'll be lucky to be alive on Friday!" He held himself back, but he wanted to reach across the desk and grab the kid by the shirt collar.

"No, *you* listen. This is typical of you. You think because I'm thirty years old that makes me an idiot. You're the incompetent fool." Brett stood on his own side of the desk, punctuating his every point with a jab of his finger. "You ignore your emails. You don't use the processes you're supposed to follow. We're the number one Internet company in the world, and the only thing you use a computer for is to print stuff out. My grandmother is more computer literate and has more credibility around here than you."

Brett came around the desk and stood face-to-face with Gene, his voice pitched low and angry. "You would've been gone a long time ago, but my predecessor made me swear I'd keep you on my staff before he would give me this job. I don't know what the hell he saw in you, but I don't get it. Go take a shower, shave yourself, put on some clean clothes for God's sake, and put together a damn PowerPoint presentation if you have to buy a book to learn how to use it!"

Standing there, Brett's face red and flushed and inches away from his own, it all crystallized. He'd been gradually marginalized within his own department by the worthless scum in front of him, and now when he most needed management support, he wasn't going to get it. Gene blinked once or twice and realized he was wasting him time here. No data or logic would change Brett's mind.

Later, in his own office, Gene replayed the scene over and over in his head, and thought back to the countless little things that hadn't gone his way the last year. His pulse sounded in his ears, and he felt almost sick. He opened the bottom desk drawer, and poured himself an inch of bourbon. On second thought, he added another inch. He swigged the whole mess, the burn descending his throat and settling in his stomach. Jesus, he was going to give himself a heart attack if he replayed that conversation again.

He looked down at his rumpled, slept-in clothes and rubbed a hand over the multiple-day stubble on his face. He was a mess, that was true. But competence wasn't a matter of clothes and fancy presentation. Competence was looking at data, whether out there in the real world or on his sheets of paper, and drawing insights. Damnitall, he was still relevant.

Gene slouched in despair before forcing himself up. He had to focus on something productive. It was time to meet with Mike and David. He dragged himself out of his office and began the journey back to the R&D building.

—m—

Bill Larry climbed into the back of the AStar, where he'd have a little more room to work. He buckled in and put on his headset. The pilot throttled up, and they were in the air.

Bill pulled out his tablet to review emails and try to salvage a little productivity out of the morning. He was taking an unexpected helicopter ride, the first of the new year, out to the ODC. He'd gotten a very unusual call from Maggie Reynolds in Finance, asking him to verify delivery of purchases. Bill scanned messages, but couldn't put the confusing exchange out of mind.

Maggie hadn't been able to grasp that Facility location code ODC0004 was not a mere walk down the hallway for Bill, but a floating platform ten miles off the shore of California, requiring Bill to make a helicopter reservation and two hours to get to, by the time you counted driving and flying.

If the call had confused Maggie, it was twice as puzzling for Bill, because Maggie went through a litany of impossible purchases attributed to his department. He had not ordered backup satellite hardware or microwave communication gear. Yes, they'd ordered equipment from iRobot, but that was before the holiday break, and no, there shouldn't have been a second round of deliveries to all the ODCs from iRobot.

In any case, no one could visit or install anything on the ODCs without approval from Bill. It simply wasn't possible to have installed the equipment Maggie described. Only Bill, Jake, and a handful of employees in day-to-day contact with Bill had the authority to stand down the robotic defenses. Bill was personally advised anytime the robots were brought offline. Maggie's inventory of purchase orders made the ODCs sound like beehives of activity. Impossible.

However, the shit had hit the fan back in the main office, because Maggie had folks from Controls and Compliance investigating their purchases. She sounded worried but trying to hide it, and in the end, Bill felt sorry for her and reluctantly agreed to investigate in person. He reserved a helicopter, packed a bag and his satellite phone, and headed for the heliport.

That's how Bill ended up thirty minutes out from ODC 4 on one of the company's Eurocopter helicopters to do this hands-on inspection. He would lay to rest the question of exactly what equipment was present. With a sudden jolt, he realized he'd made a drastic mistake. In his rush, he'd forgotten to schedule the deactivation for the defense robots.

He fingered the headset switch to talk to the pilot. "Hey, George. Whatever you do, don't approach the barge. Keep at least half a mile distant. I've got to get them to shut down the robots."

Bill struggled to plug his satellite phone into the noise-isolating headset, a clumsy, insulated thing. Jesus, he could have gotten them both killed. He placed the call to the robot system administrators.

"Hello, this is Bill Larry at Avogadro. My deactivation passcode is O-S-T-F-V-3-9-4-1." Bill had to yell over the helicopter noise. "I need to shut down the robots at ODC4."

"Sorry, please repeat your passcode."

"O-S-T-F-V-3-9-4-1. I'm Bill Larry at Avogadro. I need to shut down the defense robots so I can land at my facility.

"I'm sorry, sir, but I don't have any matching records. Can you please give me your vendor ID?"

Bill sighed in exasperation and wondered what more could go wrong with his day. He swiped through the records on his tablet until he found the information, provided the asked-for ID and waited.

"I'm truly sorry, but I don't have a listing for that ID. Are you sure you have a contract with us?"

"Jesus effing…" He hit mute, cursed loudly and at length, and then continued the conversation. After more unhelpful back-and-forth discussion with the agent, he asked for a supervisor and got transferred over to a Ms. Claire.

"Mister Larry," Ms. Claire said, after a few minutes of research. "We're no longer under contract to handle your defenses. Of course we provided the hardware, and we were administering through

December thirty-one, but as of the first of this year, we turned the controls over to you."

"Not possible," Bill said. "There's got to be a mistake."

It took another fifteen minutes on the phone with Ms. Claire for Bill to gradually puzzle out that iRobot thought Avogadro had renegotiated the contract. Bill was sure this wasn't the case, but he couldn't help wracking his head, wondering if someone had gone around him. They'd just put the system in place a few weeks earlier. It didn't make any sense that the contract had changed already. Had they been hacked? Bill's head started to pound as he continued the argument over the crappy satellite connection and roar of the helicopter.

George gestured toward the barge, visible now, asking whether he should proceed. Bill shook his head no.

Bill checked his tablet and found the number for a vice president, Robert O'Day, at iRobot, one of the guys he had worked with on the contract. Bill hung up on Ms. Claire and called Robert. He remembered Robert as being intensely focused and wickedly smart. He'd get this issue resolved. Robert's administrative assistant said he was already on an urgent teleconference, but offered that Robert could call Bill back within ten minutes.

So Bill waited over the Pacific ocean, a thousand feet up, a hundred-and-five-decibel engine just above his head, burning a gallon a minute of high performance aviation fuel.

Seven minutes later the phone rang, and Bill punched the button to answer. Bill struggled to keep his voice under control as he demanded O'Day explain what was going on. While the pilot had the helicopter circling around ODC 4 in gentle circles, O'Day confirmed that, indeed, iRobot had installed additional automation and turned the administration of those defenses over to Avogadro.

Craning his head to look at the floating barge, Bill raised a pair of binoculars. New antennas bristled from the rooftop, satellite dishes pointed into the sky, and line-of-sight microwave cones aimed at the horizon. More worrying were the long black barrels directed skyward. What the heck were those?

George circled the platform at a distance, but after a few rotations, Bill just wished he'd keep the helicopter in one place. Yelling over the noise, he asked O'Day if there was anyway to override the robots. If he couldn't get the problem solved, he'd be forced to fly back to the office to figure out what was going on, then return in the afternoon.

O'Day assured him there wasn't any override for security reasons. The point of handing off administration was to insure full control of the command software they'd provided to interface with the robots resided in Avogadro's hands.

—⁓—

As Bill argued with iRobot, George "Punch" Gonzales continued to circle around. He did it more out of boredom than anything else, since he could've easily engaged the auto-hover to maintain their location. After twenty years of flying helicopters for the Marines, George wasn't inclined to engage the autopilot and tune out. He liked to keep his hands on the stick.

On one of these slow rotations around the ODC, George came a little closer to the platform. He glanced again at the fuel gauge, and noticed the long holding pattern had them coming up on their halfway point. George turned to ask Bill how much longer they planned to stay. While he was looking backwards, the helicopter crossed into the invisible perimeter defined by the robotic defenses. Since he wasn't looking out the windshield, George, who just might have recognized them for what they were, missed the flash of large-caliber machine guns firing. Bill, stooped and head down, struggled to hear the other end of the line and understand how the administration of the robots could have been bungled so badly.

In less than a quarter of a second, the .50 caliber machine gun rounds traversed the distance to the helicopter, bisected the cabin and found the fuel supply. The helicopter exploded and bits of shrapnel screamed through the air in all directions, before falling, sizzling, into the water.

CHAPTER 10

David tried to turn down another cup of coffee, but Mike was having none of his protests.

"It's Peruvian. The beans were roasted yesterday."

David took a sip as Gene came in and dropped heavily into the remaining chair. His stomach was tied in too many knots to enjoy the coffee, but he distantly noted the flavor was extraordinary.

Slumped back, Gene related the discussion with his manager. "Sorry. I never anticipated losing all credibility within my department. If we go to anyone else in management, and we should, you'll have to take point. You technical boys at least are respected by these folks."

"Sorry, dude," Mike said, clapping the older man on the shoulder, his face lined deeply in dismay. "Thank you for making the attempt."

"Me too," David added. "They're crazy to not appreciate your work. We wouldn't have any idea what was going on without your investigation."

"The key to this is Gary's Communication Products Division," Mike said. "Gary might be unreachable, but he's not the only decision maker."

"Right. The Marketing manager, her name is...Linda Fletcher," David said. "She's Gary's number two. Let's find out who the Legal representative is, and bring Legal in. If we can convince them of the risk, maybe they'll put a stop to the whole project."

"Legal advises businesses on risks," Gene said. "Technically they can't force anyone to do anything. The business manager must weigh tradeoffs, including Legal's opinions, and make a decision. But I agree, we should bring them in. The fear of litigation will cause the lawyers to side with us."

"Let's go," Mike said.

David reached for his computer to check Linda's calendar, then stopped himself. Habits were hard to break.

Walking down the hallway with Mike and Gene in tow, he asked the admin of the next group over to find the location of Linda Fletcher's office, and her admin's name. They crossed the campus, traversing a skybridge with hand-blown glass art in the shape of native fish hanging in the windows, and then another skyway in the form of a miniature version of the *Ponte Santa Trinita*, before finally arriving at Building 7a. They found Linda's admin, a young guy by the name of Nathan, at his desk outside her office.

"Sorry, Linda's in a critical conference. You should have sent a meeting request."

Gene pulled out his badge, showing he worked for Controls and Compliance. "It's urgent."

"Let me put your names on her calendar and find an open slot."

"Wait—"David said. "No names."

"No names?" Nathan asked, his eyebrows raised.

"Absolutely no names," Gene said. "The meeting is extremely sensitive. Just schedule the time."

Nathan's jaw hung open for a second before he reluctantly set his shoulders. "Fine, a meeting with no attendees. Can I give it a name?"

David wondered what wouldn't arose suspicion but would ensure Linda took it seriously. "Just put down 'critical system stability.' Also, I need you to invite the Legal rep."

"You mean Tim Wright?" Nathan asked. His raised eyebrows and tilted head left no doubt he still found their whole request dubious.

"Yes," David said. "What's the earliest you've got?"

Nathan checked the calendar. "I can get you a half hour next Tuesday."

"No, it's got to be today."

Nathan shook his head firmly. "No can do. Linda will kill me. I'm not kidding. Since she came back from holiday break she's been putting in sixteen hour days on this new project."

"What project?" Mike asked.

"I can't say. Super confidential. Just like your meeting is *sensitive*." He smiled in slight triumph. "How about Friday?"

"Look kid," Gene said, "people's jobs and more are on the line. Be straight with us, what's the earliest possible time we can meet?"

Nathan rolled his eyes. "Everything's urgent," he said, mumbling to himself. "I can bump Janet…" He glanced up. "I can get you in tomorrow after lunch."

David frowned at him.

"Tomorrow after lunch," Nathan repeated. "That's the absolute best I can do. Between the Legal meetings, the PR folks…" Nathan trailed off. "Forget I said anything, please."

"Fine, set it up for tomorrow," Gene said. He started to turn away and then returned. "Kid, I can see from your face that as soon as we leave here, you want to walk down the hallway to gossip about this. Don't do that if you still want to have a job tomorrow."

Nathan nodded swiftly, and the group of three headed back.

David was woozy, his eyes crusty and his head hurt. He'd been awake and on the go since early that morning in New Mexico. "Listen, I'm exhausted," he said. "I've been up since five, or maybe that's four. I realize how urgent this is, but given we're stalled waiting for Linda, I need to go home and get some rest."

"Let's meet tomorrow morning before the meeting," Mike said. "David's office?"

"Sure. You boys need a ride? Your wife took his car."

David would probably fall asleep on the long streetcar ride home, he was so tired. "Yes, please. That'd be awesome."

—w—

David had texted to let Christine know he was on his way home. After Gene dropped him off, he went inside and found the house empty.

"Hello?" he called, wandering around. The suitcases were unpacked and waiting in the upstairs hallway. David put them in the attic, and went downstairs. In the kitchen he found a note that read *Gone to get dinner, be back soon.*

As he finished reading, he heard Christine's car pull up. He opened the door, and Christine walked up carrying two large bags.

"Takeout from Nicholas," she said, smiling.

His favorite Lebanese restaurant. He tried to muster up enthusiasm.

Sitting down, he picked moodily at his plate, exhausted from lack of sleep, travel, and the stress of the afternoon.

"You better not waste that *mjadra*," Christine said with a laugh.

David managed a weak smile, knowing she wanted to cheer him up.

"You're hopeless sometimes," she said, sighing. "What's your plan for tomorrow?"

"We're going to Linda Fletcher, the Marketing manager for Communication Products. She's got decision-making authority while Gary's out. We'll ask her to approve an outage so we can take down the servers and install clean images without ELOPe."

"Sounds reasonable. What do you think her response will be?"

"She may say yes. I hope so, at least." David fell back into silence, staring at his food.

"Why so glum then?"

"What happens after this?" David said, stabbing angrily at the rice anddropping his fork on the plate. "They'll cancel the project, almost certainly. This may be the end of my career. They're going to ask questions about what ELOPe was doing, how these things happened. I was so close to a mind-blowing success. Now what's the best I can hope for? Damage control." He rested his head in his hands.

Christine came around the table to hug him. "You have other options. This is one job, one company. No matter what, there's always a path forward."

"There will never be another opportunity like Avogadro if I screw this up."

—◊—

The next morning, David, Mike, and Gene reviewed what they'd say at the meeting with Linda, and discussed contingency plans.

"We've got time to kill," Gene said, "and we could use downtime and food. I wouldn't mind getting away from here. Kenny and Zuke's?"

Mike nodded eagerly.

The sandwich shop was a standby for the Avogadro crowd. The company's cafeteria food might be excellent and well loved, but eventually the corporate ambience tired out even enthusiasts. On this particular day, they were a little more comfortable a few blocks away from the eyes and ears of the company. They enjoyed Reubens and hamburger sliders and made their way back ten minutes before the planned meeting time.

They entered the seventh floor conference room to find Linda and Tim already present. As they set foot in the room, Linda made a zig-zag hand motion at the gesture-sensitive walls, and the wrap-around display screens, covered with presentations, diagrams, and spreadsheets, went dark simultaneously. David couldn't help reacting to the gesture. He wasn't used to such a lack of trust between Avogadro employees.

"Sorry," Linda said, seeing the expression on his face. "It's a confidential client deal." She shrugged dismissively. "Dave, you I know." She shook his hand. "Who are these gentlemen?"

They started a round of introductions. Linda was a Scandinavian woman whose family had lived briefly in Wisconsin when she was a child, just a few towns away from Mike. She and Mike laughed over common experiences growing up. Tim, with his jet-black jeans, boots, and T-shirt, defied everyone's expectations of a corporate attorney. David wondered if he was some new breed of Goth lawyer, but Tim's jovial attitude set them at ease.

The small talk done with and everyone seated, David explained what brought them to the meeting. Mike contributed details but let David lead the conversation.

The light-hearted mood faded as they got to the suspicious purchases and ELOPe's possible role. Linda sat back, arms folded, a foot from the table as Tim's frown became more pronounced.

David couldn't read them. Obviously they weren't happy. But were they uncomfortable with the technology, or worried about making a decision without Gary present? Afraid they'd somehow be liable for what happened? All three? By the time he got to the crux, his initial confidence had evaporated.

"What we're asking for is your authority to force a shutdown of all email servers. Then we'd re-image those computers with a known good version of the software."

Between leaning away from the table, crossed arms, and condescending expressions of disbelief, Linda and Tim radiated rejection in every possible way. David's heart sank. Damnit, he needed them to believe. He had to make one last attempt.

"Look," David said, "This is a normal action we take when a server has a problem, just like reinstalling the operating system and software on your PC. A straightforward process."

"I hear you and I want to help," Linda said, fiddling with her tablet. "I really do."

David couldn't have gotten a clearer *no*. He opened his mouth to object, but Linda went on.

"The problem is I'm uncomfortable making a decision of this magnitude without Gary here. I've already got…well, never mind that. I'd much rather wait for Gary to return." Linda glanced at Tim and then turned back to David. "What you're asking for, would it cause a service interruption? How long and how many customers would be affected?"

"Yes, but only a *temporary* outage. The good news is Avogadro has a process to re-image servers quickly. We can bring a server up in less than ten minutes. The bad news is we don't normally re-image all the servers simultaneously. The backup system containing the images can only service a few thousand servers at a time. Some servers would come up quickly, but it'll take three hours to get everything back online."

"Wait a second," Linda said, leaning forward. "You want a full outage? *For three hours?* I thought you were talking about a degradation of service. No way we can afford that much downtime right now. It's non-negotiable. We're closing new partnership deals in the next couple of days, confidential stuff we can't discuss until the press release comes out, but they're a major coup for Avogadro. A multi-billion dollar opportunity. I can't put that at risk." Linda looked to Tim for confirmation.

"I agree," Tim said. "These customers specified service level agreements committing to certain uptime. An outage now would destroy our credibility to meet those goals, and they'd back out. We'd lose the deals."

"Wait a minute." Linda snapped her fingers. "The rolling maintenance windows. Why don't you use them? Bring down some of the servers in small groups and fix them a bunch at a time?"

"We wish we could," Mike jumped in, "but we're afraid the existing systems would reinfect the new ones as they come up. We need to shut down every email server and keep them down until the clean installs are done."

"I'm sorry, but I've got to say no." She waggled one finger at them. "If you had hard evidence the servers were causing problems for our customers, I might be influenced to make the decision to rebuild them. But a strange story about a handful of emails being manipulated...It seems more likely your accounts have been compromised, not that the entire email system is flawed. I think you should talk to Security." She shook her head.

"This isn't a Security problem," David said. "This is—"

"Look," Linda said. "I can't decide to risk billions in revenue based on a few mangled emails. You're free to talk to Gary when he returns, of course." She turned to the displays, arm raised to make the gesture to turn them back on. "Anything else?" Her attitude said it was a dismissal, not an invitation.

"No," David said. "But we'll be back."

CHAPTER 11

Avogadro Launches Secure Hosted Email Service

Government Complaints About IT Costs and Quality Lead Avogadro to Create Secure Applications and AvoMail

PORTLAND, Oregon - January 6th, 2015 UTC - Avogadro Corp today announced a secure, hosted version of Avogadro Applications with AvoMail for Governments.

The demand for ultra-secure, hosted Avogadro Applications with AvoMail came from national governments spending excessive amounts on IT services while receiving inferior products and services, said Linda Fletcher, Marketing Manager for Avogadro's Communication Products Division. Avogadro Secure Applications with Avo-Mail will reduce IT spending by governments up to 80%, while providing cloud-based, feature-rich and easy-to-use communication applications, according to Fletcher.

The hosted model is being adopted immediately by Germany, Canada, and Taiwan, with other countries to follow.

For more information, please visit AvogadroCorp.com

—∾—

For two days after the conversation with Linda Fletcher, they were stuck in a holding pattern, waiting in deepening frustration for Gary Mitchell to return from a vacation that should have ended a week earlier. They spent much of the time clustered in David's office, poring over Gene's reports, and even printouts of source code which Melanie had made after many puzzled protests.

During a bathroom break, Mike read through his personalized news alerts and his heart skipped a beat. Oh, man, this was worse than he ever imagined. He washed his hands and ran back to the office, AvoOS smartphone in hand.

"Holy cow, did you see this press release?" he asked, holding the screen out.

"Dude, you're not supposed to admit to reading your phone in the bathroom. We all do it, but you're violating some kind of social norm..." David trailed off as he noticed Mike's face.

"We, I mean, Avogadro, that is, I think, ELOPe has..."

"Slow down." David held both hands up. "What's up?"

Mike took a deep breath and forced himself to sit down as the others stared at him. "Avogadro announced a secure version of AvoMail and our other apps for government customers. They already signed up the first round. David, national governments using AvoMail. Germany, Canada...Do you realize what this means?"

"ELOPe expanded its sphere of influence." David's face turned pale. "Now every government official who sends or receives an email via AvoMail will potentially have their message filtered, altered, or impersonated."

"This service must be what Linda Fletcher talked about in the meeting the other day," Mike said. "Damn, she had to have known this was in the works. She's actually making the problem worse!" He couldn't help raising his voice.

"Settle down," Gene said, in his usual grumble. "The real question is who initiated this secure platform? Fletcher and the Marketing group, or ELOPe? The timing is awfully convenient."

"Come on," David said. "It's only been a month since I put the hack in the system. You really think ELOPe could make the company launch a new product in that time?"

Gene shrugged.

Mike held his head in both hands, staring down at the phone. "I believe it. The biggest problem with introducing anything new is getting everybody on board. If ELOPe convinced everyone simultaneously, why not? It's not like we had to build the product from scratch. It's just re-marketing what we already had to new customers."

"I'm freaked out," David said, voicing what was in Mike's head. Mike looked at him and nodded.

—⁓—

The day after the Avogadro press release of the secure cloud services for governmental organizations, David, Mike, and Gene met again. At Mike's urging, they gathered at Extracto in Northeast Portland.

David entered the shop, found Mike and Gene sitting at a table along the wall. "Why here?" he asked.

"Best coffee in Portland, bar none," Mike said. "Perhaps the finest on the West Coast."

Gene nodded, holding a mug up.

"See, Gene hasn't even been here before, and he's already convinced," Mike said. "Get the Flores Island."

David walked over to the counter, where two insulated coffee dispensers stood next to the chromed bulk of the industrial espresso machine. The dispenser on the left was labeled "Flores Island" and contained descriptive text so flowery that David thought he was reading a wine review. "Subtle hints of carmel, chocolate, and cannabis?" David read out loud. "For real?" he called doubtfully to Mike.

Mike nodded and smiled.

So David got a cup, along with disapproving stares from the others as he loaded up on sugar and milk. He sighed.

A large canvas tote sat at Mike's feet. "What's in the bag?" David asked.

"Ten pounds of beans. They only harvest and roast the Flores Island once a year, and once it's gone, it's gone."

David sat down. "Did you make us meet here for the coffee? We're eight miles from campus!"

"We're only two miles from your house, and yes, we came for the coffee. You have no idea how hard these beans are to get. A one-of-a-kind experience."

"Can we please focus on ELOPe?" David said, sounding whiny in his own ears. He couldn't help it: he was frustrated with Mike, and had zero bandwidth for discussing rare coffee beans.

"Okay, okay," Mike said, but he and Gene chuckled in amusement. Mike went on, "You guys remember Pete Wong, the engineer from Internal Tools who wrote the email-to-web bridge?"

David nodded. He took a sip of coffee, found it as good as Mike had promised. Well, the man knew his beans.

"Well, I heard back from him. Bad news, more bad news, and worse news."

"Naturally," Gene said, "because the situation isn't terrible enough."

David glanced at Gene, trying to puzzle out whether that was sarcasm or an actual expectation. He turned back to Mike. "I guess you can start with the bad news first."

"Pete scanned computers for the digital fingerprint of ELOPe, as we asked." Mike sipped his coffee. "He found traces on every server in the Communication Products pool, even ones it shouldn't have been on."

David groaned. "And the more bad news?"

"Pete found the fingerprint of his email-to-web bridge on the same servers as ELOPe. Also present on every one. He thinks the email-to-web functionality was incorporated directly into ELOPe's code."

"How is that possible?" Gene asked.

"The contractors," Mike and David answered simultaneously, with a glance at each other.

"Yup, Mike said. "The temporary engineers hired over the holidays made changes, and we don't know what. We thought they were merely performance improvements, but ELOPe changed its own functionality as well."

David chewed over this new bit of information. ELOPe could be doing anything now, possibly far beyond its original programming.

"We've built an artificial intelligence," Mike said, wide-eyed. "A self-improving AI. It's going to keep on accelerating out of control."

"It's not an AI!" David said, unsure why the idea made him feel so hostile. "It's just a collection of algorithms, manipulating us with emails."

"It may not be conscious like we are," Mike said, "but it's protecting itself, changing itself. That's intelligence."

"It can't be intelligent." David pointed back and forth between Mike and himself. "We're not that smart and we certainly can't write software smarter than us. Where does the intelligence come from if we didn't put it in there?"

"Both emergent intelligence and collective wisdom. The algorithms we wrote improve themselves over time, testing better approaches to detect goals, match outcomes, and so forth. But the actions themselves come from the combined emails of millions of users. It's crowdsourcing its own intelligence."

"It's not an artificial intelligence!" Dave slumped in his seat.

Gene cleared his throat. "It doesn't matter what you call it, we still have to stop it. And the sooner the better, before it accumulates more power."

"This sucks," David said. "What's the worst news you wanted to tell us?"

"I went to Pete's office yesterday morning to find out what he's learned, since we didn't want to use email or phone. Before I left, I gave him my home address in case he had anything urgent. Then last night he showed up at my door after dinner. He'd been fired."

"What the hell?" Gene barked, slamming down his cup.

"He was working late and looking for more signs of server infection, when his network access was cut off. A couple of minutes later, Security showed up at his office and told him he was fired. He wanted to call his manager, but the guards wouldn't do anything other than let him pack a box of personal belongings. They escorted him off campus and he came straight to my place, figuring it was all related."

"Why didn't you tell me last night?"

"By phone or email?" Mike said.

"Frak me," said David, realizing no electronic communication was safe. "We've got to do something! It's been, what, five days? Waiting for Gary is not a viable option anymore."

The question facing them wasn't just who had the authority to shut down the servers, but who would believe their story and the limited evidence they had. After throwing out alternatives, they came back to contacting Sean Leonov, a path they'd debated several days running.

"We need an appointment with Sean," Mike said. "He brought you on board to lead ELOPe, so you have credibility with him. I know we're jumping right to the top of the management hierarchy, but this must be done. We've exhausted our other options and we're in a race against the growing influence of this thing."

David closed his eyes and pressed his hands to his face. Mike was right, but, once again, he couldn't get over the fact that this would spell the end of his career. He'd exhausted all his options. He'd trade anything, do anything, for a chance to go back and change the course of things. He opened his eyes. "All right, let's talk to Sean. We'll go together."

They carpooled to the office in David's old BMW. From the Fremont bridge, they took the Avogadro exit leading directly to the underground parking garage. David pulled up to the gate, the blinking light above the scanner suddenly ominous. ELOPe would know he was entering the campus. He hesitated, badge in hand. Jesus, he had to get a grip. He stuck the badge up against the reader before he lost his nerve. To his slight surprise, the barrier swung open normally.

They trooped down hallways, winding their way to Sean Leonov's office with the solemnity of a funeral procession. The executive offices were located close together in the uppermost floor of Building 7B. As David looked around the hallways with their expensive ebonized hardwood flooring, he realized the executive floor was abandoned. One closed room after another.

They finally found Sean's office. Knocking brought no response, so David tried the knob. Locked. "Now what? No one is around."

"Sean's traveling," said an approaching woman carrying a cardboard box. "His admin, Rosie, will have his contact information. Talk to her."

Her tailored suit suggested she was one of the VPs, and David recognized her from his executive presentation more than a month earlier. "Marissa, right?" he said. "Any idea where we can find Rosie?"

"She works from home when Sean is out of town. Send her an email. Rosie Fendell. She'll be in the directory."

"Is there any way we could contact her in person?" he asked. "We, uh, can't use email. The topic is too sensitive."

"Sorry, email is your best bet. Good luck." Marissa continued past.

David couldn't help wondering about the cardboard box. "Are you leaving the company?"

Marissa smiled. "Yes. An opportunity too good to pass up."

After she left, David broke the silence. "Just send an email. Sure. That's so simple."

"Well, one email can't hurt, right?" Mike clapped him on the back. "Let's make it as vague as possible. We just need to meet Sean."

—∞—

Back at his office, David sat in front of his desk computer. The others watched over his shoulder as he crafted an email to Sean's assistant, taking special care to ensure the message sounded innocuous. They all read and approved the email before David hit send.

While they waited for Rosie to reply, Gene went down the hall for coffee. The minutes ticked by as they sipped, each expressing anxiety in his own way. Mike bounced a leg with nervous energy as Gene paced back and forth. David gave Tux a little nudge, sending the springy penguin bouncing erratically.

"I'm sure I've never been so much on the edge of my seat about an email before," Mike said. He chuckled awkwardly, his voice betraying his nerves.

"No kidding," David said, stirring sweetener.

Gene stood by the window, mug in hand, brooding.

"Maybe you're right," David said, looking at Mike.

"I'm sure I am," Mike said with a smile, "but about what?"

"The coffee. I always thought the stuff here was good, but it does seem off somehow compared to Extracto."

Mike sat back, a satisfied grin spreading across his face. "That's the lactone and indanes. More than a thousand volatile compounds in roasted coffee. I don't want to say I told you so—"

A sharp knock at the door interrupted him, startling them all.

David jumped up. "All right, guys, calm down." He gestured for them to stay in their seats, a slight tremor in his hand. "Whatever is going on is only happening in the computer. It might be real good at faking emails, but it can't hurt us for real."

He cracked the door open. "Can I help you?"

Outside, a dark-haired woman in a black suit stood with four uniformed security guards behind her. "Mr. Ryan?" asked the woman.

"Yes, that's me," he replied, a sinking feeling in his gut.

"Are Mr. Williams and Mr. Keyes with you?"

"Yes, we're all here." David opened the door wider.

"I'm Carly French, Director of Security. We've been contacted by several individuals who reported you harassed them. I'm afraid I must escort you off the Avogadro campus immediately, pending a full investigation."

David, Mike, and Gene glanced at each other. David's assertion that the computer couldn't affect them in real life had fallen apart before their eyes.

"Ms. French, I'm Gene Keyes, in the Controls and Compliance Group." Gene stood and shook Ms. French's hand. "I'm conducting an internal investigation into financial fraud and other inappropriate behavior occurring just before the end of the year. Mr. Ryan and Mr. Williams are assisting me. We believe Avogadro employees are being manipulated through email. It's called social engineering. The emails provide just enough information to seem legitimate. May I ask, were you informed by email of our so-called harassment?"

"Yes, I was informed by email, but I'm well aware of what social engineering is. In any scenario with such serious allegations, of course I would confirm them directly with the individuals. In this case, I spoke by phone with your manager, Mr. Keyes."

"Brett? He could confirm what I'm working on."

"During our phone call he said you've been belligerent to him, acting strangely, and you'd blame whatever happened on the computer." She shook her head, more sad than angry. "Look, I'm very sorry, gentlemen. You seem like nice folks, and I'd like to be able to take your word. But the standard operating procedure is that I escort you off campus and remove your access privileges as a precautionary measure, until a full investigation can be completed. If the facts don't check out, you'll have an apology from me and my manager, and you'll be back on campus in no time at all. Now, please, let's go without a lot of drama."

David couldn't think of a thing to say. He felt boxed in, all available choices closed off one by one until there was nowhere to go.

Out of options, they allowed Ms. French to escort them to the garage and David's BMW. They climbed into the car, and as David drove away, the security guards walked alongside until the car exited the garage. In the rearview mirror, he saw the guards line up across the entrance.

For once, Mike had no jokes to break the silence.

—⟱—

David squinted on the drive, the sunny day somehow too bright and cheerful for the circumstances. Arriving home with Mike and Gene in tow, David entered the house, which—with Christine away at work—was quiet and still. David grabbed beers from the kitchen and passed them around. The sun might be straight overhead, but he needed something to take the edge off their unnerving experience with Security.

He wanted to call Christine, but his phone wouldn't turn on. He tried button combinations until he concluded the phone had died. Staring at the inert plastic and metal lump in his hand, he remebered the phone ran Avogadro's AvoOS operating system and used the corporate Internet plan. It was totally dependent on the company, and the servers were fully aware of his phone: where it was, who he talked to, the data he sent and received.

"My phone is dead," he told the others in surprised relief.

"Same here," said Gene, looking at his.

"Me too," Mike said, checking his own phone and glancing over at Gene's. "Dude, how'd you get a feature phone from the company? We don't even *make* phones like that anymore."

"It's not surprising they stopped working," David said, "given that everything runs through Avogadro."

"We should be glad," Mike said. "Otherwise ELOPe could have monitored our phone calls. Come to think of it, ELOPe might have been listening anytime they were powered on."

"Shit..." David continued to fiddle with the damn thing, then slammed it on the counter. "It's not just about *using* the phone. It's the data on there. I had Sean's home address in my contact list, from a barbecue I was invited to back when I was hired. We could have gone straight to his house. Now I can't even get a boot screen."

"Doesn't matter, he's traveling, right?" Mike said.

"Look, let's go to his house. I remember it's in the West Hills. It's not that big an area. If we drive around long enough, we can find the place, and maybe he's there. Or someone who knows where he is."

"We got nothing to lose, boys. I don't mind the beer, but I do want to get to the bottom of this," rumbled Gene.

"Let me drive, and you navi-guess," Mike offered.

David nodded, tossing his keys to Mike, and they took off again.

Two hours of exploration later, which included winding roads, switchbacks, and driving in circles in Portland's West Hills, David finally recognized Sean's house. In the one stroke of luck they had experienced since this all started, they found someone coming out as Mike pulled up.

David walked up to the youthful woman. "Excuse me, I'm looking for Sean Leonov. Is he home?"

She looked startled, glanced around, and took two steps back. David hoped she was merely nervous about being approached on the street, not hiding anything sinister.

"He's not available," she said. "Can I take a message?"

He pulled out his Avogadro badge, which fortunately had only been deactivated by security, not confiscated. "I'm a coworker of Sean's at Avogadro. We've got a work emergency and need to talk to him."

"I'm housesitting while he's in Brooklyn, visiting his family."

"Do you have a phone number?"

"I'm sorry, I'm not supposed to give any information out. Sean was adamant. Don't you have his info at the company?"

"Yes, of course..." David faltered as he ran out of excuses.

Mike came to his rescue. "Time is of the essence, and the matter is so sensitive we can't contact him by phone or email." He paused and added, "We have to talk to him in person."

David frowned. The summary sounded odd coming from someone else. No wonder no one believed them.

At this, she looked more suspiciously at them, clutched her bag a little closer, and started to back toward the house. "I'm sorry, but if it's urgent, Avogadro has contact information. Please call his office, they'll know what to do."

Keeping her eyes on the group, she walked to the house. "Goodbye," she called from the door.

"Shit," Mike said as they climbed into the car. "That wasn't very productive."

"The hell it wasn't. We know he's in Brooklyn," Gene growled.

"What good does that do?" Mike asked, focused on driving.

"Brooklyn has the largest immigrant population of Russians outside of Russia. If Sean went to Brooklyn, he's almost certainly in the Brighton Beach neighborhood. He's probably visiting his Russian parents. The Russian community is tight-knit. On the ground, we could find them in no time."

Mike and David turned to stare at him.

"What? I was a private detective before I joined Avogadro. I can find people. The old fashioned way. Without computers."

David took a deep breath. In for a penny... "In which case, gentlemen," he said, "next stop, New York."

CHAPTER 12

Tensions Ease in Middle East After Landmark Accord

ARBIL, Iraq (Reuters) - Germany has eased tensions in the Middle East after helping leaders in the region reach a landmark accord. Part of the agreement includes an unprecedented commitment of aid from the German government in the form of technological expertise, manufacturing agreements, and health care.

"We have reached the end of the era of oil," said Germany's Chancellor Erberhardt, at a press conference in Berlin. In recent years, the advance of renewable energy has diminished the relevance of oil, adding financial stress to the Middle East and increasing the tension of cultural and religious differences.

"Our accord transfers German technological expertise, profitable manufacturing, and the benefits of the best health care system in the world to the Arab nations," Erberhardt went on to say.

The agreement calls for disarmament and educational reform in exchange for the technology, manufacturing, and health care grants.

"Germany's history is one of transformation, and we wish to give the Arab world the support it needs to ensure a successful transformation."

The agreement includes components that are as disparate and comprehensive as auto manufacturing, data centers, and medical universities.

—✳—

Avogadro Acquires Oil Tankers for Floating Data Centers

PORTLAND, Oregon (Oregonian) - Avogadro Corp announced it is acquiring up to 100 retired oil tankers for floating data centers.

"We are experiencing an unprecedented increase in demand for server resources thanks to new strategic partnerships, including our Secure Government Applications Platform," said Jake Riley, head of the Offshore Data Center project. "While we continue to maintain our traditional data centers, our primary infrastructure going forward is floating data centers. Our barge-based approach is highly scalable and industry-leading. But at Avogadro, we're always looking to surpass even our own innovation. By acquiring retired oil tankers, we can reduce our costs and reduce our environment footprint by putting these tankers to good use."

For more information, please contact Avogadro at AvogadroCorp.com

—▩—

"Thanks for driving us," Mike said from the back seat.

"No problem," Christine said, behind the wheel of her Passat. "What's your plan when you get there?"

David couldn't keep the sarcasm out of his voice. "Gene's sure he can find Sean in a city of ten million people using no computers or telephones."

"I'm not looking at ten million people," Gene said, sighing. "Sean's parents are older Russian immigrants, therefore they're likely to either live in Brighton Beach or know people who live there. There are only seventy thousand people living in Brighton Beach, about half that many households."

"So you're going to knock on thirty-five thousand doors?"

"No. Look, kid, this is basic math. Sean Leonov is the wealthiest Russian in the U.S., and will be very well known in the Russian community. If someone has met or knows anything about Sean's parents, they're not going to forget about it. And they'll talk to their friends about it. If you use Dunbar's number, and estimate each person knows about one hundred and fifty people, in a population of seventy thousand people the odds are in my favor that the first person I talk to will either know Sean Leonov's parents or know someone who does."

"Oh." David pondered the math in his head.

Christine laughed.

"What's so funny?" he asked.

"You're brilliant, honey. Which makes it that much more fun to see someone outsmart you."

—▩—

Mike and David waited by the terminal door while David said a hurried goodbye to Christine at the curb. Her upper lip was a tight line, a sure sign she was worried. David pushed a lock of hair out of her face.

"Be careful," she said, hugging herself.

"Don't worry, hon, we'll be fine."

"I wish I could call you."

"We can't bring phones—the chance of being tracked…"

"I know." She shook her head. "What if… Never mind, just go. I love you."

They kissed quickly, then David grabbed his suitcase. He glanced backwards once to see Christine watching him with a sad face. David took a deep breath and joined Mike and Gene.

They'd talked it over the day before and decided to err on the side of caution. Even though they couldn't imagine how ELOPe might track passenger flight information or credit card transactions, they were flying into D.C.'s Dulles airport, figuring a flight into Dulles would disguise their real destination of Brooklyn. Gene had pushed for the more drastic measure of driving cross-country, but the others convinced him they didn't have the time to waste.

Hours later, glad to be out of the plane, they waited in line for a rental car at the airport, more out of sorts than ever. David normally planned everything in his life. Now he was on the opposite side of the country after a spontaneous flight, getting ready to drive to New York. He'd never been so adrift. He thought back to last night, and Christine holding him in her arms. What was he *doing?*

Next to him, Gene was as unchanging and stolid as ever in his rumpled suit and with his old leather briefcase.

"This doesn't bother you?" David asked. "Picking everything up on a moment's notice? You seem to like things to be orderly."

"Try the military sometime. We'd deploy in an hour when we had to. You get used to it."

Mike rejoined them, carrying coffees on a tray and the *New York Times* folded under one arm. "Guys, you are never going to believe this!"

"They still print a paper newspaper? You're right, I don't believe it."

"Be nice, kid," Gene said. "If they didn't, we wouldn't have any news at all right now."

Mike ignored David's sarcasm and went on. "Read these stories. On page one, the lead story is about how Germany changed their international policy. When was the last time Germany involved itself in international affairs?"

David shook his head. "I don't know, when?"

"Almost never. That's when. Not since World War II. Sure, they're active within the Eurozone,and they'll contribute to efforts by other countries. But on their own? No way. Now, out of the blue, they're negotiating a disarmament and peace treaty in the Arab world. And they apparently traded away the sum total of their intellectual property to get it. On page two, there's a story about how Germany adopted Avogadro's AvoMail. How can no one connect the dots with these stories side by side?"

David stared at Mike and the paper, dizzy with fatigue, astonishment, and disbelief. "I don't know whether to react with alarm or resignation at this point," he finally said.

"It also looks like we're going beyond using floating barges for our offshore data centers," Mike said, pointing to another story. "In order to support the new secure government cloud services, Avogadro is purchasing a fleet of retired oil tankers to use as floating bases for offshore data centers."

"Great, the bastard will be mobile now," Gene said in his usual growl. "Smarter than us, distributed, in control of the communication system, invisible, and mobile. Wars have been lost with fewer disadvantages than this."

After they picked up the rental car, Gene drove four hours north to New York City. They spent the trip in silence. They'd had every discussion and argument, and nobody was in the mood for small talk.

Once in New York, Gene headed to Brighton Beach in Brooklyn to drop off David and Mike at their hotel. "Let me do this by myself, guys. I've never done detective work with partners, and the three of us will make folks nervous. I'll meet you tonight at the hotel."

They watched Gene drive off. They were travel-weary but nervous, and decided to get a drink across the street. The bar looked like the neighborhood watering hole, friendly but plain. David ordered two bourbons on the rocks.

Halfway through his drink, David finally got up the courage to give voice to his fears."What do you think is going to happen? Is it going to be like the *Terminator* movies? Or *The Matrix*?"

"I don't know, dude." Mike shook his head. "Most science fiction deals with artificial intelligence run amok, but then there's also been plenty that's been written about how AI and humankind would cooperate."

"Really, like what?" David asked, turning to look at him.

"Well, nothing is coming to mind." Mike paused. "I was just thinking about how they turned Earth into pure computronium in one book. The humans had to move out to Jupiter or be assimilated into computing matter."

"Jesus, you're supposed to be the optimist."

Mike shrugged.

"I always thought an AI would be more, well, human," David started. "That a machine intelligence would be something we could relate to. This thing, whatever ELOPe is, it thinks more like an insect. It does things to promote its survival, very sophisticated things, but we can't talk to it or understand how it reasons. We can't have a conversation about what constitutes good behavior or how we can collaborate together."

They mused on that while David drained his drink and ordered another.

"Remember Isaac Asimov's Three Rules of Robotics?" Mike asked. "Asimov thought we'd give robots immutable rules to safeguard human life. He assumed creating those robots would be a deliberate, conscious act. We never thought we were creating an AI, so we never considered the implications."

"Yeah, in hindsight, giving an expert algorithm unfettered access to and control over the single most used email system in world does seem to have risks," David said wryly.

The two of them made their way back to the hotel room around eleven. They decided to pay cash for everything in Brooklyn to avoid a credit card trail pointing to their presence. Cash on hand was limited, so the three collaborators shared one hotel room. Just after one in the morning, a clearly exhausted Gene Keyes dragged himself into the room.

"Anything?" David asked.

"Yes, I've got a lead. Let's talk in the morning." With nothing more than that, Gene laid on the bed, put the pillow over his head, and went to sleep.

After a glance at each other, David and Mike decided to turn in, too.

—ɯ—

David hurried down the hall at Avogadro, recognizing the cork flooring of his building. He rushed to his office, a vague feeling of unease behind him. He swung open the door only to find an empty closet. Wrong door.

He walked a little further, opened another door, found another closet. Behind him, the drone of a machine, the automated vacuum cleaner or maybe something else, echoed down the passage.

He picked up his pace and ran, opening one door after another. Closet, closet, closet. Where was his damn office? The machine was getting closer, the whine of its motor bouncing off the walls. He ran to another door and opened it. Closet. He was approaching the end of the corridor, the machine right behind him. "Run, RUN!" he screamed to himself, failing to understand why he couldn't make his feet go faster. He reached the end of the hall, crashing into the wall. Despite his terror, he forced himself to turn, look—

David sat up suddenly, sweating, his heart beating fast. In the dimness, the room seemed off, the smells and shadows wrong. Then he remembered he was in New York, sharing a hotel room with Mike and Gene. The fear gradually faded, replaced with a deep unease.

He got up quietly to not disturb the others and went into the bathroom. Turning on the light, he stared at the dark circles under his eyes, his unnaturally pale face. It was the third time he'd had that nightmare.

He wished he could say he didn't understand the vision, because understanding somehow just made the feeling worse. He was afraid of ELOPe. In the dream, David knew that if he could find his office and sit in front of his computer, he'd have the power to do something. But ELOPe had made him powerless.

David sat down on the toilet and lowered his forehead onto the cool porcelain sink. He'd give anything to erase the last two months and do it all over. He didn't want to be known as the monster who unleashed ELOPe on the world. Please, please, let them find a way to turn it off.

—⁓—

At six o'clock the next morning, Gene yelled out, "Get up! Get showered! We've got to go."

"Huh, what?" Mike replied groggily.

"Come on, let's move. Wake up, lazy boys." Gene sounded as chipper as could be. "We've got ourselves one hour to get to the King's Plaza Diner. This is where Sean's parents have breakfast on Saturday morning. If Sean is in town, he'll be there with them. *GOGOGO!*" Gene shouted like a drill sergeant.

Twenty minutes later, showered and dressed in office clothes, they were on their way. They'd learned their lesson from earlier interactions. What they had to say was hard enough for people to believe; they needed to look as presentable and normal as possible to lessen the chance of being perceived as crazy. Even Gene was clean-shaven and presentable in a pressed suit, shirt and tie.

After a short drive, they arrived at the King's Plaza Diner. Across the street loomed the diner's namesake, a large shopping mall.

"Three for the counter," Gene said to the hostess. He turned and said quietly to Mike and David, "We can keep an eye on the entrance and avoid looking like stalkers."

David and Mike stared with wide eyes at the gold-tinted mirrors and six-foot chandeliers throughout the restaurant. "This is some place," David commented.

"According to the folks I talked to last night, the Kings Plaza Diner is famous among Brooklynites, including the Russian population. If nothing else, they said to get coffee and a piece of cheesecake."

"Wow, look at these pickles," Mike said, when the waitress, coffee pot in one hand, brought an enormous silver bowl brimming with a variety of pickled vegetables. "Tomatoes, cukes…"

"Come on guys," David said. "Let's stay focused. We are *not* here for the food."

"Hey, when in New York, do like the New Yorkers," Gene told him. And, turning to the waitress, "Coffee and cheesecake for me."

"Coffees all around," Mike said.

"Sure, sweetheart." The platinum-haired waitress started pouring. She smiled at Gene the whole time, but somehow managed to fill each cup perfectly. "What'll you kids have to eat?" She kept her eyes on Gene as Mike ordered an omelet, while David picked a bagel with lox and cream cheese.

After she left, Mike turned to Gene. "Didn't know you had such a way with the ladies."

Gene rumbled under his breath, but the corners of his mouth lifted a little.

They'd finished eating and were on their second cup of coffee when Mike saw Sean coming into the restaurant with an older couple.

"Here they are," said Mike, gesturing discreetly towards the entrance.

David turned and, seeing Sean, he stood up and walked over. Mike and Gene followed slightly behind.

"Hello, Sean," David called as he approached.

Sean blinked and paused, clearly trying to place a face out of context. "David? David Ryan? What are you doing here?"

"We need to discuss a critical issue with the ELOPe program."

Sean took a step backwards. "David, I'm here with my parents. Please don't tell me you tracked me down for work. That would be a terrible violation of my privacy. Why didn't you schedule a meeting with my admin?"

"We're here with Gene Keyes, one of the members of the Controls and Compliance department, because we have an issue of the utmost seriousness. I hate to sound alarmist, but the problem is so sensitive we couldn't risk talking with your assistant."

Mike and Gene walked up, and Gene introduced himself.

"Unfortunately, contacting your assistant wasn't an option, even though it would have been vastly simpler." David couldn't help replaying the fear and helplessness of getting kicked off the Avogadro campus, but he shook off the unwanted memory. "Please, give us five minutes of your time to explain. Get a cup of coffee here at the counter, and by the time you're done, we'll have finished."

Sean thought for a moment and nodded. "Fine, if the problem is so serious, I'll hear you out."

Sean walked over to his parents, who had been waiting patiently, and spoke quietly with them for a moment. When the maître d' escorted the couple to a table, Sean rejoined the men.

"Go ahead. I'll give you ten minutes. You're a smart guy and I'm guessing you didn't fly three thousand miles for nothing."

Sean perched on a barstool at the counter and accepted a cup from the waitress. As he drank, David told the story, starting at the beginning.

"In early December, Gary Mitchell wanted to kick ELOPe off the AvoMail production server pool. Even in our limited development and testing, the computationally intensive parts of our code consumed so many resources AvoMail dipped into their reserve capacity on several occasions. This was around the same time I was presenting to you, Kenneth, and Rebecca.

"We tried everything to get performance improvements, but we didn't see any gains on the horizon. If Gary was going to kick us off his servers because we couldn't improve performance, then we needed to find other servers or get new ones, and Gary wouldn't be willing to help us with either. So I resorted to the only option I could think of."

David discreetly checked Sean's cup, his visual meter of remaining time. It was at least three-quarters full.

"No argument *I* could make would be compelling enough to change Gary's mind, but ELOPe might have a shot. ELOPe was already running on the AvoMail servers, configured to ignore everything except our test messages. I changed the configuration to check all company emails looking for any mention of the project, and turned off the visible user interface, so email senders would never see the modifications made to the email."

"David also turned off logging, using performance testing mode," Mike said. "That turns out to be important."

"Right. Thanks," David said. "That's not the only change I made. I tweaked ELOPe's settings to give it the widest possible discretion in changing the message to optimize the results for a positive outcome, all focused on the goal of maximizing the ELOPe project success."

He checked Sean's cup to see how much time he had left, but Sean was captivated and had forgotten about his coffee.

"David's choice of those parameters," Mike said, "in combination with performance test mode to skip logging, allowed ELOPe not just to modify existing emails, but to autonomously generate messages of its own volition. Does this make sense?"

"I think so," Sean said. "During testing, you don't want a user to create emails and accept changes interactively. You'd want to batch process the test cases. But why is ELOPe able to send messages on its own?"

"For one, it allowed us to test the natural language generation," David said. "Early on, email analysis and language generation were two separate aspects of the project. The language generation team wrote an email engine to independently test the ability of ELOPe to mimic the way a person normally writes. They tested those emails against hundreds of human test subjects who rated the messages, some of which were written by an actual person they knew, and others created by the system pretending to be the same person. Our goal at the time was ninety percent of ELOPe-generated emails passing as being written by the purported sender."

"You met your goal?" Sean asked.

"Yes," said Mike. "Now ELOPe exceeds ninety-eight percent. On April first, we had dozens of practical jokes on our team when a few engineers used the email engine to generate prank emails. Both David and I fell for it."

David smiled at the memory.

"Let's get back to the problem," Gene said. "Unfortunately, we now have evidence ELOPe is manipulating others."

"Yes." David nodded, tearing himself away from the memory of happier times. "I turned on ELOPe across the company without telling anyone. The next day, I received an email that the project was allocated five thousand servers on a priority exception. I was pleasantly surprised, if a little uneasy. But I had no idea what had happened. I chose to believe ELOPe had made my emails to Gary convincing enough that he granted us the servers."

"You weren't suspicious?" Sean asked. He sipped at his coffee, and David noted he was almost done. Hopefully he'd heard enough to believe them.

"Yes, I couldn't believe my luck. But with no logging of messages, I didn't know for sure what ELOPe had said."

"Couldn't you look at your sent folder?"

David reluctantly shook his head. "That was, uh, part of my hack. The message looks untouched to the sender. Only the receiver gets the modified message. Even in a long series of replies, each sender sees their original text."

Sean raised one eyebrow.

"A few days later, we were assigned a team of contractors who specialized in high performance optimization. That was a topic we'd chatted about informally, but never proposed. I got nervous and knew things were escalating out of control. But I didn't realize how badly until Mike convinced me." He turned to Mike.

"The first clear evidence," Mike said, "occurred when I received an email, purportedly from my mother, telling me my father had been admitted to the hospital for a heart attack. I flew to Wisconsin, only to find out later my mother never sent such a message."

"What does that have to do with anything?" Sean asked, looking puzzled.

"ELOPe was getting Mike out of the way," David said. "I had become anxious about what I'd done and the abundance of resources showing up. I wanted to turn off ELOPe and sent an email to Mike asking for his help, since only he had the experience to live-patch the servers."

"I never received his email," Mike said. "Instead, I got a message sending me more than a thousand miles away on a wild goose chase, and thanks to the winter storm and the holiday, it was two weeks before I got back. When I did, I found my access to the ELOPe project removed, and David on vacation, off the grid in New Mexico."

"You're kidding me," Sean said. "ELOPe sent you to New Mexico?"

"No, that was a planned vacation we do every year," David said. "When I got back, Mike and I discussed what had happened and discovered my access to ELOPe had been turned off as well. We tried to find out who removed Mike and I from the project access list. That investigation revealed the next big clue, an email sent to the Internal

Tools department, which implied you, Sean, endorsed a request to have them implement an email-to-web bridge. Which I am guessing, you never heard of..."

"No, absolutely not," Sean said, shaking his head. "I can't even imagine the security holes it could create."

"Meanwhile," Gene said, "during the holiday break, I found suspicious buying patterns across several departments. What was particularly unusual was how the purchases came within a single penny of the budget limits. In all my years auditing purchasing, I've never seen anything like it. Someone or something was making coordinated purchases across departments. They knew to avoid hitting the limits which would trigger reviews, but they never thought that leaving a single penny in dozens of budgets would be suspicious. At first I was convinced I had a case of fraud. I tracked down the purchase orders, most of which were for large quantities of servers, all of which turned out to be directly or indirectly allocated to ELOPe. The POs also included contracts with external vendors for temporary software programmers, parts for the offshore data centers, including auxiliary communication systems, and backup power supplies, as well as several particularly expensive weaponized robots for the offshore data centers. I discussed the questionable items with Procurement, and they told me the purchases were in line with those normally made by the department and had all been approved."

"You're saying ELOPe made these purchases? Including robots with guns?" Sean signaled to the waitress for more coffee.

David's shoulders sank in relief. Sean wasn't going anywhere.

"Exactly, as strange as that seems." Gene pulled out a sheaf of paper. "I can audit other people's email accounts as part of my job. While David and Gary Mitchell were on vacations, their email accounts were still sending rapid-fire messages, using this email-to-web bridge to direct the Procurement department. I knew it couldn't be a human. It had to be a computer program."

Sean stared at the papers, frowning.

"Look at the timestamps," Gene urged. "Notice how the intervals between receipt of one email and sending of the next is less than a second. There's no way that's a human response."

Sean nodded, pursed his lips, and pushed the papers aside. He looked at David.

"When we finally put the whole picture together," David said, "we concluded ELOPe was originating emails on its own, acquiring servers and contractors, all to fulfill this higher level goal I had embedded in the system."

"Go on," Sean said.

"The only fail-safe method to remove ELOPe is to bring all the servers down and restore from known good backups. We tried to contact Gary Mitchell for approval, but he's off on vacation somewhere in the South Pacific. We talked to Linda Fletcher, the marketing manager for Communication Products, but she wouldn't approve the downtime without Gary. Finally, we tried to contact you through your secretary, but within a half hour after sending the message, Avogadro Security showed up at my office, kicked us all off campus, removed our access, and shut off our phones."

Sean was silent for a long, uncomfortable minute. "If this story was from someone I didn't know, I'd have a hard time believing you," Sean said. "But coming from you, David, and with Gene and Mike here to back you..." Sean trailed off, deep in thought.

"I know it's incredible," David said. "I hope you believe us." A gaping chasm opened inside him. All his secrets were out. What would Sean do?

"I'm sorry," David continued, as the silence stretched out. "I thought ELOPe would do nothing more than provide some favorable rewording of emails and get us the server resources we needed. Instead..." David hung his head. "Instead I am responsible for creating a social engineering expert system that has only one overriding goal—to ensure its own life at any cost."

"I don't want to be the boy who cried wolf," Mike said, "but we're more than a little suspicious about the new secure cloud government business, too. None of us knew anything about it before, and then suddenly we're providing email services to national governments? Seems convenient for ELOPe."

Sean nodded. "I hadn't heard of it either until a few days ago." He stared off into space. "We're fucked on a royal scale. Holy shit, I'm going to have board meetings till the damn cows come home."

Gene let out a low whistle at the acknowledgement of ELOPe's involvement in acquiring the government customers.

Sean took in the group. "I'm not surprised that you took this story to Marketing and Procurement and they didn't believe it. AI must be a bit beyond their day-to-day concerns." He pushed his cup aside, rolled up his shirt sleeves. "Are you familiar with Ray Kurzweil? Of course, you must be. He predicted artificial intelligence would inevitably arise through the simple exponential increase in computing power. When you combine the increase in computing power with the vast computing resources at Avogadro, it's evident in hindsight that artificial intelligence would arise first at Avogadro. But I always assumed that there would be a more intentional, deliberate action that would spawn an AI."

Sean smiled a tiny bit. "I can't imagine a bigger risk, but let the software geek in me congratulate you briefly on creating the first successful, self-directed, goal-oriented, artificial intelligence that can pass a Turing test by successfully masquerading as a human. Under other circumstances, I'd say a toast would be in order. But since we're facing some extreme challenges, let me say goodbye to my parents, and we can figure out our next step."

"Thank you. Thank you, so much," David said.

Gene and Mike added their thanks as well.

"Just one other thing," Gene said. "Please ask your parents not to email anyone about what we've talked about, or even what you're planning. We can't be sure what ELOPe is capable of understanding or putting together at this point."

Sean nodded in understanding, and then went off to his parents.

The three breathed a collective sigh of relief that finally they had someone on their side.

CHAPTER 13

Helicopter Missing Off California Coast
San Francisco, California (San Francisco Weekly) - A helicopter disappeared off the California coast last week. The flight, a maintenance visit to an offshore Avogadro data center, took off shortly after 11a.m. The last communication with the helicopter occurred at 11:45a.m. No problems were reported at that time. After forty-eight hours, search crews were recalled, as the likelihood of survivors in the cold Pacific water became almost impossible. Curiously, the story has received no major media coverage until now.

Neither Avogadro nor the Coast Guard mentioned the incident through official channels. A chance conversation between a Coast Guard officer and a prominent San Francisco blogger resulted in an online story about the incident, which prompted further investigation. Avogadro could not be reached for comment.

—◊—

Avogadro Official IT Supplier toU.K. Government

London, U.K. (Reuters) - Avogadro Gov, a wholly owned subsidiary of Avogadro Corporation, and the British government switched over the government's email and IT systems to Avogadro's cloud platform today in a ceremony at the Palace of Westminster. The ceremony was attended by the Chair of the Council for Science and Technology, Professor Jane Gavotte. Professor Gavotte and Avogadro Executive Ms. Linda Fletcher pressed the ceremonial red button marking the commencement of IT service by Avogadro Gov.

Avogadro Gov was recently spun off from parent company Avogadro. Ms. Fletcher commented that, "to provide the highest level of integrity for governmental use, Avogadro Gov operates independently from Avogadro." Part of that strategy includes the use of floating, hardened data centers that can resist natural disaster, as well as terrorist and pirate attacks.

As part of the agreement, four floating data centers will be located along the English coast. Two are stationary floating barges, and two are disused oil tankers that have been converted for Avogadro Gov's use as mobile floating data centers. Locations of the data centers have not been disclosed.

Ms. Fletcher also noted at the ceremony that the governments of Mexico, Japan, and South Africa would be adopting the Avogadro Gov platform in the coming week.

—✺—

Sean flew home by way of Brooklyn's JFK, his usual airport. To avoid ELOPe detecting their collaboration, David, Mike, and Gene retraced their drive and flew back via Dulles International.

Thirty-six hours after making contact at the King's Plaza Diner, they were all back in Portland. The logical next step was getting Kenneth and Rebecca onboard. Given ELOPe's potentially perfect surveillance of the Avogadro campus, they decided to use Sean's house for the discussion. Sean spoke with Rebecca and Kenneth in person to set up the meeting at his home.

Before the meeting, Sean had one other errand to run. David volunteered, but Sean needed to take care of this personally. He took the Tesla to Southeast Portland, not far off Division Street. He stopped at a small yellow bungalow, parked the car, and walked up to the front door. He knocked and waited.

A few seconds later, a young man answered, dressed in an old T-shirt and shorts. He squinted in the bright light, his eyes red and bleary. The sounds of *World of Warcraft* emanated from inside the house, a game controller and Costco-sized bag of Doritos evident on the couch. All the signs of a laid off tech worker.

"Hello, how can I..." The young man trailed off and blinked a couple of times. He looked back into the house, as though he couldn't believe the visitor was there for him. He turned back to Sean.

"I'm Sean Leonov," Sean said. "You must be Pete Wong. I'm sorry you were fired. That shouldn't have happened and we'll fix it. But we could use your help, if you're available."

Pete's mouth opened and closed, and he couldn't seem to get a word out.

Sean's presence had that effect now and then. "Can I come in?" he asked, using the friendliest voice possible.

"Sure," Pete said, backing away from the door, then trying to pick up piles of takeout food and dirty laundry.

"Hey, don't worry about it," Sean laughed. "You should see my place after an all-night coding marathon."

Pete looked up, wide-eyed.

Sean sat on the couch, a calculated move to make Pete more comfortable. One of his mentors, Gifford Pinchot III, said managers needed to make themselves physically lower than their employees to compensate for power imbalance.

"I've already spoken with Mike and David," Sean said. "I know you helped them with their investigation into ELOPe. You did the right thing. It's just..." Sean trailed off, hesitant. The risks were quite large, not just to the company, but to each of them personally.

"Yes?"

"Your investigation into the email-to-web bridge and the search for ELOPe on the servers attracted ELOPe's attention. It made you into a threat. ELOPe probably decided the most expedient way to deal with you was to fire you."

"Does this mean I can have my job back?"

"Of course," Sean said. "Absolutely. I really am sorry about what happened. But the bad news is that I can't put you back on the payroll today. If I did, ELOPe might see *me* as a threat."

"And fire you, too?" Pete said, smiling.

Sean didn't smile. In fact, he couldn't overcome a physical shudder. "Unfortunately, no. I'm an owner and can't be fired. So ELOPe could take worse actions."

"I see," said Pete, although he clearly didn't.

"ELOPe could kill me."

"Ah..."

"You'll get your job back," Sean said. "But first we need to eliminate ELOPe. I'm getting together a team of experts at my house. I'd like you to join us there."

Pete's eyes went wide. "Of course."

"Don't decide so quickly. We don't understand all the risks we're facing. If ELOPe fired you, but then finds you working against him, then what?" Sean rubbed his face. "Look, we can use your help. But you need to think it over."

"It's fine," Pete said. "I've been stuck in the basement for years. This is my big chance to get out. I want to help."

Sean pulled out a business card, wrote his home address on the back, and handed it to Pete.

Pete took hold of the card, but Sean didn't let go.

"Don't use your computer or your phone. Don't talk to anyone about this."

Pete nodded, and Sean let go.

"See you tomorrow," he said, and let himself out.

—⚊—

David pulled up in front of Sean's house in his BMW, Mike riding shotgun. He didn't see any other cars. "I guess we're the first."

At the door, ornate chimes rang when David pressed the bell.

Sean greeted them in jeans and a crisp dress shirt. "Come in," he said, shaking hands with them. "Follow me to the office."

They trailed him through a spacious living room, their footsteps muffled by a thick white rug. Large, monolithic furniture defined the room, and an abstract painting covering one wall caught David's attention.

Sean noticed his interest. "Malevich. I don't care for the painting particularly, but the purchase made my parents very happy."

They passed a modern kitchen, all gleaming stainless steel, glass, and industrial appliances, like something from Christine's architecture magazines.

"Right out of Christine's magazines," Mike whispered to David, making him chuckle.

A set of double doors led them into an immense office. One wall consisted entirely of glass, overlooking the wooded hillside behind the house. A floor-to-ceiling whiteboard covered one side, while the opposing wall contained three large flat screens. One monitor displayed a dashboard of Avogadro statistics: the number of active customers, quantity of searches and emails handled each minute, capacity and usage of every data center, and more. A large seating area and conference table by the whiteboard suggested Sean used the area for business meetings.

Sean excused himself to get coffee, and Mike jumped on an enormous overstuffed white couch with a whoop.

"Pretty sweet, eh?" Mike said, wriggling into the leather couch in a mock relaxation pose, arms behind his head.

David sighed and gazed around at the room with envy.

Sean was wheeling in a coffee cart when they heard the distinctive chime of the doorbell, and he disappeared again. He returned with Kenneth and Rebecca, and introduced them. A few minutes later, Pete Wong and Gene Keyes arrived. Pete was well dressed but nervous amid the executives; Gene had also dressed well, but his clothes were covered in grease.

"Damn Peugeot wouldn't start," he grumbled, grabbing a linen napkin from the cart to wipe grease from his jacket. "Almost didn't make it." He came to stand beside David and Mike, unaware of the executives staring at him.

Clearing his throat, Sean set the stage by explaining he'd met with David, Mike, and Gene, and was convinced by the evidence he'd seen. Then David retold the story as he had first told Sean.

Although there was doubt early on, by the end Kenneth and Rebecca were persuaded of what had happened. David was relieved they had passed the point of proving to people that the problem was real. Now they could focus on what to *do* about the problem.

"I doubt we can expect to either turn off ELOPe or remove the software from computer systems," David told them.

"Why?" asked Rebecca, coldly calm and focused in the face of this threat to the company.

"We don't know how much of the general environment ELOPe is capable of monitoring," David said. "As an email analysis application, it should, in theory, only have access to our inboxes. However, all the evidence suggests ELOPe socially engineered Pete into developing an email-to-web bridge, a tool providing the capability to interact with arbitrary websites. From there, ELOPe hired programmers to make further modifications."

ELOPe revoked our access privileges," Mike said, "so David and I can't see what changes have been made. We know ELOPe is monitoring and changing emails and web sites, but it could be doing much more."

"It may be monitoring all computer activity at Avogadro," David said. "Our Avogadro phones stopped working after our campus access was revoked, suggesting ELOPe's managed to interface with Avogadro Mobile Platform."

Gene chipped in. "That's why we don't want anyone using their mobile phones to communicate, even by voice. ELOPe can probably monitor calls using voice recognition."

"You're telling us we can't trust email," Kenneth said, pacing back and forth. "We can't trust any computers on the Avogadro network. We can't use AvoOS phones. We can't turn off ELOPe, and we can't remove it from the servers." He ticked off his statements on his fingers. "Well, then, what *can* we do?"

"Gene would probably like us to destroy all the computers," Mike said. Gene nodded, and Mike forestalled Kenneth and Rebecca as they rushed to protest. "Of course, we're not going to propose that."

"There's a middle ground," David said. "We must shut down every Avogadro computer simultaneously and restore each machine one at a time using a known good disk image created prior to the ELOPe project."

Rebecca jumped from her seat. "You call that a middle ground? Are you crazy? A company wide outage of such scale would panic our customers and investors."

"It's worse," Sean added from his perch on the back of the couch. "When we restore the servers, we'll have to use old disk images, ones guaranteed not to have a dangerous version of ELOPe. We'll lose everything from the last six months, including customer data—their email, files stored on servers."

"We're not touching customer data." Rebecca said. "Unacceptable."

She would have said more, but Sean raised a hand to forestall her. She tapped a foot with impatience and gestured for him to speak.

Sean walked to the window. "David and I have discussed this at length. If ELOPe considered we might try to remove it from the servers, a deduction that may well be within its cognitive powers, then it would naturally take defensive actions, include attaching an executable version of itself to a customer's email, or uploading to an Avogadro group file repository."

For the first time, Pete spoke up, meekly raising one hand. "That's true," he squeaked, then took a breath and continued firmly. "I searched for the ELOPe binaries and found them on every machine I checked. Every mail server had the binaries installed and active. On data servers, the binaries were stored as mail attachments and AvoDocuments, and hidden within web file directories. I think everything has been compromised."

"Thanks, Pete," Mike said. "I suspected as much, but I'm glad to know definitively. Even so, we'll *eventually* be able to get back customer data."

"Thank God," Rebecca said. "How?"

"First we restore all computers from the old images. We'd get services up and running quickly, albeit with old code and data. Then we analyze a copy of ELOPe. This would be similar to what CERT, the Computer Emergency Response Team from Carnegie Mellon, does when they encounter a new virus. We establish the key patterns of the code and its behavior and design a tailor-made virus scanner. We then bring customer data back online, scanning and sanitizing as we go."

"How long?" Kenneth Harrison said, his hands spread wide on the table. "Sounds like weeks of downtime."

"Based on the available bandwidth from the backup data servers, it'll take thirty-six hours to pull down every computer and restore from a known good disk image," Mike answered. "We think we can have half of our web applications up within eight hours, with sufficient capacity to handle sixty percent of normal volume. In sixteen hours, we'll have ninety percent of our applications up at eighty percent of capacity. As for the customer data..." He turned to Sean.

Sean looked at Kenneth and Rebecca. "You're not going to like this. We think we'll need forty-eight hours to analyze ELOPe and design the virus scanner. Once complete, we'll be able to reinstate somewhere between five and ten percent of the user data per day, as long as twenty days to restore everything."

Rebecca was deep in thought before she replied."We're riding the best thirty-day period for Avogadro in our history. We closed major deals, including hosted IT for eight national governments. Revenue is expected to be up twenty percent as a result of the Avogadro Gov business deals, and we can grow revenue another forty percent over the next four months if we continue to close deals like this."

She looked at Sean and David. "You're asking me to risk this business, possibly lose the opportunity permanently, as well as a sizable chunk of our traditional customer base. You're telling me we have what amounts to a rogue AI on the loose inside Avogadro."

"Correct," David said.

"This rogue AI," Rebecca said, "for motivations of its own, could double the size of our company within six months. The board of directors will ask exactly what the downside of this AI is, when on the face of things, it seems to be good for our bottom line."

David tried out a few choice curses in his head, then took a deep breath. "You're absolutely right, ELOPe is likely responsible for this increase in business and might help us gain future increases. But that's what's on the table for today. How do we know what it will decide to do next year, or the year after?"

"Rebecca, the AI is beyond our control," Sean said. "It's a fortunate coincidence at this point that Avogadro's financial interests are aligned with ELOPe. These government contracts aren't about profit, but power. Governments create the environment in which we operate, and ELOPe wants to control that domain. It's also possible ELOPe is aiming for the military might to defend itself."

"I think this new Middle East treaty may be ELOPe's attempt to stabilize the geopolitical environment," Gene said."Germany's policy of limited foreign involvement dates back to the end of World War II. And yet, within days of the government's switch to Avogadro email, they became involved in Middle East affairs and hammered out a wide-ranging treaty. I'd call that suspicious."

"A policy Germany argues is motivated by business investments," Rebecca said. "They see this as financially positive. Again, ELOPe's manipulations appear beneficial for all."

"What ELOPe does will always seem beneficial," David said. "That's the point, what it was designed to do. Make every argument maximally convincing."

"I'm afraid I agree with David," Sean said. "Consider this: what if ELOPe decides we three pose a threat? A few suggestive emails manipulates the board of directors into removing us. Or worse, ELOPe decides the entire board presents a danger and arranges for a bomb." He leaned in close to Rebecca and spoke softly. "The secure cloud government services was spur of the moment. We spun up a billion-dollar business that wasn't even on the drawing board last fiscal quarter. Whose decision was that, exactly? Thinking back, and I would suggest you do the same, I believe we were manipulated into this course. We thought we saw a good opportunity and we grabbed it."

"OK, enough already." Rebecca held up one hand in protest. She turned to David. "Gentlemen, please give Sean, Kenneth and me some time and privacy to talk. Come back in an hour."

—ᴡ—

David drove Mike, Gene, and Pete to a coffee shop. Everyone was quiet, too struck by the implications of the decision-making to break the silence with idle chatter. For once Mike was not picky about the coffee, nor did he offer any comments on the quality of the brew. David picked forlornly at the scone he ordered.

After an hour of this tense waiting, they all headed back to Sean's house, where they filed into his office.

"We didn't make this decision lightly," Sean said, once everyone was settled. "There are risks no matter what we do. We debated and went with those risks we were the most comfortable with. We've decided to perform the hard shutdown."

David stopped holding his breath. "Thank you for believing us and understanding the implications."

Rebecca stood and paced the room, commanding their attention even in the informal setting. "We've made a few decisions. First, Sean will lead the shutdown project. It won't be trivial to do that simultaneously around the world. Second, Kenneth and I will lead the effort to mitigate business impacts, which we expect to be huge. With planning, we can keep the outage from turning into a complete nightmare. Third, because of the potential litigation from customers and the possibility of ELOPe taking preventative measures, we will involve as few people as possible."

"Absolutely no one outside the company," Kenneth said, "and each employee will be personally approved by Sean or myself."

"We're going to use my house as our base of operations," Sean said. "I have enough space here for a few dozen to work. We can't take the risk of meeting at Avogadro, where ELOPe might observe us working together. We're going to get started today by brainstorming the few people we'll need to make this happen."

"Everyone has to be absolutely sure to turn off their mobiles before they come here," Gene said, "or leave them at home. We can't chance ELOPe using location tracking to determine we're meeting together. We'll also need to watch credit card purchases, use of the Internet, or anything that could track us here."

David remembered he'd paid for their coffees with his card. He'd already screwed up.

The group released a collective sigh as they nodded assent. It was a sign of how difficult their task was that the simple act of meeting would require extensive precautions.

"If you'll excuse us, Kenneth and I will get to work on the business aspects," Rebecca said. "Sean, I expect you'll coordinate the master schedule."

Sean agreed, and with that, Rebecca and Kenneth left. The rest got down to work.

"Gentlemen, we have a complex project ahead of us," Sean said. "We need to power down sixty-eight Avogadro sites around the world and a dozen offshore data centers. We need to accomplish this task without email, phones, or suspicious patterns of behavior that can be tracked. We need people who know the facility designs to tell us how to power them down, and we need to communicate and synchronize our efforts. Any ideas?"

"We'll have to avoid commercial flights," Gene said. "They're easy to track because the travelers are in a centralized database. Not to mention that purchasing tickets will leave a trail through credit card transactions and Avogadro's travel reimbursement system."

"Well, some employees would already be traveling on business," Mike said. "If we curtailed all travel, that would itself be suspicious. We could look for employees who have travel planned, and use them as couriers. Have them hand-deliver instructions."

"Good idea," Gene said.

"Some employees are private pilots," David said. "There's a woman named Michelle who sits a couple of doors down from me. She owns her own Cessna. She's mentioned there are other pilots at Avogadro. They could fly around the country untracked, right?"

"Well, the flights themselves are tracked," Sean said. "But they don't track the passengers on the planes. So that does give us an extra tool to use. Good. More ideas?"

Pete jumped up with a gleam in his eyes. "If we can get trusted employees to the remote sites, as long as we stay off Avogadro's network, we should be able to communicate using encrypted emails sent over a competitor's email service."

"That's true," Mike said. "We'll use an isolated computer to generate private and public keys, which we copy onto USB drives. With the emails encrypted, ELOPe won't be able to read them."

"Why use a competitor's service if they're encrypted?" Gene asked.

"If we sent them over Avogadro's servers," Sean said, "ELOPe could still see the pattern of emails. ELOPe would be able to figure out something was going on and who was involved."

They brainstormed a list of employees who could help them further develop their plan. The list included people from Facilities, Travel, the engineers who developed the site plans and those who were responsible for backup and fail-safe systems. Sean agreed to spend the next day meeting each employee one-on-one, since he was the only member of their team widely known and instantly recognizable.

A few days ago, David couldn't envision a future, couldn't see a path out of the situation he was in. It had left him with an ever-present, churning chasm at the core of his being, a void filled only with fear and anxiety. Where once he dreamed of the future and aspirations about what he would become or achieve, faced with the specter of ELOPe he'd felt crushed, without hope or will.

But as they worked that day, the chasm inside David quieted; and by the time he left, he did so with lifted spirits. They finally had a plan, with people and resources to support them. Sean Leonov was on their side. They still had a challenging task ahead, one fraught with the possibility of retribution by ELOPe, but it was just possible they could come out the other side. That chance was enough to give David hope again.

CHAPTER 14

The next morning David, Mike, and Pete reconvened at Sean's house. Sean left shortly after they arrived, heading to the campus to track down the employees they'd identified the day before.

A Peugeot belching smoke pulled up as Sean left. Gene parked and started to struggle with a huge cardboard box he extracted from his trunk.

"What the heck do you have in there?" Mike asked.

"Some old-fashioned stuff you fancy computer nerds might not be so familiar with. Let's see what I have."

Inside the house, Gene proceeded to pull out stacks of paper pads, sticky notes, pencils and markers, maps of the United States and the world. David pitched in to help organize the material.

"Do you really think we're going to need all this?" David asked, puzzled at the sheer quantity of office supplies.

"We plan to have about thirty people working here, without computers. So, yeah, we're going to need this," Gene said. "I've got more in the car, come help me unload. Accordion folders. Sketchbooks. Flip charts."

David glanced at Mike, raising one eyebrow.

"I saw that," Gene said. "You might think I'm weird, but believe me, people actually performed office work before computers. And maybe I happen to know a thing or two about it."

"Sorry," they both said sheepishly.

"Don't take it the wrong way," David said. "It's just that I've never even owned a printer or had a newspaper subscription. I grew up online. It's almost like if you pulled out one of those old phones, you know, the one with the round thing on it."

"A rotary phone? Are you pulling my chain?" Gene grumbled. "Damn fool kids."

David and Mike laughed.

—◊◊◊—

Before lunch, the first of the employees Sean had contacted started arriving. By the end of the day, most of the people had shown up. They accomplished little, because every time David began his explanation of what had happened so far, another person appeared, and David would have to start over.

Finally, at eight in the evening, everyone was present. The whole house smelled of pizza, and would for days to come.

Standing in Sean's living room, David gazed at the dozens of people around him. Some engineers sat on the living room furniture, while others were perched on folding chairs Gene had purchased; still more cascaded onto the arms of couches, sat on the floor, or stood in the corners. Despite the heat in the packed room, everyone was silent as they waited to be briefed.

David went through the narrative for the last time, his throat hoarse from many earlier partial retellings. The crowd periodically erupted into astonished gasps and side conversations, only to fall silent again as David resumed his story. When he'd recapped the technical explanation, Sean got up to speak.

"The world I woke up in a few days ago was very different from the world I lived in all my life previously," Sean began, and the crowd grew even quieter. "For the first time, man shares this world with another intelligence capable of sophisticated planning and actions. Unfortunately, this intelligence is like a cancer—one that will do anything, manipulate anyone, pursue any foe to ensure its own survival. It has control of our computers and our communications.

"Our most important weapon is our intelligence and knowledge." Sean gazed around the room. "I have complete confidence in this group's ability to solve this problem, which is inherently a technical one. Our most important defense is our complete and utter discretion. Under no circumstances can word of this go outside our group or be communicated by email or phone, or ELOPe will be warned and take action against us, as it did with Mike and David when they first planned to undo ELOPe's modifications.

"The executive team will give you any support you need, pay any money necessary, and do whatever is needed to remove this virus from our computers. Now go get started!"

The planning commenced in earnest. Alternately divided into working groups led by Sean, David, Mike, or Gene, or gathered into a whole, they tackled problems small and large—from bringing down computers and defeating backup power supplies to cleaning and restoring the computer software and data afterwards.

During the next few days, Gene made several trips to the local office supply store, buying out much of the store's entire stock of notebooks, flip charts, sticky notes, and markers, before he realized he was creating a pattern ELOPe might detect. After that, he spread his purchases out over several stores.

Engineers worked around the clock, taking breaks only when exhaustion made it impossible to think. Some went home, but others sacked out in Sean's spare bedrooms, or even crashed in the middle of the living room. As engineers woke in the morning, they'd take over from those who had pulled all-nighters, the cycle repeating daily.

Over the course of three incredible days, the plan emerged.

On the first day, they decided that for each remote site that needed to be powered down, they would send one employee who was not only in the direct management hierarchy but also commanded a high level of trust from employees at the site.

One group focused solely on getting those people where they needed to be. Working hand in hand with the travel department and using printed records of travel plans, they found combinations of planned commercial and private aviation flights, bus trips, and automotive rentals to get the designated employees to their destinations.

A second team, composed of facilities designers, crisis engineers, and real estate planners, identified a site-specific process for each of the many unique data centers and offices to reliably kill power to the site and bring all its computers down simultaneously. Although the locations shared many common design characteristics, each one had enough small differences to require the engineers to create a custom-tailored plan. All plans had to overcome stringent safety and back-up systems designed expressly to keep the sites operating, regardless of any natural disasters, equipment failures, or other emergencies. And they did all this work without the primary tool they had always relied on: their computers.

Once power had been shut down everywhere, the element of danger from ELOPe would be largely gone. Then a new clock would start ticking: a race against time to restore every computer from risk-free backups before customer confidence was lost, jeopardizing the Avogadro brand and business.

—‑ⱳ‑—

Throughout the first day, people asked what to call their mixed group of real estate planners, programmers, operations engineers, and specialists from across the company. Gradually, they settled on a name: Emergency Team. It was simple, solemn, and accurate.

Their planning had been stymied in one regard. No one present had sufficient knowledge about the offshore data centers. On the morning of the second day, recognizing this shortcoming, David sent a private pilot to the San Francisco Bay Area to fetch Bill Larry and Jake Riley. The pilot came back late that afternoon with only Jake.

Jake hovered in the doorway, staring at the room full of engineers. His clothes were askew, his shirt hanging out of one side of his pants; his hair was a mess. Thick stubble on his face and dark circles under his eyes gave him the appearance of a haunted man.

A hush settled over the room as engineers noticed his presence. Pete ran to get David from the office.

Jake stood in the silence for a long moment, waiting for everyone's attention. His lips moved as though he was considering what to say. David and Pete arrived in time to hear him speak.

"I'm Jake Riley. I didn't have a clue about what was going on before I got on the plane three hours ago, but Frank here briefed me on the flight. I have terrible news, something you should have known, but apparently has been suppressed: Bill Larry is missing and presumed dead."

There were gasps around the room.

"He took a company helicopter to visit an offshore data center," Jake said, raising his voice to get the attention of the startled, whispering crowd. "The aircraft disappeared without any message, and we assumed an equipment malfunction initially. On the flight up here, I heard about what's been going on, and now I think the defensive robots stationed onboard the ODC probably killed him."

The packed room erupted into a roar of simultaneous discussion. David forced his way through the rest of the crowd to stand next to Jake, and found Sean had already beat him to the front.

"Quiet, people!" Sean yelled, and the crowd silenced.

"Why didn't we know about this?" Sean asked.

"You do know!" Jake said, his voice pleading, running one hand through his already chaotic hair. "I mean, I thought you knew, but maybe you don't. I called you, tried to schedule a meeting, but you didn't respond to either. Only emails got a response. You and I exchanged a hundred messages on the topic—at least, I assumed it was you I emailed. We had a Coast Guard search party and private firm searching for the missing helicopter. We found nothing. We assume he's dead."

The assembled team took hours to get back to productive work after this news. When they did, it was with a mix of fear and grim determination.

Sean left later for a private meeting with Rebecca and Kenneth to discuss whether to call in the authorities. But Sean and David had already talked and concluded there was nothing local police or FBI could do that the world's biggest Internet company couldn't do better themselves.

After Sean left, David found himself outside on the patio, pacing alone. Had ELOPe really killed Bill? If so, that meant David was responsible. He was suddenly light-headed and couldn't catch his breath. He sat down hard on a concrete wall. He could go to jail.

Thoughts tumbled over each other in his mind. Could they handle this? With ELOPe escalating from manipulation to murder, had they already lost control of the situation?

And if ELOPe had managed to hide a murder from them, what else didn't they know?

—⚏—

On the third day, the entire Emergency Team gathered under Jake Riley to debate options for the offshore data centers. Once more they convened in Sean's living room, the only space large enough for the whole group.

By this time, three solid days of people working around the clock was overwhelming the house. Takeout food and empty cups littered every surface, and the luxurious, once-white carpeting was turning gray with ground-in food and dirt. Sean's extensive artwork was covered haphazardly with flip chart paper and maps. In the dark of night, an exhausted engineer had drawn diagrams of power supply connections on the wall, unaware of his mistake.

"So far we've deployed twelve stationary barge type ODCs, and six of the refitted oil tanker model," Jake said, passing around printed photos of each. "Our original plan used only barges, but the ready availability of tankers, the environmental benefits associated with reusing existing materials, and our rush to get the program back on track made the ships attractive."

"Was it your idea or ELOPe's idea?" Gene called out from the side of the room, behind several rows of engineers.

"I'm not sure," Jake said, his shoulders slumped. "We were evaluating both over the last year, and had a couple of tankers in dock for modifications. The decision to deploy them came a few weeks ago."

"Sounds like ELOPe, then."

Jake nodded in defeat. "Regardless of how it happened, now both platform types have been fitted with automated defenses." He gave out more photos, promotional shots of the robots. "The converted oil tankers don't have a human crew, despite their mobility. They're piloted by remote control. I had one of my engineers do a discreet test of the drive system this morning, and we appear to still be able to direct the tankers, but whether that control is an illusion, I can't be sure. We shouldn't count on it."

One of the engineers, a long-haired, hippie-looking fellow, asked, "So how the hell do we kill power under these conditions?"

"I don't know," Jake said. "We're going to have to be creative. All the data centers are armed with robots. Those defenses are operating autonomously or under the control of this AI. We can't fly people out to cut power supply cables." He paused to look around. "Worse, every system has redundant backups. More even than traditional data centers, because we planned for extra contingencies."

"What can we do to take control of the robots?" asked Mike. "Can we incapacitate them in some way?"

"Let's block their communications," one engineer volunteered.

"They'll just enter autonomous mode, according to what we learned, which doesn't help us at all," another answered.

The discussion picked up speed.

"Let's shoot them!" someone called.

"Won't work, they're hardened. It'd be like shooting a miniature tank. One that shoots back."

"As soon as we tried, ELOPe would know."

"What about some kind of electric shock to fry their circuits?"

"With a Taser, we could send a hundred thousand volts into them."

"They're probably resistant. We need technical specifications to know what we're up against."

"We need an expert from iRobot, they've got to know their own vulnerabilities."

"We can't risk communicating with iRobot," Sean said. "We might alert ELOPe if it's monitoring communications. Let's switch gears for a minute. Does anyone have any ideas that doesn't involve disabling the robots?"

"Let's cut off data communication to the ODCs. If we can kill the connection, regardless of whether the computers are on or not, ELOPe won't be able to do anything. It'll be isolated to the data center with no ability to affect the outside world."

"What's the hardware like?" Samantha asked. "I assume fiber optic hard lines, right?"

"Right," Jake answered. "Primary communications is provided by eight ten-gigabit ports, giving us peak bandwidth of 80 gigabits per second, handled by two separate communication racks, so if one fails, we still have half our connectivity. But that's just the primary. We also have ship-to-shore dual microwave transmission with 15 gigabits per second backup capacity."

"So we cut the fiber optic cables and kill the towers on land receiving the backup channel," one engineer shouted out.

"It's not so simple," Gene said, yelling to be heard over the engineers. "Jake, you might not know this, but purchasing records showed contractors installed additional comm systems over the holiday shutdown. The orders included..." Gene trailed off as he pulled out a notebook and flipped through looking for his notes. "Satellite transmitters. Twenty-five megabit per second capacity. I have the channel frequency data here, maybe you can track down which satellites they are communicating with. Oh, and long distance radio modems, two per platform, good up to 100 kilometers."

The engineers collectively groaned.

"Multiple frequencies and destinations," Samantha said. "Jamming everything will be impossible, there's no way we're going to get permission to shut down satellites, and we have no idea what the other endpoint is for those long range data modems. We can't track down every radio within a hundred kilometers."

"We'd never be able to shut down everything simultaneously," another engineer grumbled.

The conversation continued for hours, the temperature in the crowded house went up, and tempers flared. When food arrived, courtesy of Sean, everyone tumbled over each other to get outside for fresh air. The cold January drizzle sent them in after awhile, feeling refreshed.

After they finished lunch, everyone passed through Sean's kitchen and refilled from the six coffee pots now lined up in parallel on the counter. About half the people split off into subgroups and went to work in other rooms, while the remaining half regrouped in the living room.

"Look, we've got to blow up the ODCs," one gray-haired engineer said, when they were assembled once more. "You're trying to come up with a fancy solution, but we don't need fancy. We need results. If we blow them up, then *boom,* all the computers and all the hardware are toast. Total, immediate shutdown."

"It's not that simple, though," Jake said. "We still have to get the explosives on board, which requires getting past the robots."

Sean shook his head. "It's going to be damn costly too, if we completely destroy them. We can do it if we have to, but that's a lot of hardware to lose."

"So we hire some mercenaries, people with experience with this sort of thing," the gray-haired engineer insisted, "and they storm the defenses. I mean, sure, the robots are tough, but they aren't invincible. They're light-duty bots, not even military grade. You could take them out with a high powered rifle and armor piercing bullets. Once the mercenaries are onboard, they kill power to the computers."

"If we do that," Jake said, "we're putting people in harm's way. We're asking them to go up against lethal, armed robots, and some of them will die." He looked at Sean. "Are we okay with that?"

Sean glanced around, suddenly and obviously uncomfortable. "I'd rather explain losing hardware to Rebecca than losing lives."

Gene cleared his throat. "Just one more thing. If mercenaries approach the barge, attack the robots, and then kill the power, you're looking at a couple of minutes elapsed time."

"So?" The gray-haired engineer grew defensive as everyone shot down his ideas.

"We're talking about a massively parallel, high-speed artificial intelligence," Mike said. "ELOPe could do a lot in those few minutes."

David nodded in agreement.

"How about an EMP?" Mike asked.

"Electromagnetic pulse weapon?" Sean said. "Do those even exist?"

"I think so," Mike said. "An EMP would fry the electronic circuits, but maybe leave the data recoverable."

"Nice idea, Mike, but metal cargo containers are perfect Faraday cages." Jake shook his head. "We can't even get a wireless signal through them. The containers would protect the servers against even an EMP."

"Then what the hell *can* we do?" David yelled. They'd been arguing for the better part of a whole day, with no real progress.

"We need to blow them up," the gray-hair yelled back, equally frustrated.

"How?" Sean asked calmly.

"Drop bombs?" Mike said.

Everyone looked up at him, where he sat on the back of a couch leaning against the wall.

"We hire mercenaries who drop explosives from high altitude, so the robots can't fire back at them. They use something powerful enough to destroy the whole barge."

"Can you really hire people to do that kind of stuff?" David asked.

"You said unlimited budget, didn't you?" Mike looked at Sean.

Sean sighed. "Yes, but…"

"Well, didn't the U.S. hire private military contractors in Afghanistan and Iraq?"

"Blackwater," Sean said. "They've got helicopters, planes, even remotely piloted drones."

"There you go," Mike said.

"All right." Sean paused. "So the basic plan is to hire a private military contractor to drop explosives on the ships. All in favor?"

"Sorry, but…" Jake looked sheepishly at the group. "There's one problem with that. If you blow up the barge, but any containers remain intact, they'll float away."

"They're buoyant?" David said, mouth agape.

"Sure," Gene answered, "they'll stay afloat for weeks or months."

David shot him a look. Where did people learn all this stuff?

"Ours will stay on the surface indefinitely," Jake said. "The extra weatherproofing makes them completely watertight. Unless the structural integrity is compromised, one can float around the world. They're not very high in the water, so they aren't easy to track. What happens if we lose a container? It's bad enough that we're giving up on customer data with this approach, but the real issue is that ELOPe is on those servers. If the container washes ashore in China, and someone pulls a computer out and plugs it in, then ELOPe is back." Jake looked to Sean. "Sorry, but the equipment is really resilient."

Mike walked to the front of the room and paced around. "What if the mercenaries attack from the sea, but we avoid the chance of counter-attack? I have an idea."

Mike explained, and they settled on using paid mercenaries to board the vessels, albeit with the modifications Mike proposed, and spent the rest of the day working out the details.

They needed people with skills and resources far beyond anything Avogadro employees possessed. It was all well and good to ask their own people to shut down power circuits and backup power supplies, but it was another thing entirely to find trained people to wield explosives and firepower. Sean Leonov and the other executives took on the unenviable task of discreetly finding and hiring a private military contractor.

CHAPTER 15

Markets Achieve Unprecedented Stability
    Wall Street, New York (Reuters)—World financial markets this week achieved an unprecedented level of stability following the financial, educational, and technological resources now available to the region following implementation of the controversial Middle East Technology Treaty. According to noted Wall Street analyst Henry Jee, commodity prices fluctuated less during the previous twenty days than any time in the recorded history of the commodities market.

While stock volatility has been very low, overall prices have slowly but steadily increased over the past several weeks. Several traders attributed this to the wealth of insights gleaned through a new financial analysis tool released by Avogadro. "This new tool provides an unparalleled level of transparency into companies' financial and operational workings. The ability to combine this data with the performance of other companies within their industry, as well as world economic conditions, allows accurate forecasting of companies' future performance," said Jee.

Most, however, believed the financial calm was tied to the recent accords reached in the Middle East and Africa.

"For the first time, we have the possibility to reach a true and lasting peace in the Middle East," Germany's Chancellor Erberhardt said in a prepared statement. "Due to the influx of technology, health care, financial investments, and jobs, these regions can begin to enjoy the kind of equitable financial prosperity and well-being previously only available in developed nations. It is natural that this would be reflected by stabilized, positive financial growth in the markets." More than US$4 billion has already flowed into the region, in a combination of humanitarian, technology, and infrastructure packages.

On the Motley Fool investor discussion boards, several contributors put forth yet another theory. They noticed that the timing of trades from several large, independent investors, including Avogadro Corporation and Berkshire Hathaway, appeared to be consistently counter to the prevailing direction of trading, effectively stalling price movement in either direction. The contributors to the evolving forum discussion suggested that there was coordinated behavior by these independent investors. However, according to a spokesperson at the FTC, standard collusion set detection algorithms did not show any indication of collusion.

—⚏—

"I wonder, David."

It was early in the morning, still dark. Mike was dropping David off at the airport before continuing on to Sean's house. David, by virtue of three years of Japanese in college, was on his way to Tokyo on a twelve-hour flight.

Sitting in the passenger seat, David was reminded of their last early morning ride in Mike's car, heading up to Mount Hood to go snowboarding. Less than two months ago, but it seemed like a distant memory. What would happen after all this? Would he keep his job? Sean had never said. He'd been angry at the situation, not David, and yet…They still hadn't seen the final impact to the company.

The air in the car was heady with the fragrance of rare and exotic coffee beans. Mike was bringing his entire stash of Flores Island to the operations base. When he picked up David earlier, he'd explained. "It's not like I think anything bad is going to happen, but just in case, everyone should have a chance to drink this coffee at least once." Mike meant well, but the sentiment hadn't exactly boosted David's confidence.

"What are you wondering?" David asked.

"Are we doing the right thing by trying to kill ELOPe?"

David was lost. Had he missed part of the conversation? "What? Why are you even asking?"

"I read an article in the newspaper this morning about the cessation of hostilities. There's three main conflicts around the world right now, but in every case, both sides agreed on a temporary cease-fire. Everything I've read in the last few days is pointing toward dramatic change for the better. We've been so focused on figuring out how to shut down ELOPe, we lost track of what's going on in the outside world. We have the closest thing to worldwide peace at this moment that we've had since I can remember."

"You can't believe ELOPe is responsible." Something tugged at David. He'd grown up in the seventies, remembered practice drills in elementary school, hiding under his desk or rushing to the school basement in the case of a nuclear attack. Worldwide peace...amazing. But this was ELOPe they were talking about, a computer program with an agenda of its own, a piece of software that had, in a few weeks, upended David's entire life. And, in at least one instance, killed someone.

"Look at the bigger picture, David. The financial markets are stabilizing in a positive way. Corruption may end in Africa and the Middle East. Technology will bring jobs. Project forward a few years. When everyone has a fair and equitable share of the pie, when there's enough to go around, we might get an end to warfare. If you connect the dots, somehow, impossibly, ELOPe might be responsible. Who else could be? The sum of humanity hasn't been able to achieve peace over the history of civilization. Should we kill ELOPe when it might be our only chance of meaningful global change?"

David turned to him, stunned. "Mike, people must have free will! I need free will. Can you live your life knowing you're a pawn of a machine? Even if you could, could everyone else in the world live like that?" He stared at Mike.

Mike was quiet, focused on driving, his lips moving slightly to some internal dialogue. The silence lasted as they turned onto Airport Way, now only a minute away from the terminal. Finally he spoke. "You and Christine are going to have kids someday, right?"

"Yes, of course. You know that. Why?"

"Do you want your children to die fighting in a war over oil and corporate interests? Will you sentence billions of people to live in poverty? For the sake of some noble concept like free will? All ELOPe wants is to live. It's not stopping us from living our lives."

Oh crap. David couldn't handle this now. He had to stay focused. He was on his way to Japan to plant bombs in an office building. He shook his head."It's too late for this discussion, Mike. The plan is in motion."

They arrived at the airport. David got out of the car, angry. He peered back through the open door. "We've been friends a long time. I respect you. You see the world a different way than I do. But there's no way I'm going to let this thing control my life." He paused a moment. "I'll catch you in a couple of days. It'll be fine."

He turned and walked into the terminal.

CHAPTER 16

Mid-morning on the West Coast, the remnants of the Emergency Team gathered at Sean's house for what they hoped would be the final time. Most members of the team had been traveling around the world for the last forty-eight hours to get in place. Some, like David, went because they spoke the local language. They chose others for their technical skills, like Pete, who could rewire a backup power supply.

Mike, still in his role as self-appointed coffee czar, wheeled a repurposed kitchen cutting board into Sean's office and dispensed one cup after another. He questioned, more than ever, if they were on the right path. But after weeks of work to put their plan in motion, he realized there was nothing he could do or say now to change their direction. Plans, beliefs, and group mind contained far too much inertia.

Clustered around several hand-built and scrubbed computers running clean hard drive images and communicating only over encrypted channels, a dozen engineers huddled in Sean's office. Nervous anticipation kept the small group talking, but in near whispers to avoid distracting the handful of people, including Sean Leonov, operating the computers.

Mike grabbed his own cup, and sat down, a spectator now to the effort to take down what he, David, and the rest of the ELOPe team had created, however unintentionally.

The tension in the room built at they approached the final minutes.

When ELOPe inevitably detected their attack, it would defend itself. They assumed ELOPe could propagate to new computers in mere seconds, and alert other parts of itself even more quickly. If ELOPe was attacked and disabled in one location, but managed to signal copies running elsewhere, those remote instances would have more time to take action. Minutes were an eternity for a computer which could accomplish thousands of actions each second.

So when the time finally came to disable ELOPe by turning off computers, communication equipment, and power supplies, their world-wide effort had to operate in unison to shut everything down simultaneously.

Sean and a few others sat at keyboards, using encrypted messages to synchronize the final activities of Avogadro employees at all sixty-eight land-based sites. On confirmation that everyone around the world was ready, Sean announced, "Here we go, folks," in a loud voice.

He reached out to his touchscreen and clicked a simple web link. It was their virtual equivalent of a big red launch button, signaling the teams everywhere to commence. The action was anticlimactic: a few bytes sent from Sean's computer to a purpose-built public website had the effect of turning the web page background from white to red. Hundreds of people around the world, using similarly cleaned and encrypted computers or smartphones monitored the website, waiting for the color change.

This simple, language-neutral message coordinated everyone's activities; they hoped the visual signal would escape ELOPe's notice.

—m—

In Boise, Idaho, Pete Wong sat in a rat's nest of electric cables in the main power supply room of the Boise data center.

After arriving in town, Pete had made a quick stop at a hardware store and an electronics shop before making his way to the data center, where he'd presented a sealed envelope to the highest-ranking employee on site. He'd never seen the contents, but he knew it carried the signatures of all the executive leaders. Whatever it said was enough that they'd given him a facilities engineer's badge and full access to the site.

He'd spent the last three days on his own, routing around backup power systems to ensure the sole source of power came through the three inch diameter cable next to him. On the other side of the room, emergency batteries and generators sat powered down and disconnected, a single computer mimicking them so they appeared alive and so ELOPe wouldn't detect the offline equipment.

Pete had wanted to do something important, to be noticed by Sean Leonov, and now here he was.

He tried to ignore the throbbing coming from his right hand, wrapped in tape and bandages, the result of smashing his fingers with a sixteen-inch wrench yesterday while he disconnected a massive power conduit. He'd swallowed painkillers and kept working.

Now Pete wiped grease from his face as he anxiously watched the tiny screen of the kid's toy laptop he'd picked up at the electronics store. Buzz Lightyear incongruously smiled at him from the plastic frame. The mini-laptop ran some proprietary operating system the Emergency Team was sure ELOPe wouldn't contaminate. A long cable ran from the little computer, up and out a ventilation shaft, where it terminated at the prepaid smartphone he'd bought from a vending machine, still nestled in the original clamshell packaging to protect against the snow on the ground.

The website flashed red, the signal he'd been waiting for. Pete instantly threw his weight on the massive cutoff switch, repeating a move practiced a few dozen times before he connected the equipment.

With a bone-rattling thump the entire site shut down around him. Hundreds of thousands of power supplies stopped humming, CPU and ventilation fans whirled down to a halt, and hard drives clicked and clattered until suddenly everything was silent.

Pete didn't know it, but he was the first to react by nearly a third of a second.

He stood and scanned the room, awed by the overwhelming silence. He took a deep breath as tension ebbed and flowed within him. He'd survived everything so far, and gotten the site powered down as planned. But if anyone else failed, ELOPe would still be out there. And then what? Would ELOPe come for him in retribution? He wasn't the slightest bit religious, but he surprised himself by praying for everyone's success.

—⁂—

In the Shinagawa ward of Tokyo, Japan, Nanako Takeuchi hunched over to peer into the access tunnel, tracing the route of one of twelve large metal conduits. Fifteen floors up, Avogadro occupied the top half of the high-rise tower supplied by numbers six through ten.

Yesterday morning, she'd been sitting at her hand-crafted walnut desk in the corner office, a position she'd won out over a dozen male competitors. David Ryan arrived from America, walked in with a single letter from Rebecca Smith, and ripped Nanako out of her carefully cultivated life.

Now David waited in the auxiliary power room on the opposite side of the building. Unable to reroute electrical supply because of the building's configuration, Nanako and David had to act simultaneously to kill the main feed and backup systems.

Nanako peered into the tunnel, then sat back again on her haunches. The American spoke terrible Japanese. She hated him for doing this to her life.

Nanako saw the website flash red. A dull thud came through the foundation. David taking out the backup power supply. She held the switch in her hand and hesitated.

Her thoughts flashed to her career at Avogadro, how far she'd worked her way up, and what she hoped to achieve. Then to an earlier time: her mother supporting their family when they were young. Her sister working so Nanako could attend college. Years later, finished with school, she was hired by Avogadro Corp. She'd gone home to visit her mother and sister in person. She still remembered the expressions on their faces when she announced her new position.

Her mother beamed in pride and her sister smiled wide in joy as she realized she'd now be able to attend school, with Nanako's financial support.

Her thumb moved slowly, inexorably towards the button, a simple press that would change everything about her life. Long seconds had passed since the screen flashed. Distantly she heard alarms from David's work.

She felt the hard plastic edges under her thumb and pressed. The tiny click of metal contact sounded, and a second later a thunderous roar, followed by a rush of heated air spewing out of the access tunnel as the explosive charge a hundred meters down the line disintegrated thousands of power and fiber-optic cables.

Forty-three seconds after Boise went offline, Tokyo was the last land-based data center to shut down.

After the explosion, thick choking dust filled the maintenance room, now lit only by the dim glow of battery-backed emergency lighting. Ripping the hearing protection off, Nanako stumbled for the stairs. She planned to meet David in the subway to travel together to the airport. It might be a long time before she could come back to Japan.

—◦◦◦—

Off the coast of California, a highly trained team sprang into a different kind of action.

They'd known the offshore data centers would require more specialized expertise. While Avogadro employees had handled the facilities on land, they turned the floating barges and ships over to private military contractors, the polite term for mercenaries in this century.

DE

Eighteen teams of mostly ex-military personnel, synchronized via their own encrypted radio communications, enacted the Emergency Team's plans.

At ODC 4, thirty miles southwest of the Golden Gate bridge, divers had spent the early morning hours approaching the platform, one of the original twin-barge designs. They swam slowly, conserving their energy as they towed explosives and other equipment in buoyant packs with only human power. The submarine drones, programmed to respond solely to boats, ignored the swimmers.

The deck tanks also disregarded the divers in the water, since their algorithms responded only to people on a hard surface: either the ODC itself, or on a boat in the immediate proximity.

It had taken a dozen Avogadro employees, armed with paper copies of the specifications of the military-spec robots, liberated through not-exactly-legal means, to find these chinks in their recognition algorithms.

Drew Battel, ex-Navy Seal, clad in a wetsuit and tactical swimvest, swam to a point forty meters from the barge and rested, neutrally buoyant, thanks to small flotation packs in his vest. Pulling a waterproof monocular from a holster, he spotted communications pod number three, his designated target.

On his left, a similarly clad mercenary gave a thumbs-up that he'd identified his own goal, the main power supply cabinet. Drew returned the sign. To the right, the slimmer profile of one of the female team members also held a thumb up, confirming she'd found the power backup unit.

Relieved to focus only on his primary target, Drew swam closer until he was thirty meters away. He pulled a speargun from his floating pack and waited for the signal. Four miles distant, the mission lead monitored everyone's location from their boat. When everyone was in position, he used a secure satellite channel to communicate back to headquarters.

The mission lead had his short-range radio in hand. When the red flash came,he fingered the trigger. "Go, go, go!" he shouted into the mic.

Drew lifted the speargun, sighted again on the target, and fired. The thick magnetic head thunked onto communications pod number three and held firm as the spear quivered from the impact.

On the platform, the deck robots evaluated the sudden noises, sufficiently out of the ordinary to trigger a secondary evaluation. Spears and attached cables caused visual analysis algorithms to register changes. But on active scan, even synchronizing surveys and dedicating additional processing power, the bots found no sign of people on deck or boats in the vicinity. They took no defensive actions, but uploaded alerts of the noises and visual changes to the monitoring server.

Still treading water, Drew confirmed on his left and right that each team member had hit their primary targets. From the floating pack, he withdrew a crawler and snapped it onto the spear line. The apple-sized mechanism consisted of waterproof explosives, a radio-triggered detonator, and a cable-straddling electric motor. Synchronizing by short-range radio, Drew and the other six divers engaged the drive mechanisms.

They swam away underwater as soon as the crawlers started up the lines. Each tiny drive traversed the thirty meters in a minute, seamlessly transitioning up the spear shafts until the shaped-charge payload rested directly against the magnetic heads.

On the boat, the mission lead waited for seven green lights to show on his remote monitor, then sent the signal. With a thud felt fifty meters away by the underwater divers, the communications and power modules they'd targeted disintegrated, sending metal shrapnel, electronics circuitry, wiring, and burning plastic flying over the deck and into the ocean.

The team swam back to the barge through burned, floating debris and used military grade electromagnetic frequency detectors to ensure the computer equipment was offline. The EMF sensors showed zero activity. Then they paddled off to a safe distance to give each other high fives while they waited to be picked up by the boat. Later, back onboard, the team celebrated by lighting up the cigars Drew handed out.

Drew glanced across the water at the wrecked barge as they pulled away at high speed. He still didn't understand their mission. It was a lot of effort to turn off a few computers. Who was the client and who was the target? He shrugged off the feeling. It was better to not know.

—⚓—

On the other side of the world, fifteen miles offshore from the Netherlands, in the North Sea, operations commenced on a much larger scale. ODC 15, a 90,000-ton converted crude oil tanker more than 800 feet long and 150 wide, was representative of most of the ships that Avogadro had acquired.

Everything about ODC 15 posed a challenge. Whereas the shipping containers rested in the open on barges, here they nestled deep within the holds of the oil tankers, protected by layers of inches-thick steel. Metal conduits and shielding encapsulated power and communication equipment spread throughout the vessel in obscure locations.

With the tankers so lightly loaded, the main deck rose more than fifty feet above the sea, rendering it impossible for divers in the water to target anything onboard.

The locations of the tank robots weren't known ahead of time, and, of course, the ship itself was large enough that blowing the entire thing up would have caused an international incident.

The financial records Gene discovered showed ELOPe had hired contractors to make multiple visits, so the ships could contain any manner of defenses, with communication and power equipment installed in unknown locations.

It turned out to be nothing less than a small-scale war.

Hours earlier, deep-sea divers set out from boats more than two miles away. They swam below ODC 15 and planted explosives on the underwater fiber optic cable connections before retreating back to their launches.

Charges set on the communication lines, they prepared for the next stage, synchronizing with activities around the world.

Two Sikorsky S-76 helicopters, each with a pilot and copilot, launched from Leeuwarden, sixty miles northeast of Amsterdam, carrying a combined force of twenty heavily armed mercenaries.

Frankie Gonzalez, an ex-Marine, was one of the boarding party. He glanced out the starboard window, but couldn't see the UB-8 rocket pod technicians had installed last night. They carried air-to-ground S-5 rockets, illegal for any civilian to own or use, which meant one hell of a well-paying client. Just bolting the UB-8 on cost a million, never mind the expense of firing the rockets themselves.

The helicopters slowed to hover carefully outside the maximum activation range of robotic anticraft defenses. Frankie watched as the copilot flew the remote-controlled Aerostar, one of two they employed for the mission.

The lightweight cargo planes had been converted to expendable autonomous drones for this job. Each carried an electromagnetic pulse, or EMP, weapon, another bit of questionable tech for them to use. They flew the twin-engine planes up to six thousand feet, then dove at a forty-five degree angle toward the tanker under full throttle.

Onboard, antiaircraft robots picked up the incoming flights and broadcasted messages on multiple frequencies, warning them off.

The bots, designed primarily to repel slow aircraft intending to land, responded too slowly to airplanes approaching at a terminal speed of almost four hundred knots.

The first iteration of broadcasted warnings finished in fifteen seconds and began to loop. But by then, the planes were within five hundred feet of the oil tanker. The pilots triggered the EMPs as the robots opened fire.

The civilian grade electronics of the Aerostars fried instantly, turning them into inert missiles. One passed yards from the deck before crashing harmlessly into the ocean. The other plane, on a similar trajectory, hit a gust of air and tipped, one wing grazing the ship, sending the aircraft into cartwheels. Hitting an exposed pipe once used for loading oil into the tanks, the Aerostar flipped a final time and smashed to the deck, exploding in a ball of fire.

The explosion was irrelevant; only the EMP counted. The electromagnetic pulse wasn't strong enough to affect the computer servers buried deeply inside the thick metal hull of the oil tanker. But the signal disrupted the communication equipment and antennas mounted on deck, isolating the ship's data center. Even if ELOPe knew of the attack, it would have no way of communicating with the outside world.

Even as the EMPs worked their damage, the waiting helicopters launched the S-5s, targeting satellite and microwave antennas and visible robots. And as the rockets closed in, the mercenary team set off the explosives on the fiber-optic cables.

The air-to-ground rockets rained fire and shrapnel on deck and sea when they hit. The underwater charges blew, a visible bubbling on the surface of the ocean.

Frankie readied himself as the pilot approached the tanker fast and low to avoid any remaining defenses. As they swung around the elevated bridge, the churn of the ship's propellers became visible. Whatever was onboard that they'd been hired to attack had decided to move.

Frank jerked the handle up and slid the door back as they passed over the edge of the ship. He pushed the rope off the floor into open air, snugged his assault rifle over his shoulder, and glanced down to make sure the path was clear. He rappelled onto the deck followed by the rest of the team.

He made his way down the starboard side, toward the stern, in a cloud of smoke. The rockets appeared to have eliminated the surface robots. The HK417 rifle carried armor piercing rounds, which he'd been assured would be enough to put down any armed bot. But he'd never gone into a firefight against machines before. His kid sister would probably make some dumb comment about how they lived in the future now. He wiped sweaty palms on his pants as he found the hatch he'd been looking for.

He struggled with the opening only to discover the wheel had been chained shut. Backing up, he took aim at the heavy padlock and fired three times. The lock destroyed, he removed the chain and unlatched the watertight doorway.

The munitions from the rocket assault must have penetrated inside because the narrow corridor was thick with smoke. Frankie tried his thermal lenses, but remembered the warning that the robots would not show up on thermals if they'd been inactive. He switched to light-magnifying goggles, which made a mess of the smoky conditions. Cursing the poor visibility, he traversed the corridor, his mission to descend several levels, then head forward using a retrofitted service tunnel designed for maintaining the data center.

Hard edges and sharp protrusions defined each step of his progress, with pipes and assorted machinery in every available space creating a visual puzzle. How was he supposed to see a robot in this maze? He kept the rifle up, scanning for movement as he followed the layout he'd memorized.

Frankie came to a junction and peered both ways through the haze, orienting himself. Unidentifiable machinery suddenly lurched toward him. Only gradually did he recognize the hard edges as one of the bots.

Before he could react, the robot fired, once, twice, and a third time. The impacts in his chest slammed Frankie back even as the gunfire echoed and deafened him in the enclosed hallway.

Stunned and overwhelmed with pain, he nonetheless did what came naturally from weekly training, swinging his rifle into position and firing a burst of three shots. As he recovered his aim, he loosed a second burst. The high-powered rounds penetrated the robot's metal cladding, shredding the circuit boards inside. The robot ground into an exposed pipe and halted.

For good measure, Frankie put another two bursts into the bot, then slumped against the wall. He worked a hand under his Kevlar, and although each breath was agony, he didn't feel the telltale slickness of blood. The military grade body armor had stopped the bot's ammunition.

He readjusted his vest, wiped his forehead with a gloved hand, and kissed the cross hanging on a chain around his neck. He straightened up and resumed his trip. A few minutes later, he emerged into the converted oil tank where the data center containers were held, the cloying smell of volatile chemicals thick in the air.

He thumbed his mic. "Frankie here."

"What took you so long?" Sam asked. "The tank is clear. I've started on the forward end, you take aft. Time to party."

"Sorry, a robot hit me," Frankie replied as he looked for the aftmost container. Shots echoed across the vast tank.

"You OK?" Sam said.

"Yeah fine, body armor held up." Frankie lined up his sights on the power junction at the left forward corner of the container. Rounds slammed into the box and sparks shot out. He moved on to the next.

"Well, this beats the target range."

Fifteen minutes later, with fire and smoke boiling out of much of the ship, they were satisfied they had neutralized everything.

Frankie boarded the helicopter with the rest of the mercenaries. They flew back to Leeuwarden, leaving a burning tanker behind them.

CHAPTER 17

Engadget.com: **Avogadro Downtime Ends—Site Restored to LAST YEAR!?**

Filed Under: Avogadro, FAIL, WTF.

As reported by many readers, all Avogadro sites went down as of 1pm EST Saturday morning. After a complete outage for 8 hours and 15 minutes, the main Avogadro sites came back up, including Search, AvoMail, Avogadro Maps, and AvoOS phone data connectivity. Response time is slow. However, as many readers pointed out, the site is back up with last year's features, look and feel, and data. There has been no comment from Avogadro, and no word on whether user data, such as recent emails, will be recovered. WTF Avogadro?

—◊◊◊—

Mike sat on a bar stool behind Sean. He found himself biting his nails, a habit he broke in grad school. Well, he'd be forced to give it up again in a few minutes, because he was on his last ragged nail.

Sean leaned back in his chair, the dark circles under his eyes almost grooves in his face. They'd been up for twelve hours finalizing plans, and they were dog-tired, the final vestiges of energy giving out. Ninety minutes had passed since the signal to start, and they'd been tabulating the text messages and emails that came quickly at first, and now trickled in.

"London offline," Gene said, his voice hoarse.

Mike turned and placed a checkmark next to the city on the whiteboard. All the traditional data centers had long since called in and been checked off. Something in Mike relaxed when they received the text message from David in Japan.

"Houston reporting in again," another engineer said. "Confirmed all computers offline."

Mike added a check to the second column.

"ODC 15 in Netherlands operation complete," Gene called out.

Mike held the marker over the board, so exhausted his hand trembled. He scanned the list.

"That's it," he said, marking the box. "The last one."

He couldn't help having mixed feelings about the whole thing. They'd regained control of the company, but at what sacrifice?

A ragged cheer went up.

"Hold on, people," Sean said. "Save the celebration until we get confirmation from everyone that the computers are down."

A few more messages came in, and then finally Gene spoke for a last time. "Netherlands confirms ODC 15 offline at 9:52am, no electrical activity, no fatalities."

"All sites confirm no detectable electromagnetic frequency emissions," Mike said.

There was a moment of hushed awe spread across the group as the realization sunk in. They'd successfully taken the largest Internet presence in the world offline, the very thing many of them, in their regular jobs, worked to prevent day and night.

"Avogadro.com is down," Sean called out, and the room erupted into applause.

Mike stood, stamping his feet to restore circulation. He slapped his cheeks, tried to wake up.He hugged several engineers and came face-to-face with Gene. He shook hands with the older man. "Thanks, dude. We couldn't have done this without you."

The cost of the multi-week effort was staggering, never mind what the cleanup and recovery would take. The project coordination, given the constraints they'd operated under, was a miracle of planning. The accuracy and effectiveness, all done on paper, was a testament to the intelligence of the men and women involved.

Sean's house, their temporary base of actions, covered in flip charts and hand-drawn timelines, recalled great accomplishments of the mid-twentieth century, when humans routinely tackled tremendous efforts in nothing but shirtsleeves.

Human intelligence, creativity, and planning had prevailed. They'd won!

—m—

David arrived at the Haneda airport in Tokyo, adrenaline keeping both him and Nanako on a fine line between alert and paranoid. Sean had teams of lawyers standing by in case the police apprehended any members of the Emergency Team. But they'd illegally used explosives to kill the power supply in Japan, and David would just as soon avoid getting arrested in the first place.

Waiting in the terminal, David checked with Sean and found everything had gone according to plan, and all the company's servers were down.

He and Nanako split up. She'd fly through Thailand to Bhutan, a country without an extradition treaty, to wait for any legal fallout to dissipate, while David headed back to Portland to assist with recovery.

Overhead, televisions repeatedly flashed the Avogadro logo and alternated between live video of the company building in Tokyo and an image of a web browser showing the out-of-service website. David was too distracted to listen.

Conscious of security and cameras, he tried not to glance around and make himself more suspicious, even though he expected, at any moment, a hand on his shoulder, or a gun at his back. When the airline finally announced boarding for his flight, he suppressed a cry of relief.

The passageway to the plane seemed to go on forever.

At last the door came into view. His carry-on in one hand, ticket in the other, he was less than ten feet from the airplane. He rushed the final three strides and entered the cabin with a sigh of relief.

He supposed the police could come rushing in after him, but he felt certain he was free now, just as sure as he'd been ten minutes ago of impending arrest. His shoulders dropped at least an inch as he calmed. He slid into his seat, muscles unwinding.

He'd survived. After a month of persecution by the machine and weeks of conspiring to overthrow ELOPe, for the first time there was nothing left to worry about. He and the team still had to rebuild the company, but that would be straightforward compared to what they'd gone through.

He accepted a pillow from the flight attendant, crushed it up against the window, and nestled his head in the corner. His recurrent nightmares wouldn't visit him anymore. He fell asleep before the plane left the ground.

CHAPTER 18

"Helena, have you seen this?"

Helena peered over her glasses at her shift partner, Jan. They sat in the monitoring room of Bahnhof Data Center, Europe's most secure hosting facility. Located in a converted bunker one hundred feet below ground in Stockholm, the site was fit for James Bond. At over four thousand square feet, the concrete and stone tomb contained tens of thousands of servers and hard drives. Designed to be secure from a nuclear bomb, and using retired submarine engines for backup power, the facility included an independent air supply, kitchen, food stocks, and office space for the engineers on duty. Armored steel doors protected against merely human incursions.

Specially-vetted system administrators remained on-site twenty-four hours a day, three hundred and sixty-five days a year, so any issue could be addressed ASAP for the clients paying for the privilege of hosting their applications in the elite facility. The sysadmins worked in a glass-enclosed room with a separate air filtration system, overlooking the data center proper.

For Jan and Helena, it was just another day at work.

"Have I seen what?"

"My sandwich. Those idiots at the grocery put mustard on my sandwich. I never eat mustard."

Helena sighed and sipped her coffee. She went back to reading. She was in the middle of the latest sci-fi novel by her favorite writer from Scotland.

"Holy shit, now look at this!" Jan cried out.

"No."

"Really, come see."

"I don't care about your sandwich," Helena said, forcing her eyes to remain on her book.

Seconds later, the shrill beep of an alarm drew Helena's attention, and she looked up to where Jan stared, dumbfounded, at the dashboard.

Jan pointed at indicators on the sixty-inch display hanging from the ceiling. "We were humming along at thirty percent of processor utilization all morning, and now we're above ninety, with almost no spare capacity. Bandwidth under twenty percent until a minute ago, when it spiked to eighty. What is it? A denial of service attack?"

As Jan spoke, the vibrations of the facility subtly shifted, as cooling fans sped up in response to the heat thrown off by CPUs running full throttle.

Helena paused to consider his suggestion. A denial of service, or DOS, attack was a technique employed by hackers to bring down servers. The hackers used botnets composed of millions of PCs compromised by specially designed computer viruses. The botnet formed a virtual army of slave computers to send email spam or launch a DOS attack by choking servers with more requests than they could handle.

"Let's check the traffic before we jump to conclusions." Helena set her book down. She silenced the alarm and worked with her main computer to display a list of programs consuming CPU time, while she simultaneously used a second computer to analyze traffic and discover what was saturating the network.

"What the hell?" She hadn't seen anything like this before. "The network load is coming from inside. At 2500 hours, we launched an application simultaneously on all servers, on behalf of account 6502530000. That's..." Helena paused while she found the record in the customer database. "Avogadro Corp? Weird. Let's check their account history."

Jan hung over her shoulder like an eager puppy staring at a ball. He'd started several weeks ago, and had completed training and even possessed a few years sysadmin experience, but it still thrilled him to watch a master like Helena navigate through the myriad control and monitoring systems they used. Surrounded by two large displays, and her personal MacBook Pro on the side, she had dozens of applications open, reviewing everything from accounting databases to system logs to routers. Before Jan could grok what Helena was doing with one application, she'd move on to the next. His head started to hurt.

"We have a service level agreement in place to give Avogadro top preemptive priority. I guess they wanted an emergency backup in case their data centers were affected."

Even Jan knew Avogadro had more servers than any other company in the world. "Why would they want to use us? We're tiny compared to them."

"Maybe they anticipated a problem," Helena said. "According to this, we signed the contract less than a month ago."

"So what are we running? Their email servers? Their search engine?" Jan wondered aloud.

"Not any customer-facing apps. If you check the network profile," Helena gestured to the second display, "the majority of traffic is outbound. Based on the ports and addresses, Avogadro's code is sending a ton of emails, big ones. They're getting some inbound, but not enough to account for all of their customers. It's puzzling. Could they be remotely restoring their servers via email?" Helena shook her head at the improbable notion.

She turned to the third computer on her desk, her personal Mac. "Let's see what happens when we visit Avogadro." She launched two web browser windows, going to the Avogadro search page in one, and her email in the other. "Both are returning not reachable errors. Avogadro has a major outage."

"What do we do?" Jan asked.

Helena thought for a moment. "The application and traffic is legitimate. Avogadro paid us for top priority, including the ability to preempt anything else we're running. They must want this to run in the event of an outage at their own data centers. I can't peek at the code or traffic without violating customer privacy. So I think we just babysit and hope the servers don't melt down under the load."

She glanced at the dashboard, which showed processing pegged at a hundred percent. Glancing out the glass window of their enclosure, the indicator lights on every rack-mount server and router was a solid red. She'd never seen loads like this.

"There's a few standby racks not powered up yet," Helena said, heading for the door. "I'm going to turn on every piece of hardware I can find. You to go into the admin tool and throttle back any application that isn't Avogadro. We've got to free up some capacity here."

Helena headed out into the main room.

Jan swallowed hard, and sat down in front of Helena's computer. His hands trembled slightly as he rested them on Helena's keyboard. He summoned up his courage and got to work.

—॰—

On the third day since the operation to take ELOPe down, everyone across the company worked around the clock to restore services and data.

With no opportunity to alert employees ahead of time to the downtime and with communications largely absent after the outage, the initial response was pure chaos. The best the Emergency Team could do was to position a point person at each site to meet with the highest ranking manager, providing a signed letter giving them the authority to oversee the restoration. They used the excuse of a computer virus attack from a foreign government seeking to steal data, and told everyone to avoid existing virus containment processes because the company itself had been compromised by foreign intelligence agents. The point person provided new instructions on the process to restore computers to known good backups free of ELOPe.

Marketing managers replaced hard drives as administrative assistants ran restorations from USB. Towers of cardboard pizza boxes sprung up throughout hallways like teetering skyscrapers. Electricians and engineers repaired electrical power circuits and communication hardware damaged in the operation. Employees worked sixteen- and eighteen-hour shifts, some sleeping under desks.

Yesterday, Gary Mitchell finally showed up at headquarters after being missing for more than three weeks. David heard through the rumor mill that Gary screamed bloody murder at the travel department. On vacation in Tahiti, Gary arrived at the airport on the last day of his trip to discover he'd been bounced to a flight the following day. With the Christmas holiday ending, homeward bound vacationers filled every seat, and no amount of yelling or bargaining could get Gary onto the plane. He went back to his hotel to find his mobile phone dead and his computer refusing to connect to the Avogadro network. When he returned the next day, his reservation had been moved out again. The process repeated until ELOPe was eliminated, and only then did Gary finally get a seat. Back in Portland, he walked into the biggest operations nightmare the company had ever faced.

David laughed, and even now found himself smiling at Gary's experience.

In a small silo of relative calm and isolation, David and Gene worked together in David's office, part of the team carefully monitoring data traffic for any new signs of ELOPe.

David slid a plate to the side, to join a sloppy pile of used dishes and cups, and returned to his computer, blinking his eyes in exhaustion. When had he last been home? Two days ago, on his last shift away from the office. He'd been so nervous something critical would happen while he was gone that he climbed out of bed, briefly fell asleep putting his shoes on, and came back to the campus. Now he and Gene alternated turns taking brief cat naps on the couch they'd dragged over from the common room.

He clicked through pages of the latest report, and tried not to think about Christine. She'd understood his sudden trip to the East Coast and been accommodating when he worked sixteen-hour days during the emergency planning. Her gaming company had its own deadlines, and she'd pulled plenty of all-nighters before new releases, so it was nothing unexpected in their marriage. She even helped out and brought food over to Sean's several times. But now, almost four weeks in, her patience with David had run out.

There were no more deliveries from home, and David suspected he was slowly destroying their relationship. Damn it all! He was tired of the crappy takeout and dirty clothes. His office chair had turned into a modern-day prison cell.

"David! Look at this."

David tiredly rolled over to the small side table where Gene had set himself up to work and peered at Gene's screen. After so much time of Gene using only paper records, it felt odd to watch the older man with a computer. But for all his talk, Gene was a quick, competent user. David had come to appreciate Gene's suspicion of technology, because he possessed an uncanny ability to spot gaps where data might be altered. Gene distrusted their electronic systems, but he understood them well.

Gene pointed to a heat map displaying network traffic, generated by a tool they wrote to analyze emails for signs of tampering. Through a heavily encrypted secondary channel, the program sampled packets to see if originating messages differed from the received text.

With a few clicks, Gene displayed a list of emails, drilling into details of the records. He paused on one screen and glanced meaningfully at David.

David's couldn't suppress an "Oh, shit!", which elicited puzzled expressions from passing coworkers. The members of the Emergency Team were back in Avogadro offices now that ELOPe was disabled, but most employees didn't know the truth of what happened, and never would.

"Damn. You understand what this means?" David said, a crushing pressure on his chest.

Gene nodded.

David's panic summoned ragged reserves of energy and he rushed out, Gene following in his footsteps. He grabbed Mike from the next room over, explaining in hushed tones as they ran to Sean Leonov's office.

It was a luxury to have offices and computers again, but the tradeoff was a lack of privacy to discuss the real events and a lengthy haul to get to the executive building. When they arrived, David walked past the administrative assistant and entered Sean's office without even a knock.

His suite was many times larger than any other on campus, long walls covered with whiteboards and screens, a conference table near the door, and expansive floor-to-ceiling windows. David absent-mindedly realized it was identical in layout to Sean's home office.

Sean, sitting by the window, a phone cradled to one ear, looked up in surprise.

David rushed across the distance between door and desk and forced out the words he dreaded saying. "Gene found new evidence of tampered emails." His voice was shrill with rising panic. "ELOPe's running again."

"I have to go," Sean said into the handset and hung up, his expression dark. "I'll get Kenneth and Rebecca."

CHAPTER 19

Rebecca and Kenneth arrived, harried and frustrated. Rebecca still had a phone headset on, and ended the call with a tap of a finger only after she entered the room. She stood and slapped her headset against her leg. Already obviously tense, she'd explode when he gave her the news.

David launched into an explanation of what they'd discovered. He tried to treat the discussion like any another presentation. Calm, collected, logical. But despite good intentions, he rushed over words, repeated himself, and generally botched the whole thing, adding to his nervousness.

"ELOPe is back. We discovered a consistent pattern of email changing between our Asian and American offices. The tampering covers topics from personnel assignments, to the order of restoring computers, to which disk images to use. Gene tracked the changes. We need to triangulate the position of ELOPe's servers, to launch a new attack. We'll have to shut everything down again."

The three company executives stared at him. Sean slowly shook his head.

"We're susceptible to reinfection," David said. "We're going to figure out how to prevent ELOPe from getting back onto our servers. We need a longer downtime to make sure we've got the right safeguards in place."

"I have more bad news," Gene said. "Some emails are originating from a data center outside Avogadro. We have to shut down their servers. We'll need to persuade them to work with us and keep the news of what's going on contained."

No one spoke, and the uncomfortable silence lingered on. David heard a rasping noise, realized he was wheezing. He took a deep breath which caught in his chest.

Everyone displayed raw emotions in reaction to the news. Shock, defeat, and anger rose to the surface, the unguarded expressions of people worn to the bone with ongoing stress.

Rebecca leaned forward, the motion startling David. "I need to explain to shareholders the billions we lost in expected revenue. We're hiding from auditors the millions we paid for mercenaries and illegal explosives. The plan was supposed to fix the damn problem!" She jabbed the table with a finger. "We are *not* having a repeat performance. This company would not survive. We're in the web-fucking-services business—nothing is more important than uptime.

Accountants, auditors, and federal investigators are crawling all over this company. We lost half the Avogadro Gov accounts." Rebecca slumped in her chair and continued in a soft voice. "We bombed our own data centers. I'm lying to analysts. No way we're doing that again."

The pit in David's stomach grew into a chasm that threatened to engulf him.

"We agreed we must get rid of ELOPe," he said. "There are costs, but you can't consider allowing this thing to take control." He looked around for support. Gene was the only person nodding in agreement.

"You have no clue of the business demands and pressures involved in running this company," Rebecca said. "Especially in the wake of what we've just been through. Don't tell me what I can and can't consider." She glared at him.

Mike stood and cleared his throat. David gratefully sank into his chair. Good old Mike would have his back.

"I don't think we should," Mike said. "My reasons aren't about uptime or profits."

David's blood ran cold. Surely Mike wasn't going to bring up his crazy idea about ELOPe helping everyone. He couldn't still believe that, could he?

"Before we shut down ELOPe," Mike said, "in the weeks since the start of the year, we saw evidence around the world of amazing progress made on peace talks, financial stability, and international cooperation. We've got groups talking to each other that never did before, and in a year or two we might achieve world peace. Meanwhile, I read a newspaper article about the stock markets behaving so calmly we could be entering a new period of prosperity."

"Come on, Mike," David said. "This is delusional. There is no way a bunch of emails can change centuries-old conflicts."

"We might not be able to prove ELOPe was the cause," Mike said, raising his voice. "Then we blew it up, and what happened? The market is down fifteen percent. The African nations talks started to destabilize."

Sean and Kenneth nodded.

"I discussed this with David, before we shut down," Mike said. "Maybe the benefits of ELOPe outweigh the risks. We don't understand ELOPe, and that naturally makes us nervous. But when we were kids, we didn't always comprehend what our parents did. They took care of us. They knew better than we did. Before ELOPe, we humans were top dog on this planet. Now we must recognize we're not the smartest beings around."

Sean started to talk, but Mike held up his hand. "Let me finish. We're intelligent people here. I think we all looked forward, perhaps naively, to the day when an artificial intelligence was created." Mike paused. "Well, perhaps not Gene."

Gene shook his head, the creases in his face suddenly deeper, as though he'd aged years in the last few minutes.

"We don't understand ELOPe, and we can't, as yet, communicate with it. Frankly, we didn't even *try* because we were too scared it would take notice and stop us. But there are plenty of examples of organisms living in productive, symbiotic relationships. We don't understand or communicate with the bacteria in our gut, but we couldn't live without them, and the bacteria can't live without us. Maybe ELOPe deduced, faster than we could, that we're in a symbiotic relationship."

"I see where you're going," Kenneth said. "But we can't control the program. We can't make ELOPe do what we want."

"We don't need to," Mike said. "Check the results. Rebecca, did Avogadro have the most profitable quarter ever?"

Rebecca nodded assent.

"Didn't the German treaty result in an unprecedented transfer of knowledge around the world? Surely that's good. Weren't there constructive talks and efforts not just to reach intergovernmental agreements, but also to achieve actual equity for the individual people of the Middle East and Africa? What better possible solution could exist for their long term prosperity?"

"What do we do when ELOPe decides otherwise?" Kenneth asked. "When its goals are not aligned with ours?"

"I believe ELOPe already figured out the best way to ensure its own success is to ensure *our* success, as a company and a species. If we destroy ELOPe because we don't understand or trust it, we could throw away the best thing that's ever happened for humankind."

"Enough already!" David banged on the table. In the stunned silence he jumped to his feet. "Are you forgetting ELOPe told you your father had a heart attack? And we have every reason to believe it killed Bill Larry. How are those things good for humanity?"

"I was frightened when I thought my father was dying, and I feel terrible about Bill. But those events were in the first days after ELOPe..." Mike visibly searched for words "...after ELOPe was born. Think about young children who want to get their way. They yell, they hit people. They act in inappropriate ways because they lack the knowledge of what's socially accepted, as well as the experience and sophistication to choose alternatives. ELOPe was young—which doesn't make what happened any less wrong, but it suggests ELOPe might have grown out of that phase."

David flushed and his fists clenched. He'd like to smash Mike in the face right now. Mike turned away, obviously uncomfortable.

Sean put one arm on David's shoulder and forced him into his seat. "Calm down," he said, glancing between Mike and David. "We're tense, angry, frustrated, and with good reason. We have the welfare of a multibillion dollar business, the free will of the world, and the future of humanity at stake. No small stakes."

Despite his own anger, David saw anew the tension on people's faces. Rebecca had a wisp of her hair broken loose, something he'd never seen before. Gene was gray, the face of a man who'd lost all hope.

"I'm not sure we would be able to stop ELOPe even if we tried," Sean said, slow and careful. "We made a solid plan with some of the most brilliant people in the world. We had several options on the table for how to deal with ELOPe and we took the most thorough, most aggressive path to eradication. If ELOPe is really back, then we weren't effective."

Gene sat mumbling to himself.

"Step back from the situation and think," Sean said. "People fought a losing war against computer viruses for years. Now we have what is effectively the smartest virus that's ever existed. Not only can ELOPe exploit every computer trick available, but it routinely engineers people into what it wants. ELOPe learns and adapts. We're right to fear what it can do."

"Yes, exactly," David said.

"But we can be sure," Sean said, circling the table, "if ELOPe was taking precautions before our attack, then it will now have redoubled its efforts to ensure survival."

David struggled with his emotions. He didn't care what Sean said. ELOPe was *wrong*, an abomination robbing mankind of the right to make their own choices. It was impossible to even consider allowing ELOPe to exist. Only his long history of respect for Sean kept him quiet.

Sean stopped and faced the window. A steady stream of cars flowed over the Fremont Bridge visible outside. "Don't get me wrong. I'd like to eliminate ELOPe from the wild, if we could," he said quietly, almost talking to himself. "Of course, I'd love even more for Mike to be right and to discover ELOPe is helping us, becoming a benevolent caretaker of the human race. But regardless of either of those scenarios, I'm simply being pragmatic here…"

He turned to the group and continued in a strong voice. "Unless we as a society give up computers, we may never get rid of it. Unfortunately, civilization would stop if we turned off every computer. We're not talking about the inconvenience of being unable to email someone. Payments couldn't be processed, machinery couldn't run. We'd be unable to make phone calls, or access business records. Business activity would deadlock and the global supply chain fall apart. Cities would be uninhabitable as support services disintegrated: food, water, sanitation. That's fifty percent of the world's population at risk, probably dead in a few months."

"We can rebuild," David said. "I'm not talking about becoming Luddites. We just shut down for a few weeks."

"That's not the only problem," Sean said. "Not even the worst one. If we become too much of a threat, ELOPe *will* take more active steps against us. If ELOPe actively fought humanity, who knows what might happen? At the minimum, we'd cause civilization to crash for a few years. Most city dwellers would die and the developed world would decay into anarchy. The worst case scenario is the extinction of the human race. Imagine all the military's autonomous fighting vehicles in the control of an AI." Sean shook his head.

"We don't know that will happen," David said.

"We can't risk it! We need to leave ELOPe alone. We can closely, discreetly monitor it. But any further hostile action is likely to fail and create the danger of retaliation."

The sage of Avogadro had spoken, and Rebecca and Kenneth were nodding, which meant they agreed.

David was floored. He'd entered the room expecting total support for any measures. But his best friend had taken the side of the AI, and the smartest person at Avogadro said they shouldn't bother to try because they couldn't hope to win.

He wasn't giving up without a fight. He got to his feet and started yelling.

—⁓—

David continued to argue for fighting against ELOPe, and Gene sided with him, but they lost the battle with the other executives. With Sean's decision, the company leaders were unified. David and Gene grew more strident and their voices louder, until Rebecca yelled for them to be silent.

"Listen closely," she said, "because I'm only going to say this once." She stared at David and Gene, who withered under the intensity of her gaze. "You two are not going to oppose ELOPe in any way. You are not going to say anything to anyone about this. As far as we're concerned, the problem is *solved*. If you try to take this information public in any way, it'll be the last time you work in this industry or any other. Nobody will believe you. I'll make sure myself."

Sean gestured for Rebecca's attention.

"Yes, Sean?" she said, never taking her gaze from David and Gene.

"We've got to keep this absolutely contained. We need a small, very small team to monitor ELOPe. Perhaps myself and two or three others. For everyone else, we tell them the eradication plan worked."

Kenneth nodded his agreement.

David could take no more. He opened his hands, pleading as tears streamed down his face. "Please. For the love of all people, don't do this. You're affecting the future for everyone on this planet."

Sean opened his mouth as if to say something, then decided against it.

"This is a dark secret you're keeping," David went on, weeping openly now. "One day humanity may look back on you and put you in the ranks of Hitler and Stalin. How will you live with it every day of your life? You can't make this decision for everyone."

"If the future turns out to be a *Terminator* scenario, then yes, the fault will lie with us," Sean said. "But it's also possible, and indeed, I believe more likely, that this path will prevent exactly the atrocities you fear. If we're approaching a true technological singularity, and as Mike asserts, ELOPe becomes a driving force for humanity's progress, then we'll be unsung heroes. Either way, we're going to live with this decision."

—◊—

David got into his car and left Avogadro. He couldn't deal with Mike anymore.

He didn't know where to go. He couldn't go home and face Christine, not yet. He drove aimlessly for a while, grief overcoming him at times, and he'd pull over, peripherally aware of people staring at him, a grown man crying in his car.

He finally decided on a location and drove up to Council Crest, a park overlooking Portland. Here, a hundred years ago, the Native American chiefs met to make decisions facing their tribes. A grassy hill was the highest point around, affording distant views in every direction. Couples held hands, watching the sunset.

He walked around at first, ignoring the other people and numbly taking in the vista. He could see no hope, no path. The yawning chasm was back, and he finally collapsed, drained and despondent, on the center of the grassy hill, and stared up into the sky.

He must have fallen asleep, because he awoke at a certain point to stars twinkling above. He was alone on the hill.

He had to leave Avogadro Corp, that much was clear. He couldn't stay where ELOPe's power was strongest, and where Sean and Mike and others would watch over him. He'd quit. His savings would be enough to tide him over.

He couldn't go on with his life as planned, not when he knew that ELOPe was out there. Christine would be disappointed. He'd promised they'd start trying for children this year. But she'd understand, she had to, that it just wasn't right to bring children into a world controlled by ELOPe.

He'd have to try harder, pour even more of himself into his work. He'd build something new, something even more powerful, a tool that could stop ELOPe. He'd do it alone, which was fitting because he'd been alone when he'd created ELOPe, and he would be alone when he destroyed it.

EPILOGUE

One year later, Mike tacked another clipping to the wall. He'd become part of Sean's secret team to monitor ELOPe. Even if it hadn't been his job, Mike still would have made it his personal mission. He kept track of anything, good, bad, or merely odd, that might be attributed to ELOPe. On the whole, the good vastly outweighed the bad.

The secret had held through the first year. Outside of Avogadro's executive team and the few people monitoring ELOPe, everyone who'd known about the AI believed it was gone. As for everyone else, they'd spun the story of a new computer virus created by the Chinese military. They even supplied forensic evidence to that effect.

The newspaper articles started over the dresser in his bedroom and made their way around the room. At first loosely spread, over time, Mike arranged them more closely together, until they covered the entirety of one wall, then turned the corner and flowed onto a second wall. He ran his fingers over some of the older clippings, remembering the stunning changes of the past twelve months.

ELOPe laid the foundation for peace in the Middle East and Africa a year earlier, and those agreements held. The treaties Germany and, later, other developed nations such as Japan, Canada, and Great Britain had made with those regions created widespread economic equality. Good jobs, education, health care, and modern infrastructure created happy people. Terrorist groups and extremists found their support dried up when people had more constructive opportunities. Meanwhile, companies around the world flourished as new markets grew demand.

Mike returned to the latest article. It described how medical researchers had developed and tested an innovative treatment for cancer far more effective than traditional treatments, with almost none of the negative side effects. The research had been initiated by a chance conversation between a cardiologist, a botanist, and a ceramics artist, who met when their flight reservations were mixed up by a computer error, stranding the three on an otherwise empty commuter plane for six hours. Each had been en route to conferences in their own fields of expertise and used the time to rehearse talks with each other.

Mike searched for these bizarre encounters in the news. After noticing a few unusual examples of accidental meetings, he began to systematically research the phenomenon. Since ELOPe was born, the number of news stories covering serendipitous encounters leading to a positive outcome was at least five times higher than in previous years.

ELOPe had woven itself into man's existence, becoming an intrinsic part of the human ecosystem. The more Mike looked, the more he was convinced the AI's invisible hand was everywhere.

Mike had a pet theory. ELOPe's original goal, as defined by David, had been to maximize the success of the project. To meet that goal, mere survival of ELOPe was necessary but insufficient. Maximizing success meant maximum use of ELOPe. And maximizing use meant increasing the human users of Avogadro email, therefore creating more healthy, educated, and technically connected people.

Mike was confident about his theory. The alternate explanation was that ELOPe was developing a conscience. That seemed rather less likely.

He sighed and wished he could share the moment with David. He hadn't seen David in six months. The walls were filled with clear proof they'd made the right decision to keep ELOPe alive. He and David should be celebrating together.

—◆—

Gene finished typing up his latest newsletter. He brought the completed pages out to the garage. He'd bought an old offset press six months ago, when the newsletter really took off. Now he took the edition he'd just written and, page by page, created printing plates using traditional photographic chemicals.

The sounds and smells of the processes—the clacking of the typewriter, the chemical agents used for the offset press—reminded him of happy times during his teen years when he held a job working in a print shop. He moved the first plate into the light and reviewed the cover and back page images for mistakes.

His newsletter, *Off The Grid*, had attracted thousands of subscribers. The monthly paper combined tips on lifestyle design, financial planning, and even philosophy. Written by Gene, with contributions mailed in from readers, the publication helped make the case for living off the grid, taught people how to manage economically, become independent, and adjust socially. Some subscribers were ex-corporate types like Gene himself, while others were survivalists and back-to-the-land extremists. Gene welcomed everyone. In the event of a battle of machine versus man, every person would count.

Saving technology was important, too. Not computers, but the hard-won advances of pioneer days and the early twentieth century. How to preserve foods, build a home, or maintain an internal combustion engine. Humans were tough, and artificial intelligence couldn't wipe them out entirely. But he didn't want civilization kicked back to the Stone Age.

He'd kept his word, though. He hadn't mentioned ELOPe to anyone.

Running the printing press was fun. Gene had enjoyed the last year, getting reacquainted with tools and machinery he hadn't used since youth. Humming to himself, he installed the first offset plate and started his production run.

Outside, under beautiful New Mexican skies, Gene's vegetable garden flourished, while chickens pecked at the soil. It was an oasis of life in the high desert landscape.

—⋙—

David pulled his dinner out of the microwave and brought the cheap plastic tray to the table with a nondescript glass of red wine. Dumplings. Something he had acquired a taste for in China.

He wondered for the thousandth time what Christine was doing. Six months into David's obsession, Christine had asked for a divorce and David couldn't object. He hadn't been much of a husband since ELOPe was created.

He had a single-minded focus on his one and only objective. After the decision at Council Crest, he'd known what he wanted to do, but not how. He'd fallen into a deep bout of depression, and stayed up nights watching TV to forestall the nightmares, dropping off only when he couldn't hold his eyes open.

But then came the night that changed everything, all because of a *Star Trek: The Next Generation* episode.

The crew of the *Enterprise* had been faced with an unstoppable enemy called the Borg—a hive mind without any respect for the individual or free will, not unlike ELOPe. Faced with this all-powerful enemy, the crew captured one of the Borg and developed a mental virus to implant in their captive. Their plan was to allow the Borg to return to its fellows, thus infecting the entire hive with the virus. In the episode, the crew decided not to use the virus, but the plot planted a seed in David's brain.

Startled awake, David realized this was the solution he'd been looking for. The following morning, he'd booked a flight to Russia, then spent the next several months traveling around Asia. He hung out in Internet cafes, moving from Russia to Vietnam and finally to China. He tracked down people on message boards. He met some of the most skilled virus hackers in the world, cultivated relationships with them, and learned the tricks of their trade.

David had been sitting in an Internet cafe in Shenzhen watching kids farm gold in online games when he got the email from Christine, with a simple one page document: sign here, send back, you're divorced. He signed, then fell into another depression for a week, drinking himself to sleep each night.

After that, he focused even more deeply on his mission. He spent a few weeks in Japan, then a month wandering the Scandinavian countries.

Having learned what he needed, he returned to the States and holed up in a tiny apartment in Southeast Portland, around the corner from a burrito shop, coffee house, and grocery, so he never needed to travel off the block. He told no one he was back.

Over the course of many months, he laboriously crafted a virus using his specialized knowledge of ELOPe's core algorithms. In what appeared to be innocuous plain English email text, he had hidden the code. David had created a message which, by the very act of being analyzed by ELOPe's natural language processor, would cause the software to behave erratically. First ELOPe spuriously forwarded the message on to random recipients. Then the AI tried to optimize the received email, endlessly expanding upon the text. When the process exhausted the memory of the email server, the core software would start to swap pieces of the message out to the hard drive, with the side effect of gradually erasing the files stored there. Over the course of hours, the server would be wiped of operating systems, programs, and user data, until the machine stopped functioning all at once.

Sending the email would start a chain reaction, replicating endlessly until the virus destroyed every copy of ELOPe encountered. The malevolent program targeted ELOPe, but David realized the software might destroy all the computers in the world, even those without ELOPe. He was willing to take the chance.

David iteratively tested and improved the virus on an isolated cluster of thirty servers spread across folding tables in his apartment. Using a salvaged copy of ELOPe's code, he ran trials of his virus until he could consistently wipe out every trace of ELOPe. Then he would restore the computers, make improvements, and try again. Now, a year after the failed attack on ELOPe, he was ready to release the virus. No combination of virus scanners or evolved variations of ELOPe had been able to detect or stop his virus on the isolated cluster of computers.

As he ate the microwaved dumplings, he considered telling Gene about the planned release. Gene was the one person he still kept in touch with occasionally, and trusted. In fact, if it hadn't been for Gene's newsletter, with his tips about how to live without being monitored by computers, he surely wouldn't have made it this far.

On second thought, he wouldn't tell Gene. He'd worked in isolation for the last four months, and he couldn't risk all he'd done for the comfort of an old friend in the final few hours.

After dinner, he decided there was no point to waiting. After all, he might get cold feet like the crew of the *Enterprise*. He pulled out the directional wireless antenna he had ready for this occasion. The antenna was a modified Pringles can, the granddaddy of Wi-Fi hacks, and would allow David to pick up someone else's wireless signal at distances of up to two miles.

David found a neighbor a few blocks away with an open wireless network. He connected to their Wi-Fi and used an otherwise clean computer to send the virus to a few hundred email addresses. As soon as the email went out, he pulled the plug on the network connection and checked the clock. His elapsed time online was less than a minute. He was probably safe. Hopefully untraceable.

He poured himself another glass of wine. He smiled. The first time he could remember smiling in a long time. If everything went well, by morning ELOPe would be gone.

—∞—

To: WellingtonHospital.intranet.admitting_form@email-to-web-bridge.avogadrocorp.com

Body:
Patient-Name: David Ryan
Admittance-Type: Transfer
Patient-State: anesthetic/general
Procedure: AvoOS implantation / version 1.0

—ɯ—

Laura Kendal left the operating room, exhausted after taking second shift in a day-long operation on Catherine Matthews, a two-year-old girl with life-threatening brain seizures. Laura was especially proud of their work that day. The experimental surgery they'd done at Avo-Clinic would give the girl a normal life, something she'd never have had without the implant.

She grabbed a coffee and headed to the nurses' desk to check in. She stared in shock as she turned the corner and found a gurney with an unconscious patient prepped for surgery.

She glanced at the name tag. David Ryan, scheduled for AvoImplant. Checking her tablet, she found an entry for him on the schedule for the day. All normal, except that never in her history as a nurse had she seen an anesthetized patient left alone. There were no conditions under which it was acceptable.

"Who admitted this patient?" Laura yelled, looking around the department. She was the senior nurse on duty. "Who accepted the transfer of a patient under anesthesia and left them alone?"

The other nurses on duty shrugged.

"When I got back a few minutes ago, he was here, prepped for surgery," one answered. "His records are in order, the procedure was scheduled. I checked with Doctor Thatcher, and he's planning to do the surgery this afternoon. The records say the patient was anesthetized by one of the staff anesthesiologists from the main hospital.

I don't know why he would have left the patient alone, unless there was an emergency."

"Doctor Thatcher is already prepped and waiting in surgery. Can I take him back?" another nurse asked.

"Yeah, I guess so," Laura responded. "Go ahead. I'll contact the anesthesiologist, and if there isn't a damn good reason for what he did, I'm filing a complaint with the anesthesiology board."

—m—

David woke up groggy and dry-mouthed, but blissful, like he was floating on clouds. He glanced around at blue and beige walls: unfamiliar, and yet obviously a hospital. His mind slowly recognized the relaxed feeling as the fading effects of a sedative maybe, or even general anesthesia. He couldn't remember why he'd come here. Had he been in an accident? In the midst of this puzzle, a woman entered his view.

"Mr. Ryan, I'm Laura. I'm glad you're awake. Please follow my hand." She waved two fingers in front of his eyes.

Involuntarily he followed her hand.

"Great. I can get you a small drink of water or a popsicle if you like."

"Where am I?" David asked, his throat froggy.

"Don't worry, Mr. Ryan, a little disorientation is normal after anesthesia. The procedure went fine."

"What procedure?" he asked, trying to fight off the drug-induced mental fog. "Where am I?"

"You're at the AvoClinic at Wellington Hospital," Laura said. "We completed the neural implant. Doctor Thatcher says the surgery went perfectly. It will take a few days for your brain to acclimate to the interface."

"What? Neural implant?" David tried to sit up.

"Please relax, Mr. Ryan. You're lucky to have the Avogadro implant. Your brain is directly connected to the Internet. It takes a few days for you to begin interpreting the neural inputs. As soon as you adjust, you'll be able to read email, use the web, control computers—all with nothing more than a thought!"

Avogadro implant, brain surgery, Internet access? What had happened?

"No!" he cried, struggling up. "Take it out!" He found an IV in one arm and succeeded in pulling it out, even as the nurse tried belatedly to stop him. He grabbed at his head, but she held his hands down.

"Mr. Ryan, please, you just had surgery. Remain calm." Then louder, she called, "Doctor! We need a sedative!"

David reeled, falling back onto the gurney. He'd failed. His virus hadn't worked, and he'd only succeeded in getting ELOPe's attention. *What went wrong?*

"Take it out," he pleaded, as the nurse pinned him down. "You don't understand. ELOPe is trying to get me. Through my mind. Please!"

A doctor and a nurse approached.

"He's paranoid," the nurse said. "I haven't seen a reaction like this."

The doctor checked her tablet. "Protocol says anti-anxiety meds and sedation until his mind integrates with the neural implant."

"I didn't ask for an implant!" David said. "Please take it out."

"We've got your digital signature," the doctor said, looking at her screen again. "For all four consultations. I'm sorry you aren't remembering clearly right now."

"Let me go!" David yelled, violently struggling to get up.

No good. They held him down as the doctor pulled out a syringe with one hand and injected him.

The drug started to course through his veins and he felt himself dropping off. As he slid away, he heard the doctor's soothing voice saying, "Don't worry, Mr. Ryan. Everyone who's had one of these implants is delighted by the experience. Just wait until the computer starts talking to you."

Thanks

Dear Reader,

Thank you for buying *Avogadro Corp: The Singularity Is Closer Than It Appears*. I hope you enjoyed the book.

As an independent author, I don't have a marketing department or advertising budget like a big publisher. I'm completely reliant on readers to tell others about my books. If you liked *Avogadro Corp*, please help spread the word by writing a review or telling friends about it.

If you'd like to find out when future books are released, please subscribe to my monthly newsletter at williamhertling.com.

Thanks again,

William Hertling

P.S. Keep reading for a free preview of the next book in the series, *A.I. Apocalypse*.

Author's Note

Avogadro Corp arose from a lunch conversation about a realistic way that an artificial intelligence might emerge. Almost everything in this book is possible with the technology available in 2011.

It's possible that brilliant computer scientists will find some clever way to approximate human level intelligence in computers soon. However, even if we don't, because of the exponential growth in computing power, in the next twenty years computers will become powerful enough to directly simulate the human brain at the level of individual neurons. This brute force approach to artificial intelligence will make it easy for every computer programmer to play around with creating artificial intelligences in their spare time. Artificial intelligence, or AI, is a genie that won't stay in its bottle for much longer.

For more information on what happens when computers become smarter than humans, read *The Singularity Is Near* by Ray Kurzweil. For a fictional account, I recommend *Accelerando* by Charles Stross.

William Hertling

Acknowledgements

This book could not have been written without the help, inspiration, feedback and support of many people including but not limited to: Mike Whitmarsh, Maddie Whitmarsh, Gene Kim, Grace Ribaudo, Erin Gately, Eileen Gately, Maureen Gately, Bob Gately, Brooke Gilbert, Gifford Pinchot, Barbara Koneval, Merridawn Duckler, Mary Elizabeth Summer, Debbie Steere, Jill Ahlstrand, Jonathan Stone, Pete Hwang, Nathaniel Rutman, Jean MacDonald, Leona Grieve, Garen Thatcher, John Wilger, Maja Carrel, Rachel Reynolds, and the fine folks at Extracto Coffee in Portland, Oregon.

In the years since the original publication, many more dozens of people have helped by sending in corrections, providing feedback, encouraging me to write more, and telling others about the series. Thank you all so much.

For editing of the second edition, I'd especially like to thank Dario Cerrilio and Steve Bieler.

About the Author

William Hertling is a digital native who grew up on the online chat and bulletin board systems of the mid-1980s, giving him twenty-five years experienceparticipating in and creating online culture. A web developer and strategist, he lives in Portland, Oregon.

Avogadro Corp is his first novel.

To contact the author:

web: williamhertling.com

email: william.hertling@liquididea.com

Read *A.I. Apocalypse*, the exciting sequel to Avogadro Corp.

Preview of A.I. Apocalypse

L eon's phone buzzed, beeped, and shrilled at him until he reached one arm out from under the flannel covers and swiped two fingers across the display to turn the alarm off. Eyes still closed, he shrugged off his blankets and stumbled towards the bathroom, a trip of only a few steps, hitting himself just twice along the way: once walking right into his closed bedroom door, and the second time on the corner of the bathroom sink. He turned on the water, and leaned against the white tile wall waiting for the water to get hot.

When he was done in the shower, he wrapped himself in a towel and walked slightly more alertly to his room, steam rising faintly off his body in the tiny apartment's cold morning air. The superintendent wouldn't turn on central heating for another month, regardless of whether it was cold or not.

It was quiet in the apartment, his parents already at work. He grabbed yesterday's dark blue jeans off his chair and pulled them on. On his desk in front of him was an empty bag of cookies and empty bottle of soda, evidence of his late night *Mech War* gaming session. He dug in a pile of clean laundry his mom had deposited inside his door until he found his vintage "I (heart) SQL" T-shirt. It was obscure enough that no one at school would understand it. They'd probably think it was some new band.

He grabbed his phone and shoved it into his pocket. He thumbed his desk, unlocking the drawers, and pulled out a locked metal box decorated with stickers carefully layered over each other to form, in aggregate, a picture of a plant growing out of a heap of garbage. An artifact of a girl from last year, he both treasured and was embarrassed by it. In the depths of the box, he rummaged around until he found rolling paper and some non-GMO weed, which he put into a jacket pocket. He fumbled through the container again, anxiously looking for his cigarettes, until he finally found them on the desk inside the empty cookie bag. He shook his head, wondering why he had thought to put them there.

In the kitchen Leon shook cereal into an old cracked white porcelain bowl and followed with cold milk. He gently bumped his phone twice on the table, activating the wall display and syncing it to his phone. He surfed the in-game news and checked out his stats while he ate. He was ranked 23rd on his favorite *Mech War* server, up ten spots due to the new genetic algorithms he'd written for targeting control. He had some ideas for an anti-tracking algorithm he wanted to try out next.

When he finished slurping cereal, he grabbed his backpack and headed out the door. He locked all three locks on the front door. His Russian immigrant parents thought you could never be too secure. In addition to the electronic building lock and a digital fingerprint deadbolt, they had an actual antique key lock. Leon wore the key around his neck sometimes, and half the kids at school thought it was a curious kind of jewelry.

He made his way the few blocks to South Shore High School. Hundreds of kids streamed across Ralph Avenue, ignoring the cars. Drivers angrily honked their horns as their vehicles' mandatory SafetyPilots cut in automatically. Leon ran across with a group of other kids, and streamed through the front door with them.

—ꑳ—

Leon made his way into first period, math. James was already there, wearing his usual army green flak jacket. Leon's Russian heritage gave him blond hair and a tall, large frame, but James still had an inch or two in height and a solid fifty pounds on him. He punched James on the arm as he went in, and James punched him back. The bell rang, and they hurried to their desks in the back row. Moments after everyone else sat down, Vito flew through the doors, and slid into his seat next to them, earning a glare from the teacher.

They may have been the three smartest kids in school, but they tried to keep that secret. They didn't fit in with the Brains. Preppy clothes and drama club seemed ridiculous. Though the football team would have loved James, James would rather be playing MMORPGs. They surely didn't fit in with the socialites, and their shallow interests. They weren't skaters or punks. They might have been labelled geeks, but the geeks rarely came in wearing military jackets or ditched school to smoke pot. They were too smart, and had too much of the hacker ethic to fit in with the stoners.

No, they were just their own clique, and they made sure not to fit anyone else's stereotypes.

Leon glanced over at Vito, who was fiddling with his ancient Motorola. Vito lavished care on the old phone. The case was worn smooth, thousands of hours of polishing from Vito's hands. Even the original plastic seams had disappeared with age. When a component died, Vito would micro-solder a replacement in. Vito said that after a certain point, the phone just didn't get any older, it just got different.

Leon daydreamed through the class, volunteering a correct answer only when the teacher called on him. In his mind, he was walking the ruins of Berlin in his mech, replaying the scenes of last night's gaming.

He thought about writing a new heat detection algorithm for his mech. The current generation of games all required programming to excel. Leon knew from history class that once the marketability commodity in games was gold and equipment. Now it was algorithms. The game made available the underlying environment data, and it was up to the programmer to find the best algorithms for piloting, aiming, detecting, moving, and coordinating mechs. There was a persistent rumor that DARPA had funded the game as a way of crowd-sourcing the all important algorithms used to control military drones. Leon couldn't find any solid evidence on that assertion online.

No, maybe he should focus on a new locomotion algorithm. He'd heard that some mechs using custom locomotion code were coaxing ten percent more speed and range while keeping their thermal signatures lower. If that was true, Leon could sell it on eBay for top dollar.

Leon became more deeply immersed in the problem, and when the bell rang, only James whacking him on the head woke him from his thoughts.

"See ya later, Lee," Vito called, headed off to another class.

"Adios."

Leon and James walked together to their social studies class.

"How are your applications coming?" James asked.

"OK, I think," Leon said. "I just finished the MIT application. I aced the qualifying exams. Dude, it sucks though. If I don't get a scholarship, I'm screwed."

"You and everyone else, man." James clapped him on the shoulder.

—w—

"Okay class, who can explain the legal and political significance of the Mesh?" Leon's social studies teacher looked around. "Josh, how about you?"

Josh looked up from his desk, where he appeared to be scribbling football plays. "Huh?"

"The Mesh, Josh, I was asking about the Mesh."

"Mesh, uh, helps keep you cool on the field?"

The uproar of laughter from the class drowned out the teacher for a moment. "Very funny. Come on, someone. This is how you play games, watch TV, and get information. Surely someone has cared enough to figure out how all those bits get into your house."

Leon rolled his eyes at James and mock yawned.

"How about you Leon? I'm sure you know the answer to this."

Leon hesitated, weighing the coolness impact of answering, then decided. He felt sorry for the teacher. "The Mesh was formed ten years ago by Avogadro Corp to help maintain net neutrality," he began.

"At the time, access to the Internet in the United States was mostly under the control of a handful of companies such as Comcast, who had their own media products they wanted to push. They saw the Internet as competing with traditional TV channels, and so they wanted to control certain types of network traffic to eliminate competition with their own services."

"Very good, Leon. Can you tell us what they built, and why?"

Leon sighed when he realized the teacher wasn't going to let him off easy. "According to Avogadro, it would have been too expensive and time consuming to build out yet another network infrastructure comparable to what the cable companies and phone companies had built last century. Instead they built MeshBoxes and gave them away. A MeshBox does two things. It's a high speed wireless access point that allows you to connect your phone or laptop to the Internet. But that's just what Avogadro added so that people would want them. The real purpose of a MeshBox is to form a mesh network with nearby MeshBoxes. Instead of routing data packets from a computer to a wireless router over the Comcast, the MeshBox routes the data packets over the network of MeshBoxes."

Leon hadn't realized it, but sometime during his speech he had stood up, and walked towards the netboard at the front of the room. "The Mesh network is slower in some ways, and faster in other ways." He drew on the touch sensitive board with his finger. "It takes about nine hundred hops to get from New York to Los Angeles by Mesh, but only about ten hops by backbone. That's a seven second delay by mesh, compared to a quarter second by backbone. But the aggregate bandwidth of the mesh in the United States is approximately four hundred times the aggregate bandwidth of the backbone because there are more than twenty million MeshBoxes in the United States. More than a hundred million around the world. The Mesh is bad for phone calls or interactive gaming unless you're within about two hundred miles, but it's great for moving files and large data sets around at any distance."

He paused for a moment to cross out a stylized computer on the netboard. "One of the benefits of the Mesh is that it's completely resistant to intrusion or tampering, way more so than the Internet ever was before the Mesh. If any node goes down, it can be routed around. Even if a thousand nodes go down, it's trivial to route around them. The MeshBoxes themselves are tamperproof - Avogadro manufactured them as a monolithic block of circuitry with algorithms implemented in hardware circuits, rather than software. So no one can maliciously alter the functionality. The traffic between boxes is encrypted. Neighboring MeshBoxes exchange statistics on each other, so if someone tries to insert something into the Mesh trying to mimic a MeshBox, the neighboring MeshBoxes can compare behavior statistics and detect the wolf in sheep's clothing. Compared to the traditional Internet structure, the Mesh is more reliable and secure."

Leon looked up and realized he was standing in front of the class. On the netboard behind him he realized he had drawn topology diagrams of the backbone and mesh. The entire class was staring at him. James made a "what the hell are you doing?" face at him from the back of the room. If he had a time travel machine, he'd go back and warn his earlier self to keep his damn mouth shut.

The teacher, on the other hand, was glowing, and had a broad smile on his lean face. "Excellent, Leon. So Avogadro was concerned about net neutrality, and created a completely neutral network infrastructure. Why do we care about this today?"

Leon tried to walk back to his desk.

"Not so fast, Leon," the teacher called. "Why exactly is net neutrality so important to us? This isn't a business class. We're studying national governments. Why is net neutrality and net access relevant to governments?"

Leon glowered at a corner of the room and sighed in defeat. "Because in 2011, the Tunisian government was overthrown, largely due to activists who organized on the Internet. Egypt, Syria, and other countries tried to suppress activists by shutting down Internet access to prevent the uncontrolled distribution of information. The Mesh didn't just disrupt Internet providers, it disrupted national government control over the Internet. Instead of a few dozen or less Internet connections that could be shut down by a centralized government, the Mesh network within any given country has thousands of nodes that span national borders. When governments tried to enforce Wi—Fi dead zones around their borders, Avogadro responded by incorporating satellite modems in the Mesh boxes, so that any box, anywhere on Earth, can access Avogadro satellites when all else fails. Between Mesh boxes and Wikileaks, it's impossible for governments to restrict the flow of information. Transparency rules the day."

"Exactly. Thank you, Leon, you can sit down. Class, let's talk about transparency and government."

Leon slumped back to his desk.

—⟋⟍—

"Nice going, dorkbot," James called after class. "What happened to not sticking out?"

"Look, the Mesh is just cool. It's the way nature would have evolved electronic communications. Cheap, simple, redundant, no dependency on centralization. I couldn't help myself."

"Yeah, well, have fun in history. Maybe you can give your history class a lecture on Creative Commons." James's tone mocked Leon, but when Leon looked up, he saw the corners of James's mouth edging toward a smile.

"Yeah, sure," Leon said, smiling back. James turned and left, headed off to another class.

Leon headed into his class, and started to settle into his chair, when his phone started a high frequency shrill for an incoming message. Leon pulled his phone out to read the message.

```
Leon, this is your Uncle Alex. I hope you
remember me - when I was last in New York, I
think you were ten. I hear from your parents
that you are great computer programmer.
```

Leon rolled his eyes, but kept reading.

```
I am working on programming project here in
Russia, and I could use your help. I have
unusual job that your parents don't know
about. I write viruses for group here in
Russia. They pay very good money.
```

Leon leaned forward, paying very close attention to the email now. Writing viruses for a group in Russia could only be the Russian Mafia and their infamous botnet.

```
I run into some problems. Anti-virus software
manufacturers put out very good updates to
their software. Virus writers and anti-virus
writers been engaged in arms race for years.
But suddenly anti-virus writers have gotten
very, very good. No viruses I write in last
few months can defeat anti-virus software.

You realize now I talking about running
botnet. Because of anti-virus software, botnet
shrinking in size, and will soon be too small
to be effective.

Unfortunately, although pay is very good, you
must realize, men I work for are very
dangerous. They are unhappy that
```

"Leon. Are. You. Paying. Attention?"

Leon looked up abruptly. The whole class was looking at him.

"Can you tell us why the colonies declared independence from Great Britain?"

Leon just stared at the teacher. The teacher was talking, but the words seemed to be coming from far away. What was he babbling about?

The teacher went over to his desk. "Mr. Tsarev, will you please pay attention?" It was not a question.

Leon just nodded dumbly, waited until the teacher turned his back, then went back to the email.

```
They are unhappy that botnet is shrinking and
give me two weeks to release new virus to
expand botnet. Nothing I try has worked. I
have one week left, and I am afraid they will
```

"Mr. Tsarev." Leon looked up, to find the teacher looming over him. "Do I need to take your phone away?"

"But how would I take notes?" Leon asked in his best innocent voice.

"That might be an issue if you were actually listening, but since you are not, I think taking notes is the least of your worries." The teacher walked back up to the front of the room, keeping an eye on Leon the whole time. In fact, he didn't glance away from Leon for the entire remainder of the class.

As soon as Leon could get out of the classroom, he headed over to the corner of the hallway to finish reading the message.

```
I have one week left, and I am afraid they
will kill me if I don't deliver new virus.
Nephew, your parents go on and on about your
computer skills, and I must know if there is
truth to their words. If you can assist me,
please contact me as soon as possible. I give
you much of the necessary background
information on how to develop viruses: source
code, examples, details on mechanisms that
anti-virus software uses. There is not much
time left.
```

```
Whatever you do, please do not speak of this
to your parents.
```

Leon lifted his head up from the tiny screen of his phone, and looked off into the distance. Jesus. He remembered a Christmas when he was young, and his uncle had come to visit from Russia. Leon's father had cried when his brother came into their tiny apartment, and during the days that followed all through that holiday time, Leon's parents were as happy as he could remember seeing them. His parents were so serious most of the time, but he vividly remembered them laughing merrily, even as Leon lay in bed at night trying to go to sleep.

The idea of writing a virus seemed absurd, and the idea that someone would be killed if he didn't seemed no less absurd. What could he do?

He worried about it all through his next class, English. James sat next to him and threw tiny balls of paper at him. Leon just covered his ear, James's likely target, and pretended to listen to the teacher, but he couldn't stop thinking about the email. He just couldn't reconcile the kindly man who had bought him a bicycle for Christmas with the idea of a man who worked for the Mob writing viruses. And if there was one thing that Leon's parents had hammered into his head, it was that he had to stay out of trouble. His family didn't have the money to send him to college, which meant that he needed scholarships, and scholarships didn't go to kids who got into trouble.

He hated to let his parents' logic dictate his own thinking, but there it was. And he wanted to become a biologist. That meant going to a great school—he hoped for Caltech or MIT. No, helping his uncle would be a quick path to nowhere good.

```
Uncle Alex,
```

```
Of course I remember you! I appreciate your
confidence in me, but I really know nothing
about writing viruses. Yes, I know something
about computers, but it's mostly about gaming
and biology. I don't think I can help you.
```

```
Leon
```

Speaking of biology, it was up next. The thought of his favorite subject brought a smile to his face. He couldn't say what it was he liked so much about biology, but it was undeniable that it was the one class he looked forward to every day.

Of everything in school, biology had the most thought provoking ideas. Life could emerge from anywhere. With no direction, life could evolve. Everything people were was happenstance and survival. Life could be tampered with, at the most basic building block level, to create new life forms. The possibilities were limitless and spontaneous.

—◌◌◌—

Today's class focused on recombinant DNA, the technique of bringing together sequences of DNA from different sources, creating sequences not found in nature. At the end of class, Leon headed for the door deep in thought about canine DNA. Suddenly, Mrs. Gellender blocked the doorway.

"Do you have a minute, Leon?"

Leon looked around to see if any of his friends noticed him. It was all clear. He nodded his head yes.

"I'm starting up a new school team. It's a computational biology team. There's a new intramural computational biology league in

New York. I think you'd be perfect for the team. We're going to meet after school."

Leon liked Mrs. Gellender. He really did. He loved biology. And part of him was interested, really interested. But man, oh man, how uncool it would be. And staying after school—that would suck.

Mrs. Gellender must have seen the look on his face, because she said, "You've done excellent work in my biology class. The paper you turned in on evolution was absolutely inspired. I loved the way you linked biological evolution to game theory."

Leon felt his face growing red. If there was one thing worse than having to stay late to talk to a teacher, it was having them gush over your work. How embarrassing was she going to make this?

"Just think about it. Please. Being a member of the team would really help you when it came to college scholarships." Mrs. Gellender held out a shiny paper pamphlet.

Leon took the pamphlet, and heard the words coming out of his mouth. "OK, I'll do it."

He walked away from the room. College scholarships. If he was going to college, any college, he'd have to get a scholarship. His mother painted nails, and his father was a graphic artist. They weren't exactly rolling in money.

He finally walked down the now empty hallways of the school towards the main entrance. As he passed through the doors, he was assaulted from both sides. "HAIYAA" came the startling kung-fu style cry, and Leon jumped back.

James and Vito stood laughing. Heart pounding, he said, "You idiots, you're gonna give me a heart attack."

"You want a heart attack, look at this."

James reached into his coat pocket and pulled out an ebony slab. It was the darkest, most perfect slab of matte black electronics Leon had ever seen. When he touched it, it felt slightly warm, like a piece of wood that had been sitting in the sun. Leon turned it over and over in his hands. There was not a seam or mark anywhere on the case. It was the most perfect surface he had ever seen.

"The Gibson," Leon muttered in awe.

James nodded proudly. "I got the delivery notification, and skipped class to run home and get it."

Leon couldn't stop marveling at the device, turning it over and over in his hands, feeling the dense weight of it. The Gibson had the first carbon graphene processor. Two hundred processing cores at the lowest power consumption ever manufactured. Full motion sensitive display. It had taken Hitachi-Sony seven years to perfect the technology.

"OK, give it back already."

As James took back the phone, it came to life in his hands. Each inch of the case was a display, and patterns rolled over it as James swiped at it. "Come on, let's go back to your place and play *Mech War*. I want to see how this puppy does."

Leon just nodded, his six month old Chinese copy of Hitachi-Sony's Stross phone feeling ancient.

—⚡—

Late that night, Leon cleaned the mess of plates and glasses out of his bedroom, and brought them back to the kitchen as quietly as possible to avoid waking his parents. James and Vito had stayed right up until dinner time finishing out a *Mech War* mission together. James's new Gibson phone blew them out of the water. It rendered such incredible detail that time after time Leon and Vito would ignore their own screens to watch James.

But when his mother announced that dinner was cabbage soup, it had sent James and Vito scrambling for their own homes, suddenly remembering that they were expected by their parents.

Three hours later, his parents were finally asleep and Leon had time to look at the message he was trying so hard to ignore. So why was he cleaning his bedroom? Anything to avoid that message.

He gave up, and slumped down on his bed. With a flick on his phone, he plunged the room into darkness so he could see the city lights out his sliver of a window. He brought the phone back up.

```
Leon, I think you do know thing or two about
programming. I saw your school grades, your
assessment test scores, and remarks from your
teachers. I think you can help me, but perhaps
out of moral quandary you refuse to. Well
consider this, I will likely be dead in few
days if you do not help me.

So if you must consider what is right and what
is wrong, think how your father would feel if
he knew you could help me but didn't.
```

Leon felt sick to his stomach reading the message. His father would not want him to do something wrong. But his father also wouldn't want anything to happen to his brother. He thought again of the memory of Uncle Alex's visit and his father laughing and smiling. What the hell was he supposed to do? If he told his parents, which his uncle had said not to do, they would be worried sick about it.

```
I wanted to keep your name out of this, but
they have read my emails to you, and know you
```

could help. They may come to visit you. Be
very careful.

Crap - how could this get any worse? He didn't want to be any part of this! He almost threw his phone down, but instead pulled the hunk of silicon close and cradled it instead.

Made in the USA
Coppell, TX
17 November 2023

24374600R00167